Gilbert touched her arms lightly. "I'm what."

Miss Beasley wet her lips. "Well, you're obviously very intelligent and…"

Gilbert cursed under his breath as his body reacted to the flick of her tongue across her lips, and the praise. He desired her, though he couldn't pursue her until the murderer had been captured.

Still, there was no reason why he couldn't reveal his interest and see what happens. "And?"

"What else is there to say?"

He leaned close. Recklessly close, and he heard her breath hitch. "I think you're very attractive, too. I notice you," he whispered. "When you arrive, when you leave. Who you talk to. Who you dance with."

Miss Beasley trembled when he set his hand to her shoulder. "You do?"

HEATHER BOYD

BESTSELLING AUTHOR

MARRIED by MOONLIGHT

Distinguished Rogues

DISTINGUISHED ROGUES SERIES

Book 1: Chills (Jack and Constance)
Book 2: Broken (Giles and Lillian)
Book 3: Charity (Oscar and Agatha)
Book 4: An Accidental Affair (Merrick and Arabella)
Book 5: Keepsake (Kit and Miranda)
Book 6: An Improper Proposal (Martin and Iris)
Book 7: Reason to Wed (Richard and Esme)
Book 8: The Trouble with Love (Everett and Whitney)
Book 9: Married by Moonlight (Gilbert and Anna)

MARRIED BY MOONLIGHT

Edited by Kelli Collins

DEDICATION

The people we meet make an impression. Some good, some bad. Our mentors help shape the people we are, and the things we do, but they may never realize how big a mark they leave on us. So this book is for Tammy F. We may not have spoken for a really long time, but I still hear your advice as I write. You're shaping the stories I tell every day. Much love and respect due to you always.

CHAPTER 1

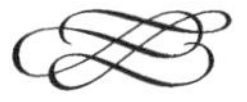

London,
May, 1815

Gilbert Bowen, Earl of Sorenson, burst through the swirling fog into the torch-lit rear courtyard of Lady Berry's home in a violent temper a little before six o'clock in the morning. Mr. Albert Meriwether deserved to be horsewhipped, and so did the Runners for going along with this arrest.

A tall, narrow fellow, probably one of them, too, peeled himself off a wall by the servants' entrance and moved to block Gilbert's path.

Gilbert wasted no time on pleasantries. "Where is he?"

The man looked him up and down, taking in his fine clothing and superior size. "Who are you?"

"A man not to be trifled with." He passed over his card and letter of introduction from a mutual acquaintance, hoping the man knew how to read.

Apparently, he did, for the Runner's eyes widened and he swallowed hard.

The man handed them back, hand shaking a little. "We were not told to expect you, my lord."

Gilbert scowled. "My presence should not have been needed if reason had prevailed. Take me to Mr. Meriwether, now."

"Of course, my lord. He's still interrogating the suspect inside." The man smiled quickly. "The name is Davis."

Gilbert recognized the name but made no further comment. Bow Street Runners were generally good men, thorough and effective at their jobs on most occasions. Except this one. They had little reason to rub shoulders with members of the *ton* or they would not have detained the man inside at all. He hated to think what had happened overnight inside Lady Berry's home.

Davis may be one of the best. But Albert Meriwether, the investigator wrongly holding a suspect inside for interrogation, was definitely not of that quality, from all he'd heard tonight. Gilbert was here to put a stop to his interrogation before any lasting harm was done.

Davis led him swiftly down halls overflowing with chairs, folded tables and piles of soiled linen ready to be taken into the country for laundering. Gilbert should have attended the ball held here last night. Unfortunately, fate had not been on his side.

He stepped into a disordered drawing room and took stock of the situation.

Lady Berry was sobbing on a fainting couch by the far window, a maid hovering ineffectually at her elbow wearing an expression full of fear.

Gilbert swung his gaze to the man tied to a chair in the center of the room like a criminal. His temper did not improve to see fresh blood spotting his friend's shirt front. His cream knee breeches were soiled by old blood too, likely the victim's.

"Meriwether!"

The investigator looked up slowly, his expression annoyed. "Sorenson? What the devil are you doing back in London?"

Gilbert raked his gaze over Meriwether, noting his bloodied

knuckles and the sheen of sweat glistening on his face. "I'm here to rectify the grievous mistake you've made tonight before it is too late."

"There is no mistake," Meriwether insisted, circling his innocent captive.

"There most certainly is," Gilbert insisted, withdrawing his orders from Bow Street and holding them out. "Read this."

The investigator snatched them up and read every line—twice, he suspected. Gilbert moved to check that Lord Carmichael still breathed. He turned his friend's face up to the light, appalled by what he saw. "Dear God. What has been done to you?"

Carmichael shuddered. His left eye was swelling shut and his lip had been split from a beating and was dripping blood down his chin. Meriwether had not been gentle or within his rights to do this. The magistrate would not be pleased.

"No. This case is mine," Meriwether complained. "He's all but confessed to the murder. He's covered in her blood."

"Old blood, judging by the state of his knees." Gilbert grimaced, reaching into another pocket for a week-old letter. "You should read this, as well, before you say another word to implicate him further."

Meriwether read the letter Gilbert had recently received from Lord Carmichael and Miss Berry, announcing their impending wedding, and their request that Gilbert come to London for the announcement last night. Rain had prevented Gilbert from reaching London in time.

"Lord Carmichael was in love with Angela Berry, and she with him. He would not kill her when he was about to announce their marriage, of that I am certain."

"This gives him motive if she refused him," Meriwether crowed. "Look at him."

"Did you not read her own words in the letter?"

"Anyone could have written it."

"Show her mother and have her disprove it is her handwriting."

Meriwether rushed to Lady Berry and thrust the letter at her face. "Is this your daughter's writing?"

Lady Berry sat in shadows, but the maid rushed to bring a candelabra to her so she could read. After a long wait, she began to nod. "That is her penmanship. I would recognize it anywhere."

Meriwether swung around, scowling at the maid.

Gilbert shook his head. "It is known he was found with the body and was nearly incoherent when questioned. He would have attempted to revive her, which is why his clothing is soiled with her blood, you fool."

"She was cold when I found her," Carmichael mumbled, clearly in pain, judging by the slurred nature of his speech. "Never even had a chance to announce we would wed…"

Carmichael sobbed and turned his face away from everyone.

Meriwether sneered. "Isn't that a convenient tale?"

"Actually, he's never been a good liar. *I'm* the reason he had delayed announcing they would marry last night. He wanted me here—which the magistrate believes too," Gilbert told the fellow. "Now, I have Bow Street's approval to release him, and you may go and track down a *real* criminal in any other case you have on your hands. You are done here. Leave the Runners behind. They are under my command now."

"Damn nonsense! You titled bastards always protect your own," Meriwether complained as he began to straighten his clothes. He pulled on his wrinkled coat in a furious rush, scowling like thunder. Clearly the man was unhappy but that was just too bad. "I'll speak to the magistrate about this immediately."

"Good. He's expecting you," Gilbert told him, glad to have the investigator gone.

Gilbert gently untied Carmichael's bonds, noticing red stripes had formed around each tightly bound wrist. Meriwether would have a hard time explaining to the magistrate why he'd treated a peer with such contempt. "Carmichael?"

Carmichael turned his head, squinting at him through his long hair. "What kept you?"

Gilbert brushed his hair back, continuing to assess the damage Meriwether's fists had caused to his face. Nothing so far suggested Carmichael would bear any scars. "The roads from Kent were muddy," he apologized. "I had only just arrived in London when a Runner I know well came with the news you were being held as a suspect in Miss Berry's death."

Carmichael carefully dabbed at his split lip with his shirt-sleeve. "I'm innocent, Sorenson."

"I believe you, but Meriwether does not know you like I do. He will be reprimanded for this, I swear."

He put his arm around Carmichael and hauled him up onto his feet. Carmichael was unsteady and Gilbert held him tightly. "Let's get you out of here, all right? My carriage is waiting in the mews to take you away."

"I want to help catch Angela's killer," Carmichael protested.

"You're in no condition to do anything but what I say, my friend. When you're rested, we'll talk again. Bow Street has given me complete autonomy in the matter. I'd like to keep this quiet for now, to protect your reputation and Bow Street's. I am sending you to my home, where my man will tend to your injuries in privacy. As soon as I finish up here and sort through this mess, I'll return home to take your real statement and discuss what will happen next."

Carmichael nodded but then turned. He looked across the room to where Lady Berry watched their slow progress through puffy eyes. She still had the letter from Carmichael and her daughter clutched in her hand. Her expression was decidedly ashamed.

"Thank you for believing in me," Carmichael whispered to Gilbert.

"Don't thank me yet," he warned. London policing was an imprecise business at best. "Meriwether is fond of beating confessions out of his suspects, whether they be true or not. He could still cause trouble for you."

Reputations were made or lost because of harmful gossip, and Carmichael's standing in society was in jeopardy now.

Lady Berry drew herself up and thrust out the letter to Gilbert. "He said it had to be him," she whispered. "He said there could be no one else."

"I loved her," Carmichael protested. "We were going to marry next week by special license and go home to Edenmere. Angela had already chosen the bedchamber that would become yours. I swear to you, I could never harm her," Carmichael promised the older woman. "I'll find out who took Angela from us if it's the last thing I do."

The older woman seemed to crumple back onto the fainting couch, covering her face as she began to cry again. Gilbert tried to hurry Carmichael away but the man was barely able to move.

"Be gentle with her," Carmichael begged of him once they were a distance from Lady Berry. "As prickly as she's always been with me, she adored Angela. Meriwether is a convincing bastard. I almost believed his arguments myself."

"No, you didn't," Gilbert disagreed. But he would need to ask some hard questions of her and everyone in the household again. There was no telling what sort of nonsense Meriwether had coerced the household staff to say to implicate Carmichael. Getting to the truth might take a while.

He pulled Carmichael through the rear door and paused to catch his breath.

"Can I help you, my lord?" Davis asked, rushing forward.

"Indeed you can," he said as Davis took on Carmichael's extra weight. "Carmichael has attended too many lavish dinners this season."

"So I could be with Angela," Carmichael added with a groan. "Any excuse."

Tears flowed from Carmichael's eyes now and mingled with the blood smeared on his face.

Although he should say something to comfort his friend in his grief, he couldn't delay out of sympathy or concern for his well-being. There was a crime scene to inspect before anyone else disturbed the remaining evidence.

He loaded Carmichael into the carriage with Davis' help and sent him on his way through the subdued foggy streets of London's early morning traffic.

Gilbert looked around and then up. The fog was thinning but the clouds overhead suggested the bad weather had followed him from Kent. It would rain soon if he was not mistaken. "I'll need you with me at all times, so there can be no question that my loyalty is to the truth," he told Davis as he turned toward the house again.

"Very good, my lord," Davis said as he hurried to catch up. "I was itching to get inside from the get go, but Meriwether kept us all away."

He looked at Davis in surprise. "Every single Runner was kept out?"

"Yes, my lord. Meriwether preferred to work alone on the interrogations, as he always does."

Gilbert cursed under his breath. Beating a man to a false confession of guilt was abhorrent to him, and very easy to do without witnesses. Thank God he'd arrived in time to rescue Carmichael from Meriwether's ham-fisted tactics. "That is not how it should be done. You will witness every interview from now on so the evidence brought before the magistrate is without reproach. Form your own opinions and we'll discuss our conclusions in private afterward. Agreed?"

"Sounds fair." Davis frowned though. "I am sorry about Lord Carmichael, my lord. It didn't sit right with me the way he was held like that, but Mr. Meriwether wouldn't hear reason."

"He wanted the conviction, not the truth." Gilbert handed over Carmichael's last letter to Davis. The Runner would have all the information Gilbert uncovered, and help spread the word that Carmichael was wrongly accused and an abused mourner, should any gossip arise.

"Well, I'll be damned." Davis nodded and handed the letter back. "That's clear enough for me. The poor woman is this way."

Gilbert stepped into the conservatory, noting the room was well lit and quite crowded. There were cushioned settees, little side tables, and a few books scattered about the room.

He dropped his gaze to the floor. As Carmichael had alluded to in his many letters about the woman, Angela Berry had been pretty.

Dark auburn hair curled wildly around a pale, lifeless face. She'd been stabbed in the chest, a blow that most likely pierced her heart. Death would have been inevitable, if not instant from a wound like that.

"Hello, Angela," he murmured. "I'm sorry we never had a chance to meet."

Davis drew close. "What was that, my lord?"

"I was just introducing myself to the victim. I never had occasion to meet the deceased while she lived. She used to add a few lines to Carmichael's letters occasionally, but that was the extent of our association. I should have come to London more often this past year."

Davis made a noncommittal sound.

Gilbert drew in a breath and then got to work, noting the arrangement of her limbs, the location of the wound, and the blood smeared around her on the Indian tiles. "Did you read the initial reports?"

"I did. Maid found them together on the floor, Lord Carmichael holding her in his arms. She thought she'd stumbled on a tryst until she noticed the blood."

"What brought her to this part of the house at that precise moment?"

"A cry for help."

"From whom?"

"The report did not say."

"We'll need to question the maid again and ask about the cry." He turned to look around. Angela Berry had fallen not far from the doorway. She might have been waiting here for Carmichael, or someone else perhaps.

Gilbert moved away from the door and the body and investigated the perimeter of the room. There was a narrow path behind the potted palms lining the walls. It was possible to walk completely around the room behind them, he discovered. Along the way, he tested every window and doorway latch. The last glass panel gave way with a gentle push, revealing a hidden exit.

"Well, I'll be!" Davis said as he joined Gilbert. He slipped outside and looked left and right. "Access to the street, and to the mews at the back."

"I take it Meriwether did not discover this?"

"He looked nowhere but to Lord Carmichael once he arrived." Davis scratched his head. "There are other suspects in my opinion, my lord…if you'd *like* my opinion."

"I would, but first things first. After the maid, tell me who else Meriwether might have spoken to. We need to re-interview everyone about Miss Berry's movements from the moment she was found to the last time she was seen alive, to be sure they have not been influenced."

"At least a dozen. There is a footman who is missing though."

"We need to find him as soon as possible," Gilbert said, making notes for himself in his pocketbook. "Tell me what else you know."

"Miss Berry was last seen alive around eleven last night during the height of the festivities of her mother's ball. There were thirty-three members of the *ton* invited, most present, and a dozen extra staff hired for the event."

A hoard of suspects but the wrong one detained. "I'll need Lady Berry's guest list as soon as possible. Bring me the maid, and then the housekeeper and the butler, separately."

“Right you are.” Davis stood straighter. “It’s good to have a proper investigator back in London, my lord.”

“Thank you, but I’m not happy about this at all.” He shook his head and looked down upon the deceased again. “I came for a wedding, not a funeral.”

CHAPTER 2

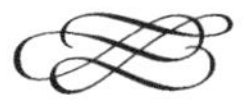

Almack's Assembly Room

Anna Beasley fanned her hot face as she was led from the Almack's Assembly dance floor on the arm of a knight in shining armor.

"Thank you for the dance, Miss Beasley," Lord Wade murmured to her through the slit in his visor.

Anna did her best to ignore the way his armor clanked horribly as he brought her back to her father's side and offered a bow—shallow, most likely because he couldn't bend any lower. Dancing in armor hadn't been easy for him, and she again wondered why he'd asked her to stand up with him in the first place. "Oh, no. Thank you, my lord."

Lord Wade, a plain-speaking viscount of modest fortune, wasn't perhaps the partner other ladies might have wished for, but he bore the stamp of approval from the patronesses of Almack's and that was enough to satisfy Anna. Besides, it wasn't as if anyone else had asked her to dance that night. She was running out of time to impress, and she couldn't bear to pass another night as a wallflower, so she had accepted without hesitation. "I had a marvelous time," she promised him.

Anna adjusted the straps that held her heavy bow and arrows into a better position across her shoulder and smiled warmly at the viscount. Dancing so encumbered hadn't been easy for her, either. Why hadn't she just worn a simple mask like her friend Portia had suggested? Something without weapons perhaps might have appeared less threatening, too.

Lord Wade nodded politely to her father and released her. Iron screeched as he turned awkwardly to face the other direction, and then he clanked off into the crowd. She hoped Lord Wade left early tonight—only so he might be spared of the weight of the heavy armor sooner rather than later.

Anna wished for release, too. She had hope that supper would be announced soon, because only then could she divest herself of her costume's weapons with the patronesses' blessings.

"Was it dreadful?" Miss Portia Hayes asked in a whisper as she rushed over to join Anna. Miss Hayes, attired all in white, carried a harp upon her hip that she strummed softly as she waited for Anna's response.

"Of course not," Anna promised, smoothing her forest-green waistcoat over her gown of similar hue. She was meant to be a woodsman's lady, rustic and wild. Anna hadn't been brave enough to leave her dark hair unbound in public, so her maid had braided it so that the long rope of its length draped forward over her shoulder. Surely someone would find her appealing in this costume and look past her habitual blushes to see the woman within.

She fiddled with the long plait and settled it again. "Lord Wade is a competent dance partner, even in armor."

"You know what I mean." Portia leveled her with a knowing stare.

Anna did, unfortunately, remembering past conversations with the viscount that had made her uncomfortable for their bluntness. Given her lack of other dance partners, Anna had resigned herself to more of that and was determined to overlook anything untoward he said. Lord Wade never said anything truly beyond the pale yet. Nothing she hadn't thought herself, really, but would never say out loud. It just wasn't politic to speak your mind when you were hoping to catch the right sort of husband. Kind, handsome, and sufficiently plump in the pocket. "He said nothing improper to me."

"He makes my skin crawl whenever he stares at me," Portia complained.

Anna had heard that statement many times from Portia. She was an heiress with a great belief in her own worth. Anna hadn't the confidence to refuse to dance with anyone. Portia even believed Lord Wade's inclusion in the invitations to attend Almack's from the patronesses a shocking mistake.

Anna feared her own inclusion was an error sometimes, too. But she had a supporter in the *ton*, a very valuable mentor for a motherless girl in search of a proper husband, and with another birthday fast approaching, Anna needed all the help she could get. Her twentieth year, and the specter of spinsterhood, was nothing to celebrate and everything to fear.

"I think supper is about to be announced," Anna whispered to change the subject.

"I think you are right," Portia agreed, staring around them with a serene smile. "Have you seen Lord Carmichael tonight?"

"He wouldn't ever be admitted," Anna warned. Lord Carmichael, the very horrid Price Wagstaff, was her father's godson—and a devil when it came to breaking the hearts of ladies, she'd learned.

"Shall we go down to supper, daughter?" Father asked.

"Yes, of course," she said obediently. She glanced at Portia. "Shouldn't you return to your parents, too?"

"I suppose I must," Portia said, sighing. Portia's parents were oddly behaved for chaperones—standing at least ten feet away facing the other direction to their daughter. Portia squeezed her fingers quickly. "Are you attending the Williamson ball on Friday?"

"Indeed I am," Anna exclaimed, holding her father back a moment. "I've been looking forward to the ball since knowing our invitation had arrived. Will you be there too?"

"Of course. I'm wearing my new blue silk gown. You should wear your pink muslin." Portia waved her fingers and finally went off to rejoin her parents.

Father clucked his tongue in disapproval at Portia's parting advice and drew Anna toward the great stone staircase of Almack's. "Wear whatever you like to the ball, daughter."

Anna laughed softly. "I had already decided on the pink, but it's good to know Miss Hayes will be wearing another color."

There was nothing worse than appearing to imitate a close friend.

They descended to the ground floor, left her weapons with a footman to collect later and slipped into the supper room. They found the only vacant table, next to a tall gilt pillar, and soon had tea and a plate of little sandwiches each laid before them. Not that Anna was particularly hungry, attending Almack's always made her too nervous to eat, but she was thirsty and her aching feet were grateful for a respite.

Her father looked at the plates with a forlorn expression. "One must bear the expense to attend, I suppose, but it's always such a poor offering at supper, isn't it?"

Anna sympathized. The food was no better than what could be had at home but there was so little of it. She eased closer to him. "Did you remember to eat before leaving home?"

"I did not find the time, unfortunately." Father looked at her sideways. "You danced well tonight with Lord Wade."

"Thank you."

His brow wrinkled. "That is the fifth night you have danced with him in as many weeks, is it not?"

"Sixth."

Father made a small sound as he bit into a sandwich, something that might have been approval or perhaps merely hunger appeased at last. "You haven't set your heart on an offer of marriage from him, have you?"

"Father!"

Anna glanced around guiltily, hoping no one had heard his question. It was one thing to talk about suitors in the privacy of home, but another entirely to discuss the matter where anyone might hear.

It appeared no one close had overheard them, but her mentor, Lady Scott, a widow and stickler for propriety, was watching them from across the room. Anna smiled at her quickly. "Lady Scott is here," she whispered.

He nodded. "She always is."

"I do hope I have a chance to speak with her tonight."

Father squinted at the woman. "For what reason?"

"Nothing too important, I promise." She wanted to ask Lady Scott about Lord Wade's situation. Lady Scott knew everything about everyone, which had proved very useful so far this season.

Her father shook his head and resumed eating.

She was just starting to feel comfortable when a shadow loomed over them.

"Ah, Miss Beasley," a familiar, masculine voice mocked. "I thought I saw your beacon-like blush guiding me across the supper room."

Anna looked up, appalled at his appearance. Carmichael had been fighting at Gentleman Jackson's again, and clearly had not been the winner this time. His lower lip had a healing cut and there was a yellowish bruise circling one eye. "What are you doing at Almack's?"

"Why shouldn't I be here?" He tossed off a loud laugh and turned to greet her grinning father. "I have as much right as anyone, don't you think, sir?"

The Earl of Carmichael was quite unworthy of treading these hallowed halls, she was sure.

Anna had known him, suffered him, since their parents had

forced them into close proximity as children, and she'd endured his company stoically on each and every occasion since she'd made her come out in society.

Father, unfortunately, loved Carmichael like the son he'd never had. He would say nothing about him returning to fight at Gentleman Jackson's, even if Carmichael had promised that he never would again. "There you are, my boy. I trust you had no trouble when you presented yourself tonight."

"None at all, and thank you for your assistance in applying to the patronesses." Carmichael glanced about the supper room, his expression bored. "Not quite as I pictured it."

"I did warn that you might be underwhelmed, my boy," Father said with a soft laugh. "Better entertainment in the ring than here."

Anna glanced between Father and Carmichael, startled that her father would actually help the earl gain entry to Almack's. Why, the foundations of society must be crumbling beneath them. "I thought you said you hated the very idea of attending Almack's?"

"You were misinformed." Carmichael's expression darkened a moment. "Oh, and here is the friend I was telling you about yesterday, Mr. Beasley. May I present Gilbert Bowen, Earl of Sorenson, to you?"

Father stood, leaving Anna sitting at the table with her cooling tea as he was introduced to a Lord Sorenson of Kent. She'd heard that name before. The older man's reputation preceded him, and she didn't care to be introduced to a known scoundrel.

"May I offer condolences on your father's passing and your elevation to the title?"

"Thank you, Mr. Beasley," Lord Sorenson murmured in a voice that sounded a bit younger and more vibrant than she'd expected.

Anna stilled. She had not known the Sorenson title had

passed to a son. Apparently, there were some things Lady Scott had not told her.

But Carmichael's friends were in general an unruly and forward lot, most with a known disinterest in pursuing matrimony but would gladly chase any lady in skirts. The apple wouldn't fall far from the tree.

Despite knowing her interest would be fruitless, she turned her head slightly to glimpse the newcomer discreetly.

Almost out of her line of sight, Carmichael's friend appeared to be costumed in tight-fitting tan leather breeches, a jerkin of sea green and, to her shock, he wore a bow and quiver of arrows strapped to his back just as she had worn earlier.

He moved slightly, and she could suddenly see Lord Sorenson very clearly. He was young, perhaps younger than Carmichael even, and handsome in a severe way. Carmichael's friend was not just handsome—he was downright devastating.

Sinful.

His hair, worn long enough to brush the collar of his crisp white shirt, was the color of an angry sunset, his eyes an unusually bright shade of green exactly matched to the shade of her own costume. He laughed suddenly, revealing even white teeth and a wickedly inviting smile that must charm every woman he met.

Anna nearly swooned herself when he pursed his lips the next moment.

She turned back to her plate quickly, suddenly far too warm for even a fan to do her any good. She reached for it anyway and beat air at her face.

"Anna, my dear girl. Forgive me. Where is my mind tonight?" Father caught her hand and hauled her up on shaking legs. "Lord Sorenson, might I present to you my only daughter, Anna."

Anna lifted her eyes slowly and quaked anew under the force of the earl's wicked gaze.

"A pleasure to make your acquaintance, Miss Beasley," Lord Sorenson said after a slight pause.

His deep voice sent a burst of pleasure racing all over her skin. He had a dark voice, the tone of which made her shiver.

The blush that never seemed to go away around handsome men heated anew, and she lowered her eyes quickly. This was a man she ought not to encourage if she wanted to keep her virtue intact. "My lord," she managed to say before becoming utterly tongue-tied.

Carmichael poked her shoulder. "Lord Sorenson is quite new to Town, Anna, and hasn't a clue of the fun he's been missing all these years," he stated. "Can you believe him once a dull vicar?"

Anna glanced at Lord Sorenson swiftly. He could *not* be a vicar. Not with those looks or that voice. "No."

"All true, I swear," Lord Sorenson promised, his expression amused by her denial.

Anna's skin heated even more and she glanced down again.

"Sorenson's been rusticating in the countryside for far too long. I mean to show him the ropes around Town and educate him on the pleasures to be found here. I'm sure you'll be seeing a lot of him in the coming weeks."

At most, she'd likely see his back as he slipped away to seduce some bold and foolish woman. Carmichael was notorious for showing his friends a very good time in the capital. He would take Lord Sorenson under his wing and lead him to places Anna should never know about. Poor Lord Sorenson wouldn't stand a chance of avoiding corruption and vice during his visit. Even a week of Carmichael's company was bound to ruin him.

"Will you be staying in London long?"

She hoped not, for his sake.

"Not the whole of the season. I must stay as long as required, on business, before returning to Kent for the summer, no matter what mischief my old friend is planning for me," Lord Sorenson promised with a lofty stare for Carmichael. He looked at her again and his smile returned. "How are you enjoying the season, Miss Beasley?"

Her body seemed to be quivering with each word Lord Sorenson uttered. She took a moment to collect herself before answering.

"Very well, thank you. My friends and I look forward to seeing you at future events."

Was that too forward? She hoped not.

She looked at Carmichael quickly. "Have you by chance seen Miss Berry tonight?"

Carmichael paled.

"Who?" Lord Sorenson asked.

"She's a very good friend of mine." She looked at Carmichael expectantly. He had been flirting with Angela for weeks and months. Anna expected an announcement of an engagement any day now, or to hear he'd broken Angela's heart.

"Haven't seen her," Carmichael mumbled. "Now that introductions have been completed, we'd best return to the ballroom," he announced suddenly. "Sorenson has promised to dance with Miss Hayes for the next set after supper."

"Please excuse us," Lord Sorenson murmured, but threw one last smile toward Anna before he followed after Carmichael.

Anna let out a shaky breath as she watched them go, her stomach twisting with jealousy and longing. Portia Hayes would be just what Lord Sorenson might like. Bold. Daring. Flirtatious. Anna wasn't at all like that. She didn't have the knack for turning heads like her friends could.

The pair strode from the supper room side by side, a wide path clearing before them as they made their way toward the staircase.

A little despondent now, Anna sat again and finished her cold tea in silence. Some nights she felt so very insignificant when compared to others on the marriage mart. She had a dowry but it was a modest sum. Her family was distantly related to the Earl of

Windermere, which meant she could count on being invited to the most important *ton* events.

But her dance card was empty more often than not.

That was entirely her fault. Blushing at every introduction tended to be off-putting for many gentlemen.

A little bell rang, signaling the end of supper and the commencement of the next round of dancing. Although she had not been asked to dance another set tonight, she would watch and console herself with enjoying the music.

"I must do better," she told herself in a whisper, darting a glance around her at all the unattached gentlemen passing her by without a second glance.

Although her chances were slim of impressing anyone tonight, she squared her shoulders and followed her father to collect the pieces of her costume.

CHAPTER 3

"The worst is over." Gilbert slipped a glass of port into Lord Carmichael's hand, studying his friend's pale face with concern. His wounds were healing slowly, the cut on his lip no longer bled and the bruises on his body were fading. But the wounds on his heart would take a great deal longer.

It had been a dreadful evening for Carmichael, a man who should have been mourning the loss of a loved one instead of flirting all night long with the young ladies attending Almack's Assembly Rooms.

Gilbert had ruthlessly forced him back into society to catch a killer because he had no choice. The Berry household servants save one had been cleared of suspicion. Bow Street wanted a swift capture of Miss Berry's killer, and the best way to gather evidence discreetly was to speak to every guest who had attended the Berry ball.

Gilbert had worked with Bow Street many times before, and had hunted villains as a vicar, too, earning the respect and gratitude of Bow Street in the process. When Gilbert had taken over his father's title at Christmas after his sudden passing, he'd expected to leave his former life as an investigator behind him. His quarry then had been mostly local riffraff and outcasts.

Carmichael shook his dark head and settled with a groan onto the leather settee in Gilbert's cluttered upstairs parlor. He had kept this house in London for years, an infrequent resident. Gilbert had rarely needed to visit London but a few times a year.

Carmichael's pale blue eyes were glassy, bright with unshed tears when he eventually looked at Gilbert. "How can you say the worst is over? Angela is dead, and you forced me to pretend I didn't care one whit about her whereabouts whenever her name came up in conversation tonight."

Gilbert exchanged a glance with Davis, who leaned against the doorway, seemingly ready to soak up every word they said, as was his right. However, he didn't need to see Carmichael break down in tears again. "If you could leave us now."

"I'll see if there is any news about the footman," the man suggested before sauntering out.

"I like him better than Meriwether," Carmichael murmured.

"Meriwether is no longer involved in this investigation," Gilbert promised.

Meriwether was in deep water with Bow Street for his behavior toward Carmichael, a peer and engaged man, and had been assigned a new case and a levelheaded partner to work with. The London investigator was too impatient to be fair, and no longer taken seriously by those who mattered. He would accuse first and acquit later, but by then, irreparable damage would be done to reputations.

Meriwether was a bull in a china shop, he'd love nothing more than to tell society he was tracking a killer just to bask in their gratitude.

Carmichael scrubbed at his eyes as weariness crept up on him.

"I understand it is difficult to hide the truth from so many acquaintances, but to succeed, we must act as if nothing is wrong," Gilbert promised, resigned to the necessity of playing everyone false a little while longer.

"*Everything* is wrong." Carmichael downed the drink and then stood abruptly. "I could have spoken to Angela's killer tonight and still never known it."

"It is possible," Gilbert conceded as Carmichael paced the room. "And yet it is entirely plausible her death had nothing to do with you or anyone connected to you in the *ton*. My men are searching the city for Lady Berry's missing footman, and we will question him once he is in my custody. Have no doubt we will get to the truth."

"I cannot credit that her death was an act of violence by a mere servant. It makes no sense. She was generous and kind to all. But she died coming to meet with *me,* and now we've learned that two other young women known to me died during the last season under equally suspicious circumstances."

"If you continue to bandy about this new theory of yours, you could find yourself a suspect all over again. Davis is a fair man but others might not be. I am trying to help you so listen to me very carefully. You are not to blame for Angela's death, or the death of any other lady. You dance with many women. Talk with them. Not all of them are dead."

"I kissed all the dead ones!" Carmichael cried.

Gilbert sighed, crossed the room to Carmichael and, after slinging an arm around his shoulder, led him back to the chair he'd vacated. Carmichael had once had a reputation for stealing kisses from debutantes new to Town, but Gilbert had trouble believing he could ever be the provocation for such a violent killing spree, if one existed. Carmichael needed to calm himself before he was overheard by someone not quite so levelheaded.

"I know these deaths, hers particularly, are difficult for you to not feel some misplaced guilt over, but you must set aside your suspicious nature and concentrate on facts. We will find Miss Berry's killer together, and we will not rest on our laurels until we have a conviction. I need your assistance. I don't have the right connections yet to make headway on my own. I need to interrogate people without anyone realizing I'm doing so. I need you at my side."

"Is that how you caught Jane Peabody's killer in the end? Pestering good people all day and all night?"

As always, Gilbert's stomach clenched with hate when he thought back to the first murderer he'd chased and captured—a woman who had stalked another young lady in his parish and lured her from the protection of her family to kill her. Gilbert had known both girls reasonably well from their attendance at services. The disappearance had shocked his parishioners, the discovery of Jane Peabody's broken body on a windswept hillside above the village had enraged them—turning friend against friend. Gilbert had gone door to door, striving to restore peace, and discovered quite by accident that he had a knack for uncovering hidden truths. The girl had been murdered by a jealous rival.

"I was more discreet than that."

Bringing Jane Peabody's killer to justice had been only briefly satisfying.

He had seen the signs of envy the other girl had felt toward her victim, but like everyone else, had brushed them aside as unimportant initially. Gilbert knew exactly how powerless Carmichael was feeling right now. He'd blamed himself, too.

"Someone knows or deep down suspects the culprit isn't quite right. They always do on some level. We just have to ask the right questions of the right people."

"I wonder if you missed your true calling. You shouldn't have spent so many years delivering sermons when there are monsters on the loose to catch here in London."

Gilbert shrugged. If he'd stayed in London, he might have become a degenerate rake—chasing women and gambling for high stakes every night like his father. He was grateful his sire had been a terrible man, gambling and whoring for most of Gilbert's life. Vice and corruption had been his natural elements.

His poor example had set Gilbert on a better path and turned him on to a profession and life he was proud of. "I chose my profession well. The solving of crimes was borne out of a desire to help others. An extension of my life in the church."

Carmichael squinted at him. "Surely the army was a more appealing career for an earl's only son than the church."

"We've gone over this a dozen times." Gilbert poured Carmichael another drink and handed it to him. "It might have been if I wasn't an only son. Father forbade me from serving my country."

"I couldn't picture you a vicar until the moment I heard you sermonize about the evils of idle occupation and vice last year."

Gilbert had come to like his life as a country vicar very much, save for the call to investigate some tragedy or other. His had been a quiet life of introspection and polite gatherings otherwise, quite in contrast to his new life in Kent, where all sorts of temptations awaited him. Father had nearly kept a harem of women lying idle about the estate. It had taken all of the first month to pack up their belongings and get them to leave.

"I wrote that one with you specifically in mind," Gilbert teased with a laugh.

"That was the old me," Carmichael promised morosely.

"That is you from top to bottom even now," Gilbert promised. "Falling in love with Angela Berry didn't change you that much as far as I can tell. I need you to behave as you always would have before her death. No one must know you are heartbroken over this loss."

Carmichael downed his drink. "Beasley knows something is wrong. I could see it in his eyes tonight when we spoke."

Gilbert sat forward, keen to know more about the Beasleys. Anyone connected to Angela Berry was a suspect until proven otherwise. "Will he say anything to his daughter?"

"No, but Anna and Angela were close. They'd been whispering to each other for weeks about me."

Quietly spoken Anna Beasley hardly seemed the type of girl

to be friends with an outgoing lady like Angela Berry was reputed to be, or to gossip. "How do you know Miss Beasley was speaking of you to Angela?"

"Angela berated me for teasing Anna not long ago. She said I should grow up and stop being mean to her. A 'monster,' and that's what Anna always said I was to her when we were young."

He pictured the girl he'd been introduced to earlier that night. Anna Beasley appeared very shy on first glance. As he recalled the way she'd kept peeking at him, dark, gentle eyes drawing him closer, he found himself smiling for no good reason. "Why on earth would you be mean to Miss Beasley?"

"Habit." Carmichael pulled a face. "We were children when we first met. Our parents were plotting a marriage between us. I protested quite strongly against the idea. I also made sure Anna would look elsewhere for a potential husband when she came out. Thankfully she took every remark to heart and doesn't trust me even now."

Gilbert shook his head. "You'd never do for her anyway."

Carmichael finally laughed. "Spoken like a man who couldn't stop stealing glances at her all night. If I didn't know you were looking for a killer, I'd say you've been struck down by instant lust."

"Don't be ridiculous." Gilbert scowled, despite knowing he had not been able to stop looking at the young woman even before their introduction. "I am committed to finding Miss Berry's killer."

Given the late hour they were introduced, Miss Beasley would not have had room on her dance card for him anyway, so he had not risked a rebuff by asking her to dance. "I was merely interested in her costume and trying to work out how she managed to seem so graceful with a bow strapped to her back. Mine was a damn nuisance to wear all night. Why the devil did you choose it for me?"

"Seemed appropriate, given we're on the hunt together." Carmichael peered at him closely. "Are you sure that's the extent of your interest in her? I warn you, her costume was entirely accurate. She's definitely hunting a husband this season. Her father cannot stop mentioning it."

"Understood." Gilbert rubbed his brow. He was not used to the hours kept by Londoners and his bed was calling to him all of a sudden. "I am here to catch a killer, not find a wife."

A small smile ghosted over Carmichael's lips. "Anna's not a bad sort, for all that she blushes all the time."

"I noticed that."

"Everyone notices that first, and it drives countless fellows away, I fear." Carmichael frowned again. "It would be a believable excuse for you though—you searching for a bride and singling Anna out for attention. She has a lot of friends in common with Angela and those other murdered girls."

"I'd not use her, or anyone, like that," he warned.

Carmichael looked down at his hands. "Angela and I made a pact last year—to pretend an interest in each other to quiet her mother for this season."

"I know you feel guilty that you waited so long to ask for her hand," Gilbert said gently.

"I should have asked after our first kiss." Carmichael squinted up at him. "It wouldn't have to be a successful courtship between you and Anna. Just enough to convince others that you're assessing the field. Anna's quite the shy mouse, but she'd go along with the deception for a good cause. If you let me explain to her father what we're doing, I'm sure he'd help us, too."

Gilbert laughed. "Wouldn't it be better if *you* were the one to court Miss Beasley, since her father already wishes for a match between you?"

"And put her in danger?" Carmichael grimaced. "No. Besides, no one would believe she'd have me. Not with our history. It has to be you."

Gilbert held fast to his principles. A false courtship would be cruel to Anna Beasley…even more so if she knew the direction his mind had traveled as he'd looked upon her last night. If she had some fellow in mind for her husband, a false courtship might harm her chances of receiving a proper proposal. "No. I won't do it to her."

"Come on, man. You're an unknown, and who knows how long the excuse of being in London on 'a business matter' will remain convincing? Besides, if you're believed to be courting Anna, it will be easier to keep an eye on her, and other young women too, without accidentally getting yourself leg shackled in truth."

Carmichael had a point—only *if* his wild theory held some truth. If Carmichael's suspicions were in any way real, only a few ladies could be in danger, those with a romantic interest in Carmichael himself. Anna Beasley might certainly be at risk by association, but only if guilt wasn't making Carmichael assume connections that were not there.

Still, he would not entirely dismiss the motive Carmichael ascribed to the killer. He'd investigate first and dismiss it later.

"Think about it," Carmichael pressed. "She's not entirely without reason, and we will have to tell her what happened to Angela Berry soon."

Gilbert shook his head. "Absolutely out of the question. Not yet. You say she was close to Angela. Have you considered she might be acquainted with the killer too?"

Carmichael paled.

"Keeping her in the dark is better protection," Gilbert promised. "We can question her discreetly and that will be the end of her involvement in the case."

"Then before I forget, I should give you this." Carmichael produced a letter. "You need a reason to be at Friday night's ball. Lady Williamson is breathless with anticipation for your attendance in her ballroom. She remembers your father fondly and cannot wait to become reacquainted with his handsome son. Her words not mine. Make sure you ask her to dance as payment for including you at short notice."

"Thank you, I think." Gilbert looked up just as Davis

appeared at the door. The Runner nodded and disappeared again. Their quarry had been captured. Gilbert got to his feet. Duty called.

Carmichael stood too, raking his hand through his hair. "I want this over."

Gilbert clasped Carmichael's shoulder. "You should get some rest. Do you want to stay again?"

Carmichael wasn't sleeping in his own bed anymore. The only way he seemed able to rest was to drink to excess in his study or sleep here in Gilbert's home. Gilbert preferred the latter and didn't mind the company.

Carmichael nodded. "Home seems so very empty of late."

Carmichael lived alone but for his servants. So did Gilbert, for that matter. He was better off staying the night.

"The guest room is prepared and waiting for you as usual," he promised. "I'll send my man to fetch you clean clothing again for tomorrow."

"Thank you, my friend. I don't really know what I'd do without your support."

"Think nothing of it. I'm happy to help," he promised. "Be off with you, and call for breakfast when you wake."

Carmichael pulled a face suddenly. "She fancies you."

"Who?"

"Anna, of course." Carmichael grin turned sly. "That blush of hers is always a dead giveaway for how she feels."

"Go to bed, Carmichael. Your tiredness is making you delusional."

Carmichael laughed softly. "I know what I saw written all over your faces," he promised. "The sooner you admit it, the better for me."

Gilbert didn't believe in love at first sight. But instant attraction he knew to be very real. He shrugged the desire for companionship away. There would be time to consider Anna Beasley later.

As soon as Carmichael could no longer be heard on the stairs, Gilbert slipped downstairs to the wine cellar.

Davis was waiting, a pair of hulking men at his back. "Bold as brass, this one. Waltzed right up to the Berry's kitchen door with a spring in his step," he said.

"Confident," he murmured. Or innocent. Only asking the right questions would tell. "Good."

Davis turned to give the order and his men moved aside.

Gilbert stepped into the wine cellar, Davis on his heels. "Mr. Toombs."

The pale-haired footman stopped pacing and turned blazing eyes on him. "What right do you have to hold me here?"

"I am Lord Sorenson, and I am commissioned by Bow Street to investigate a crime committed at your employer's residence on the night of May five." He took a seat opposite Toombs, noting the man showed immediate signs of concern for his employer. "My first question, where have you been, Mr. Toombs?"

The footman frowned. "Am I in trouble?"

He nodded slowly. "How much will depend on what you say to me today. Most likely you will at least lose your position."

"But I had leave to go home," the man protested. "I cannot marry without a position."

A marriage in the works was news to him. The household staff had not hinted the fellow had any romantic entanglements. "Neither Lady Berry nor her senior staff gave any such permission."

The fellow shook his head, and his arms dropped to his sides. "But her ladyship's daughter gave me permission. Just ask her."

Gilbert leaned forward to stare at Mr. Toombs. On the surface, he seemed oblivious to the crime under investigation but many criminals excelled at lying. "That would be difficult, as Angela Berry is no longer alive to collaborate your tall tale."

The fellow's eyes bulged. "What?"

"Murdered."

The man stared, mouth agape. He closed it suddenly and

looked about the room a little wildly. "I swear she was breathing when I left her! Is Sally all right?"

"Sally?"

"Miss Berry's maid." He swallowed hard. "We are going to marry. Miss Berry promised us both a place with her when she married Lord Carmichael."

"You knew about Carmichael's proposal?"

"Only that it was expected on the night of the ball," Toombs promised. "Everyone in the household was waiting for it. The poor man."

Toombs' shock and sympathy seemed genuine and completely convincing to Gilbert. "No one else was harmed, and Lord Carmichael had no chance to propose at all that night," he murmured. "Convince me of your innocence, sir."

The fellow came and sat opposite Gilbert, hands between his knees. "I spoke to Miss Berry at four in the afternoon," Toombs began, and then blurted out every moment of his following days in such detail as to be entirely convincing. "Sally, my intended, had finally agreed since we found out we could go with her mistress and stay together.

"I went home to tell my father the good news, obtained his permission to marry, and returned to London after speaking with Sally's parents on the way back. We had grown up two villages apart, never knowing each other until we entered Lady Berry's service."

Gilbert exchanged a glance with Davis, who was nodding slowly. Innocent, but still…it would do to keep this one close. "Lady Berry will be leaving London soon to bury her daughter. She has dismissed all but a few of her London staff."

The man looked shocked.

"You will undoubtedly be without a position, should you return to Berry House under a cloud of suspicion."

"I would never hurt Miss Berry. She was the kindest in the household. What about Miss Berry's lady's maid? Does she still have a position?"

"Dismissed too."

The fellow burst to his feet. "I have to find her. Anything could happen to her if I'm not there to protect her."

"Sit down," Davis warned. "Lucky for you, Lord Sorenson has a tender heart."

"What have you done with her?"

"Employed her. Not as a lady's maid of course, since I am not married, but she has a respectable position in the kitchens for now." Gilbert stood, straightening his waistcoat. "I do not condone the rash dismissal of staff in times of grief. There could be a permanent position for you, as long as you've been honest today."

"I was. I am. Thank you, my lord."

He gestured to Davis to lead the fellow away. Toombs trotted after Davis eagerly, and then Davis returned alone.

Gilbert studied the fellow. "Tell the staff to keep an ear open. Make sure his story holds up over the next few days. If it doesn't, we will question him again; if it does, I will find him a better position elsewhere."

CHAPTER 4

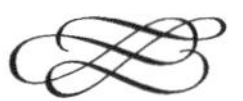

The Williamson ball would be the event of the season. Everyone who mattered was in attendance tonight. Anyone with a daughter worth marrying had come. So, too, had all the most eligible gentlemen. But there was one face missing from the crowd of ladies gathering together to look over the bachelors, and that absence nagged at Anna. "Have you seen Miss Berry tonight?"

"No," Portia answered, hardly hiding the fact her interest lie in the gentlemen across the room. For the whole of the evening, Portia had been ogling the nearest bachelors and had barely paid attention to a word Anna spoke to her.

"I haven't seen or spoken to her at all this week," Anna confessed to Portia as she kept an eye on her father's location. Father had grudgingly allowed her to take a turn about the room with Portia, provided she went nowhere else.

Portia met her gaze with obvious surprise. "I thought she was only avoiding *me*."

Portia's statement was not surprising. Portia and Angela Berry did not always see eye to eye. There had even been two weeks last year when they'd exchanged harsh words over their mutual interest in the same gentleman. However, as far as Anna knew, their squabbling days were behind them. Angela had singled out Lord Carmichael for attention, and promised the rest of the *ton's* most eligible and titled bachelors were free to wed either Portia or Anna.

"She's never been at home when I call."

"That is so strange." Portia rose on her toes and looked about them. "She's no reason to snub either of us. And how terrible for her that Lord Carmichael is in attendance tonight, too. How disappointed will she be to have missed another opportunity to dance with him. That makes twice now this week. I still cannot believe they admitted him to Almack's Assembly Rooms, can you?"

"I expected the ground to open up beneath him and swallow him whole, to be honest," Anna whispered in Portia's ear.

Portia choked on a laugh. "You are so bad."

Anna winced. She wasn't bad, she just occasionally blurted out what she really thought to her closest friends without thinking of the consequences properly.

"Of course London's most eligible bachelor is here," Lord Wade remarked from directly behind them. "This is where only the most delicious ladies will be found."

Anna blushed at the brash remark and turned. She did not believe Lord Wade meant *her* in that description, but Lord Wade often looked upon Miss Hayes as if she were worth devouring.

Portia, however, glared at him. "It is not polite to invite yourself into a conversation."

"Merely passing by," he murmured, bowing slightly before disappearing into the crowd without a backward glance.

Portia watched him go and then turned toward Anna. "I hate how that man creeps around."

Anna hid a smile. She thought Lord Wade's spur-of-the-moment conversation was purely aimed at unsettling Portia Hayes, who could be prickly sometimes. His arrivals were always unexpected. "Are you engaged for the next dance?"

"Indeed I am. Lord Carmichael has asked for the waltz tonight. I know Miss Berry has a prior claim on him but she's not here, and I do like the way he dances." She glanced down at Anna's empty dance card and pulled a face. "I'm sorry to leave you."

"Do not worry about me. I will return to my father and enjoy the view."

Across the room, she spotted Carmichael and, at his side, his friend, Lord Sorenson. Carmichael would be coming this way soon to collect Portia. Where Lord Sorenson was headed was anyone's guess. He'd seemed everywhere in the room tonight.

She sighed softly, enamored of the earl's looks still. Although he was dressed soberly, quite a contrast to Carmichael's more flamboyant tailoring, she still believed she was better off forgetting all about him.

The pair seemed to be claiming dances from two other young ladies now—Miss Goldwell, daughter of a shipping merchant, and Miss Myra Lacy, daughter of a prosperous spice merchant. They were not her particular friends but kind enough to speak to Anna whenever they met. Both were amply dowered and attracted much attention from the unattached bachelors of London. They were also rather more forward than Anna thought they should be. Something the pair of gentlemen smiling down upon them must have found very appealing.

"You should return to your parents before the set is called," she whispered to Portia.

"Yes, of course. Give my love to Miss Berry when you finally see her. Tell her I have all sorts of news to share," Portia asked before gliding away toward her parents to await Carmichael.

Resigned to watching others dance the next set from afar, Anna turned on her heel to return to her father.

But came to a complete stop before taking one single step. "Lady Scott!"

"Miss Beasley."

She smiled widely at Lord Carmichael's godmother. "How lovely you look tonight, my lady."

"Pshaw," the older woman replied with a wave of her hand. "I'm old, not foolish."

Anna smiled. "Never old."

"You should not be alone and unescorted," Lady Scott admonished her in a stern voice. "Do you not care what people say about you?"

Lady Scott worried about propriety all the time, sometimes to excess.

"I was just returning to my father." She gestured behind them. "He's not three yards away. Would you like to join me there and speak to him?"

The lady seemed to consider it a moment, but then shook her head, eyes fixed on the dance floor. "Perhaps another night."

"Very well," Anna replied. She delayed a moment longer. Conversations around her father's friends tended to be either about dull politics or, even worse, about their aching limbs. "Did you enjoy Almack's on Wednesday?"

"Of course." She peered across the room. "Who was the gentleman introduced to you that night? The one standing beside my godson now?"

"Oh. Do you mean Lord Sorenson?"

"Sorenson? That is not the Earl of Sorenson."

"The elder Lord Sorenson passed away, I understand, and the son claimed the title recently. He's only just come up to London, but before that he was a vicar in a country church." Anna considered whether to relay her suspicions about Carmichael's plans for the new earl but decided against it. Lady Scott would never believe her beloved godson could be a bad influence on anyone. "I believe he and Lord Carmichael have been acquainted since their schooldays."

Lady Scott's eyes narrowed as she looked past Anna's shoulder. "We are not acquainted."

"He seemed a very polite and amiable gentleman when we

were introduced," Anna declared, although having spoken only a few words with him hardly made her an expert. "My father seemed to like him well enough."

Lady Scott harrumphed. "You must return to him now."

"Yes, my lady," she said dutifully. "Until the next time we meet."

"Be good," Lady Scott warned.

Anna nodded and made her way to her father's side, resigned to her fate of a long and likely boring evening. Father made room for her and she was soon lost in the frustrating world of political maneuvering.

The next dance ended and Anna tried not to envy the couples too much. When she heard a throat being cleared behind her, she sighed with pleasure.

Grateful for any interruption, Anna turned immediately, hoping Lord Wade had returned to save her from another night of not dancing.

However, it wasn't Lord Wade smiling at her with sinfully wicked eyes.

Anna almost couldn't breathe. "Lord Sorenson?"

He bowed, and the interest in his eyes flared. "Miss Beasley, I wondered if you might have room on your dance card for me."

A dance! Anna didn't need to look at her blank card to know that she did. She clenched it tightly in her fist and refused to show it. "I would be honored."

He looked at her expectantly, one brow raised, and held out his hand so he could write down his name.

She wasn't about to spoil her chances by letting him see the blank card she held. "The, ah, next set is available."

"Oh. Well, thank you. That seems to suit us both then." He glanced at her father. "If I have your permission, sir."

"Indeed. Enjoy yourselves." Father gave her a warning look that said *behave* in no uncertain terms because he'd be watching like a hawk.

Lord Sorenson held out his arm and Anna placed her hand

upon his sleeve, noting the fine material under her gloved fingers. For a former vicar, he had excellent taste in fabrics.

Her heart skipped a beat and a blush heated her cheeks as they moved toward the dance floor. The waltz required Lord Sorenson to hold her close in his arms. Spaces were slowly filling up and they found a place at the rear. She flicked a quick wave toward Portia, where she stood with Carmichael, and turned back to her partner.

However, her partner was looking beyond her head at the other guests.

They bowed to each other, and then Lord Sorenson moved close.

Anna took his hand but was so overwhelmed by him that she couldn't think of a thing to say. Her face heated and she concentrated on dancing and not tripping over her own feet.

After a few turns about the floor, Anna glanced up at him, puzzled by his silence. Many men talked as if they never noticed her blushing.

However, he wasn't paying her any attention. He was looking over the top of her head and smiling into the crowd. She risked a peek beyond his wide shoulders and noted a great many ladies, married and not, had stopped their conversations and were openly watching them dance together.

She risked another peek at him, noting his interest in the crowd hadn't waned.

That stung.

Watching other women as he danced with her was very rude and humiliating. If dancing required nothing more than skilled footwork and a charming smile, no one would bother with the effort.

She began to look forward to their dance ending.

Lord Sorenson suddenly drew her closer against him. Closer than was strictly allowed for the waltz. Anna looked up in surprise to find him beaming at her as they made the final turns of the dance. As the music died, signaling the end of the set,

Anna's heart began to race. Her cheeks grew uncomfortably warm.

Lord Sorenson's eyes widened a touch more but he released her and stepped back to bow. Anna faced the musicians, face flaming, and clapped along with everyone else. What had that look meant?

Lord Sorenson touched her elbow softly, reclaiming her attention, and when she looked at him, he held out his arm for her to take. "You dance delightfully."

"So do you, my lord." Yet, Anna felt she had no choice but to compliment him in return. Her one moment of pleasure in the evening had become such a disappointing event. He hadn't really danced *with* her. Merely twirled her about, reveling in the attention from others. She had to wonder why Lord Sorenson had really asked her to dance tonight when it was clear he was more interested in everyone else.

Carmichael brushed past with Portia on his arm and winked at her. He was gone before she could react, and she was left with his distracted friend's company once more. Had Carmichael suggested Lord Sorenson take pity on her and ask her to stand up with him?

Since he'd done it before, Anna believed he would again.

She reluctantly took Lord Sorenson's offered arm and they strolled the entire length of the ballroom back to her father's side in awkward silence. Once there, Anna quickly separated herself from the earl. "Thank you for the dance, my lord."

He reached for her hand, and she reluctantly raised it. His grip was gentle as he bowed over it. "Miss Beasley," he murmured. "I very much look forward to seeing you again."

Why?

She did not say that out loud though. He departed, skirting the room, and stopped at Carmichael's side a moment. The pair exchanged a few words before each turned toward a different corner of the ballroom. Carmichael claimed Miss Lydia Goldwell as his next partner, and Lord Sorenson collected Miss Myra Lacy for his.

Myra Lacy was something of a chatterbox, and that seemed agreeable to Lord Sorenson. As the next set began, Sorenson was attentive to *her* as they danced, rarely glancing away from his new partner once.

Anna began to feel unwell, especially so when she discovered Carmichael watching her intently, a slight smirk on his face. Anna wished she were young enough to still poke her tongue out at him or perhaps throw something heavy in his direction. Dear God, that man would never change. He would forever plague her.

Carmichael winked at her again, and she turned her face away from him and the happy couple chattering on the dance floor. She was beyond mortified to have her nemesis suspect her of disappointment. He would say she deserved it for blushing so often. She did not need him to point out her flaws. She knew them all very well.

Face flushed with the evidence of her mortification, Anna barely heard another word of her father's conversation, or dared to look at those lining up for the next two dances that followed. When supper was announced she finally looked around. Carmichael and Sorenson must have already gone into supper. Father kept talking, unfortunately.

After five minutes, she tapped his arm. "Would you excuse me?"

Her father glanced around, frowning. "Supper?"

"Not exactly," she murmured.

"You will return straight away, with no side excursions," he demanded.

Anna nodded, allowing him to believe she was headed for the retiring room. "Thank you, Father," she murmured.

She felt only a little guilty for deceiving him. He was so strict sometimes it was stifling. She wasn't answering nature's call, as he'd assumed, but moved toward the quiet of Lord Williamson's library instead.

Lord Williamson's library was customarily off limits during any ball, but she knew he wouldn't mind her visit if she made it seem she was only interested in inspecting the large globe of the world that resided before his desk, something he was proud of showing off to everyone.

Anna slipped inside the dark room, noting there was only a low fire burning in the hearth. She shut the door behind her and leaned her whole weight against it as darkness swallowed her up. "Damn, damn, damn."

She covered her mouth over a frustrated scream. She had thought she might like Lord Sorenson at first, but he was obviously interested in everyone else.

Anna wallowed in self-pity a moment then nodded to herself. There were surely other gentlemen just as appealing somewhere. Eventually one would notice her and then…who knew what might happen.

She took a deep breath and stood straighter, determined to forget the disappointment of his disinterest. Her father waited for her. As the hall clock stuck midnight, Anna resolved not to care if she danced again tonight.

However, just as she was reaching for the doorknob to rejoin the ball, the door opened and a tall figure slipped inside the room with her. "It's as dark as hades in here."

Anna recognized the voice. *Carmichael.* Her nemesis come to torture her some more.

A second figure joined him. "Be quick in checking the desk."

That was undoubtedly Lord Sorenson's voice. She shivered, realizing that they didn't yet see her standing there. She eased farther behind the door, considering her chances of slipping around them and out of the room without having to speak to either one.

Unfortunately, Lord Sorenson closed the door suddenly. The darkness became a little thicker as one of them knelt by the fireside, and she had no chance to escape unnoticed. She inched toward the door anyway, hand outstretched.

Carmichael lit a taper, casting greater light about the room.

Lord Sorenson spotted her instantly, eyes widening in surprise.

Anna froze.

"Devil take it, Anna," Carmichael complained, as he rushed across the room toward her. "What are you doing sneaking up on us fellows like that?"

"You followed *me*. I was just leaving," Anna promised.

She did not want to be caught alone with that pair. She took two steps toward the door—then Carmichael's hand suddenly closed over her wrist and squeezed cruelly.

"How *could* you, Anna?"

Lord Sorenson approached. "Unhand her, Carmichael," he warned.

"No, Sorenson! Don't you see?"

That was the last straw.

Anna fought off Carmichael by kicking his shin. "Let go of me, you horrible man. I don't need or want your help."

"The hell you don't!" He scowled then tipped his head to the side and looked down, his jaw clenched.

Anna, still trapped in his unyielding grip, twisted to look behind her.

She immediately scrambled away from the fourth person in the room.

CHAPTER 5

Gilbert caught Anna Beasley against him because he feared she might scream. Even before her first gasp, he'd known she was innocent of the crime. And after her reaction, too real to be mistaken for anything but utter surprise, he kept hold of her because he couldn't seem to let her go.

It was a grim scene she'd stumbled upon in Lord Williamson's library. Another woman had been murdered.

There was blood everywhere this time. A young woman in a royal-blue muslin gown was splayed across a settee. He knew her identity even without seeing her face. He had danced with her earlier that night. "Miss Goldwell, if I am not mistaken," he murmured.

Carmichael crouched down, avoiding the pooling blood on the carpet, and touched Miss Goldwell's face and then her wrist. "She's still warm but quite dead."

At Carmichael's words, Miss Beasley struggled, attempting to flee the gruesome scene. Gilbert turned her into his chest and held her tightly against him with one arm, so she wouldn't have to witness anything more. "Wait a moment," he whispered to

Miss Beasley. He had some questions to ask of her even if she wasn't guilty.

Carmichael was pale but he skirted around the body carefully without touching anything. "Throat slashed from behind I think."

Miss Beasley's fingers scrambled at his waistcoat and a soft whimper came from her throat. "Miss Goldwell can't be dead."

Gilbert lifted Miss Beasley's face to his, holding her by the chin gently. The poor girl was so afraid, she was shaking like a leaf. "Do you happen to remember who Miss Goldwell spoke to after dancing with Carmichael?"

"I don't. I remained with my father. He lingered in the ballroom, talking with his friends until after the supper bell had rung."

She glanced over her shoulder, toward the late Miss Goldwell and Lord Carmichael, and shuddered. Gilbert turned her face back to his quickly as she sucked in a sharp, anguished breath. "Don't look. Whom did you dance with for the last set?"

"No one." Her gaze dropped to the vicinity of his chest.

He drew in a breath, drawing her sweet perfume into his lungs. The subtle lemon scent was preferred to the copper taint of blood in the air. "Why no one?"

She swallowed and looked away, drawing her hands to her chest and clenching them tightly. "I wasn't asked to dance a second time. Carmichael must have only one friend he felt he could force me upon."

Gilbert gaped. Carmichael had hinted Anna Beasley wasn't considered popular but he couldn't for the life of him understand why. She was a graceful dance partner and very easy on the eye. He'd enjoyed their dance very much, even if he'd been watching the guests for signs of guilt around Carmichael. "I'm sorry to hear that."

Miss Beasley shrugged. "The last time I saw Miss Goldwell was when she was with you, Lord Sorenson. I didn't notice her again."

He looked at Carmichael. "She cannot help."

Carmichael nodded so Gilbert propelled Anna Beasley gently toward the door. "Return to your father and say nothing of this."

Miss Beasley fought to stay. "But Miss Goldwell is dead."

"Carmichael and I will inform Bow Street."

She looked up at him, eyes huge. "I cannot leave. I'm a witness, am I not?"

"You must. You are completely innocent." In other ways too, he decided. He wouldn't be surprised if Miss Beasley had never had an ardent suitor before.

Gilbert cracked open the door to the hall and put his eye to the gap. The hall was deserted but not for long, he suspected. The time allotted for supper must end very soon. He turned to Miss Beasley, caught her by the elbow and brought her closer to the door. "When you return to the supper room, try to act as if nothing is the matter. You must think of your reputation."

"I'm innocent," she promised. "Ask anyone."

"I'm sure you are." He saw her frown and chuckled. "But you are alone now with two titled bachelors. Promise me you'll say nothing. If anyone learns of this private meeting there could be consequences, damage to your reputation."

"I'd not like anyone to misunderstand."

"I would not, either. Go now."

He pushed Miss Beasley out the door before she could say another word. She stood a moment, and then turned to stare at him. She looked utterly terrified, and as much as he wanted to reassure her everything would be all right, there was no time. The best place for Anna Beasley was with her father.

"By the by, Carmichael never did ask me to dance with you. I wanted to."

Her eyes widened prettily in surprise but Gilbert shut the door in her face and turned the key in the lock. He waited a moment, listening until he was certain Miss Beasley's footsteps were hurrying away from the library before he turned to view the murder scene again.

Carmichael had retreated from the late Miss Goldwell, holding his stomach as if he was on the brink of casting up his accounts. He stood at the fireside, staring into the flames a few moments more before he spoke again. "Another death on a Friday."

"So it seems. We will have to be quick and quiet about this," Gilbert whispered. "We must summon Davis to take over while we seek out Mr. Goldwell before he alerts others to his daughter's disappearance."

"You should be the investigator."

"That will not be my decision to make." However, Gilbert took in the murder scene and the poor dead girl across the room as if solving the case was his responsibility. Miss Goldwell had been left as she had fallen most likely, with her hand stretched out toward the door and holding her open dance card. He peeked at the names listed. The last man to dance with her before supper was known to him already. "We need to find Lord Wade before he can leave."

"Wade? Surely not him."

"Wade was her last dance partner."

Carmichael came closer and looked at the card too. "But Wade was not invited to the Berry ball. We cannot accuse a fellow peer without proof. You find him, and say I need to speak to him about a house he owns on Hanover Square. He'll think nothing untoward about that. He's been trying to sell the place for months without revealing his true reasons."

"The two deaths may be unrelated. It is best to assume they are not and keep an open mind." Gilbert did not know Lord Wade but could recognize him in a crowded ballroom. "What are Wade's reasons for selling?"

"He's lost quite a lot gambling of late, I hear."

Gilbert winced. "If Wade is short of funds, I would have thought he would be marrying heiresses rather than murdering them."

"Exactly. It may not be him but you must find out. I'll stay here to ensure the scene is not disturbed until we can send for Davis," Carmichael promised. "You find Wade now and speak to him."

Knowing time was of the essence and discretion called for, Gilbert left not via the locked set of doors but through a set of terrace windows so he could return to the ballroom without anyone wondering where he'd been during supper.

The moment he entered the room, Gilbert sighted Anna Beasley. She stood with Miss Hayes again and appeared to be laughing at some jest the other young lady made. Her cheeks were flushed with hot color and he breathed a little easier that nothing had changed with her. He was pleased that she'd taken his advice to heart and seemed to be acting completely normally.

But in her shadow, close to the entrance hall doorway, Lord Wade watched her and Miss Hayes talking together. The man was not smiling.

Gilbert stalked toward Lord Wade, aware he felt protective of Anna Beasley. He wasted no time drawing the man's attention to him. "Good evening, Lord Wade."

"Ah, Lord Sorenson, is it?" Wade murmured, lips twisting into a welcoming smile. "I thought you must have dashed off somewhere with your last dance partner. A private supper for two, perhaps," he whispered.

"No," Gilbert ground out. "I thought *you* might have, though."

Lord Wade's smile slipped, replaced by wariness. "Miss Hayes would never consent to leave the ballroom with the likes of me."

Gilbert was unconvinced by that statement. "Your last dance partner was Miss Goldwell, wasn't it?"

"Miss Goldwell was not to be found when the time came." Wade shook his head, clearly disgusted with the fact he'd been forgotten. "Miss Lacy had found herself in want of a partner. Lord Grindlewood had suffered an injury and begged me to take the floor with her instead. How could I refuse?"

"I see." He studied Lord Wade. His waistcoat was cream silk

and pristine, his coat dark and his knee stockings a bright white. There was no sign of blood upon his clothing. However, if the killer had attacked from behind, there might be blood on their fingers. Lord Wade's hands were hidden beneath a pair of white gloves.

The fellow looked behind him. "Yes, Aunt. I'll stay right here until you've said goodbye to our hosts and then we'll go home together."

An older lady shuffled past them, using a cane to forge a path through the crowd. Lord Wade rolled his eyes once she was gone. "My aunt, Mrs. Lenthall. I swear, she still thinks of me as a boy of ten when it is *she* who must be worried about," he grumbled. "Don't dare slip away with a pretty face for even ten minutes."

"Is your aunt ill?"

"Only old and entirely too fond of drink," Lord Wade complained with a smile. "No wine cellar is safe with her around, but she is family, so I make allowances for her indulgences," he said, a fond smile curving his lips.

Gilbert flicked his gaze down to Lord Wade's hands again momentarily. Something about his demeanor seemed entirely wrong for a killer. He needed to see his hands before the fellow left the ball with his aunt. If there was the slightest hint of blood under his nails, Gilbert would detain him.

Lord Wade arched a brow. "Are you in the market for a new glove maker? I got this pair, and a dozen others, from a little shop in Ramsgate last summer. Excellent fit from the very first wear."

"May I see one in closer detail?" Gilbert asked, aware it was an odd request to make in the middle of the ball. However, Mrs. Lenthall was standing opposite them, wobbling like a drunken sailor as she spoke with their host. He did not want to alert anyone unnecessarily by causing a scene as he dragged her nephew in for questioning if it was not necessary.

Wade peeled one glove from his right hand and passed it over. "The others are as well constructed. Took less than a day for the kid gloves I chose for riding to fit my hands perfectly. Butter soft and only a few shillings each, quite the bargain."

He pretended to inspect the construction of the glove, examining the white material for telltale staining from blood. Pristine, if a little damp from being worn all night. He looked at the fellow's other hand.

Wade peeled that off too with a laugh. "You take glove construction very seriously, my lord."

"Indeed I do."

Nothing at all. But soiled gloves could be replaced, and Lord Wade had admitted to owning a prodigious amount of them. Gilbert held the gloves out, noting Lord Wade reached with his left hand. He inspected the cuff of Lord Wade's left shirt sleeve carefully. Nothing there, either.

Which probably lost him his first suspect in Miss Goldwell's murder. He chose to remain with Lord Wade and see what else he might reveal about himself.

Wade's attention shifted to the dance in progress. "Are you always so interested in the dressing habits of others?"

"I am tonight," he muttered under his breath.

Lord Wade leaned close. "Do you want the name of my tailor, too?"

"No. I am quite content with my own."

Lord Wade looked him up and down then smiled. "An excellent decision, and an excellent tailor, by the look of what you're wearing tonight. We must discuss boot makers next time we meet up at a ball. I do love odd conversations like this."

"I'm glad I can offer you a diversion."

"I make do as I can," he promised. Wade leaned close. "I should warn you though, Sorenson. You are in danger."

A chill swept through Gilbert at the threat but he'd been warned off before. "From whom?"

"From about a dozen nearly panting ladies with or without husbands, of course." Wade chuckled. "Step lively, man, and keep moving before the wrong one catches you. Most of them are not worth your time."

Gilbert was about to leave there and then, but that last remark stirred his interest. He hadn't mingled in London society often, but if he had to fit in, or convince others that a marriage might be on the cards, he'd like to know where to begin to look and who to avoid. Wade had an advantage he could make use of. "Who would be worth my time?"

"You already know her."

"Do I?" Gilbert knew very few ladies in London. Perhaps a dozen at most even now, but none he'd consider pursuing. Well, maybe only one, really. He did all he could not to turn and stare at Anna Beasley.

"I will not say her name and risk adding to her anxiety. You will figure out her ways in due time, I'm sure," Wade suggested, and then followed with a bawdy laugh. He recovered and nodded, still smirking. "I do love this part of a couple's courtship. People try so hard to hide their interest but a little threat or healthy competition usually does the trick to spur on a serious pursuit."

"Do you usually toy with the affections of others?"

"Only when they are being very foolish." Lord Wade chuckled again and stepped forward to intercept his relation. "Ready to leave, Auntie?"

"Indeed I am." Mrs. Lenthall winked at Gilbert as she took her nephew's arm and then said in a soft, disgusted voice, "Williamson waters his wine. So undignified."

Lord Wade patted her hand and, after bidding him good-bye, they left the ballroom together, chatting the whole of the way.

Gilbert glanced around, noting he was indeed an object of interest to a number of ladies, including Miss Beasley.

Gilbert smiled at her despite his disappointment. None of the information he'd gleaned tonight was particularly useful in pursuing Angela Berry's killer, or Miss Goldwell's, either.

He made his way back to the library, encountering Davis on the way, dressed in servants livery. "What are you doing here?"

"There's more than one way to attend a ball."

"Good thinking." He checked that no one was around. "We have a situation in the library and since you're here, I need a man and older lady followed. The name is Lord Wade. They are just leaving the ball."

"I'll see to it and join you in a moment," Davis promised, slipping away as quickly as he'd come.

Carmichael rushed toward him as soon as he entered the library. "I think it's the same killer."

He stared at his friend. "How did you reach that conclusion?"

"The slice angles downward to the right," he said, while making a cutting motion.

"So."

"The wound. The killer used their right hand to cut from behind. Angela was stabbed from the right, too."

It wasn't wise to leap to conclusions, he was wary of adding fuel to Carmichael's theory at first. "Lord Wade is left-handed I think."

Carmichael clenched his jaw a moment. "You know what this second death means, don't you? It could be the fourth, if you count the earlier two I know of."

Gilbert studied his friend's worried face, and then sighed. A multiple murderer might be running amok in society. If that were true, they had to be found and stopped. "It is possible it could be the same man."

They were silent a long time and Gilbert shivered. Carmichael's wild theory might not be so implausible after all. Miss Goldwell tonight, Miss Berry last week, and the two other deceased women known to Carmichael—found almost at the same time of night. On a Friday before midnight. The chances of such a coincidence must be astronomical.

"The papers will dub the fiend the Friday Killer," Carmichael warned as he closed his eyes tightly. "I used to like that night of the week best of all."

He grasped Carmichael by the shoulder. If the killer acted only on a Friday, then they had another week to catch them before the story made the papers and the *ton* erupted in panic.

CHAPTER 6

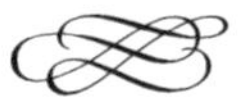

No matter the weather, Anna could always count on Lady Scott being at home when she called in the morning.

Anna and her maid entered Lady Scott's modest dwelling in Mayfair at precisely ten o'clock on a dreary Wednesday morning, and she breathed a sigh of relief that she'd reached her destination without bursting into fresh tears.

After what she had seen at last Friday's ball, fear was never far away, too. The passage of days had not altered her memory about how Miss Goldwell had been murdered. The violence of her demise haunted her. The worst of it was, she had no one to comfort her about it. No one but Lord Sorenson and Lord Carmichael, and she did not want to seek out either of them. She couldn't admit to them that she was afraid.

Her maid, Jane, was aware she was out of sorts about something, but left her alone to find her own peace. Jane was good that way. She didn't pry or prattle to Anna's father, either.

Lady Scott's home was blessedly quiet after the chaos of Anna's newest nightmare last night. She had not been able to forget what she'd witnessed in Lord Williamson's library, and her dreams had twisted the encounter horribly so she'd barely been able to close her eyes at night.

The butler announced them and Anna bade her maid wait behind in the hall. She entered Lady Scott's private sanctum and all her fears of lurking danger vanished into thin air at the countess' welcoming smile. Nothing bad could ever happen around Lady Scott. The countess would never allow a single rule to be broken in her presence.

Her mentor was waiting for her, a serene smile on her face. Dressed in black day and night—she'd been widowed years ago—she always appeared elegant and regal. Anna could only hope to be half as well turned out later in her life. "Lady Scott."

"Miss Beasley. How good of you to call on me this morning."

Anna curtsied and seated herself when directed to a chair. She folded her hands neatly into her lap, tucking her feet close together beneath her. She straightened her spine and refused to slouch even a little despite being with a close friend. "It is good to see you again."

"And you. You are up very early today and appear uneasy. I trust nothing is wrong at home."

Lady Scott was always perceptive. "No. Nothing is wrong at home," she assured Lady Scott, gulping back a sudden desire to blurt out everything she shouldn't say. She'd given her word and could not break it.

Lady Scott's eyes narrowed suddenly. "I saw you with Lord Sorenson Friday night."

"Yes, we waltzed. A single dance only."

Lady Scott studied her carefully. "I trust his company was pleasant. My godson speaks highly of him, but a lady can learn so much more of a man's true nature by the way he dances."

"Yes, indeed I agree with you on that subject." Lord Sorenson had had other women on his mind but she couldn't really complain of that to Lady Scott. "He danced the waltz very well."

Lady Scott sat back and smiled. "Good. I've heard nothing but praise for how Lord Sorenson conducts himself in society from those who should know. A far cry from his father's scandalous reputation of years ago. What does your father say of the young earl?"

"My father hasn't mentioned the earl again since the night they first met at Almack's Assembly," Anna told her honestly. Father had shown little interest in discussing the few gentlemen Anna might have an interest in, as evidenced by his constant mention of Carmichael.

Lady Scott tapped on the armrest of her chair with one elegant finger. "I could not help but notice you and my godson were absent from the supper room Friday night."

"I cannot speak for Lord Carmichael's whereabouts that night, of course," Anna assured her, but she had her explanation ready and rehearsed in case of questions. "But I felt a little unwell for a time after the waltz, all that spinning about I suppose, and when supper was announced I escaped to the retiring room until the sensation passed."

Lady Scott frowned. "I trust you recovered swiftly."

"Oh, yes indeed. Fit as a fiddle now, in fact," Anna promised.

But she had cast up her accounts Friday night as soon as she'd reached the relative privacy of her bedchamber, and any food she saw even now made her queasy. "Father is well, too."

"I am very glad to hear it."

Lady Scott's servant interrupted them, bringing tea and a plate of little cakes. Anna knew better than to accept one.

Lady Scott passed over her tea, black and unsweetened. "What brings you out so early today, my dear?"

Anna bit her lip and then straightened her spine. It was time to stop being so timid about gentlemen. Life could be short and so unfairly taken away. "I wanted to ask you for advice about a gentleman of my acquaintance."

"Which one?"

"Lord Wade?"

Lady Scott shook her head swiftly. "No. He is not for you."

Undeterred, Anna continued. "He's been very attentive these

past weeks. Father has noticed how often we dance, which makes me believe I should consider him, and at least learn more about him. I wanted to seek your opinion, too. He is a viscount and his family is well connected."

"And so you should apply to my judgment of any suitor." Lady Scott seemed to consider the matter for a few moments. "I am well acquainted with Lord Wade and his aunt, and am quite sure a marriage into the Wade family would *not* suit your family."

"But he's accepted at Almack's," Anna reminded her. "His aunt was perhaps a little intimidating when we first met, but she does speak to me now without first inspecting me with her lorgnette. You also said the man I consider to marry must be one who could gain admittance to the assembly rooms."

"I do agree that *is* essential," Lady Scott replied. "I had expected you to have set your cap a little higher than a mere viscount, my dear."

She knew that. Unfortunately, the earl she'd admired last season had surprised everyone by announcing he was married quite suddenly. Other than Lord Louth, she'd seen few gentlemen who appealed to her as much. Perhaps it was time to forget the importance of titles altogether or a gentleman's physical appeal. She did not wish to live out her days as an old maid.

Anna smiled. "All I want is to marry someone who will be kind to me. Gaining a title is not as important to me as it is to other women of my acquaintance."

"That I will never accept." Lady Scott was about to continue when the butler tapped on the door again. "Forgive the intrusion, my lady, but Lord Carmichael wonders if you might have a moment to spare him?"

"Carmichael?" Anna's discomfort returned.

Lady Scott glanced her way with a delighted smile. "He must have known. How pleasant to have my two favorite young people call on me at the very same time. Do send him in to us."

Anna basked in her praise, ignoring her mention of Carmichael. Lady Scott had once claimed Carmichael singled her out because he liked her, that his once childish pranks and taunts disguised his real interest. Anna hadn't the heart to correct Lady Scott's delusions. They would never see eye to eye about the Earl of Carmichael. Regardless of what Carmichael may or may not think of her, Anna would never like him after all he'd done.

Carmichael burst into the room, full of exuberant energy as he greeted his godmother. "There you are—the most beautiful woman in all of London," he gushed.

"Charmer," Lady Scott murmured as Carmichael kissed her on both cheeks like the good little boy he always pretended to be around his godmother.

He faced Anna next and drew close. "Anna, what an unexpected surprise to find you here, and out of bed so early. You're usually still abed at this hour."

"I'm always awake at this time of day. I just pretend not to be so I don't have to speak to you," she informed him as softly as she could so Lady Scott would not understand her words.

"Children. Now gather about me," Lady Scott begged. "It is so good to see you both together and looking so well."

Carmichael seemed startled by his godmother's request, but then he smiled warmly as he sank into a chair a good distance from Anna. "Did you and your father leave the ball early Friday night?"

"Yes." Anna marveled that he appeared unaffected by the horror of a murder. She wasn't as lucky as he seemed to be.

"A pity. I had hoped to speak to your father before you both left. Haven't found the time to call on him at home since. Why did you both leave early?"

What a foolish question to ask of her. It had taken all of her persuasion to convince Father not to stay until the very last set without explaining why she wanted to go.

Lady Scott clucked her tongue at Carmichael. "There is nothing to worry about but your concern for Anna does you credit. Anna suffered a slight headache but is very well now, as you can see. The noise of the crowd can put one out of sorts very easily. Lady Williamson's ballroom was far too crowded. She should know better than to invite so many guests by now."

"True. But I do love the noise and chaos of the Williamsons' events myself," Carmichael professed as he finally settled back into his chair, slinging one leg over the arm as if he lived there. "And what of you that night, my dear godmother? You were at home and tucked up in bed by one o'clock with your nightly sherry, I suppose?"

Lady Scott touched her cheek. "A woman my age must do all she can to take care of herself. You could benefit from an early night or two, young man. You need a wife to look after you too, I think."

He shook his head swiftly and his laugher filled the room. "You've always retired too early for my taste, but it is always at night when the most exciting things happen to me," he promised, winking. "As for taking a wife, I'll tell you about my latest misadventure another day and you'll see why I would make anyone a poor husband."

Anna frowned at him. "What of Miss Berry? I take it you've forgotten you made her fall in love with you."

Carmichael appeared taken aback by mention of Miss Berry, but then he smiled brightly. "Such concern for my love life, Miss Beasley! You wound my heart!"

The mention of wounds made her think of poor Miss Goldwell, and how awfully she'd died. She blanched and considered casting up her accounts there and then.

Carmichael must have finally seen her distress, because he turned his attention to his godmother quickly and dominated the conversation. They spoke of the people they had met at the previous Friday's ball. He even slipped in a mention of poor Miss Goldwell, but managed not to reveal he knew of her death. After a few moments, Anna gathered her wits. She was in danger of overstaying her welcome in Lady Scott's drawing room, and that would provoke another lecture on manners at a later date.

As soon as the pair paused for breath, she quickly said, "I should be going."

"It is always a pleasure to have you come to call, my dear." Lady Scott smiled warmly at them both. "Carmichael will escort you to your carriage, Miss Beasley," she murmured.

"Yes, indeed. But I must be going too, unfortunately. I have more errands to run and Sorenson is expecting me. I cannot let him down. I promised to dine with him at the club and I need all the time I can spare to dress for the occasion." He kissed the woman's cheeks yet again, smiling widely. "Goodbye, fair lady."

"Try to be good, Carmichael," Lady Scott begged.

"I'll do my best," he told her. "But as always, there are so many pretty distractions that I can make you no promises."

Carmichael held out his arm but Anna pretended not to see the gesture as she fetched a handkerchief from her reticule and walked to the door. She brushed her nose with it and descended the front stairs with her maid at her side without waiting for him to catch up.

Carmichael followed her all the way to the carriage door. "How are you really?" he whispered.

"I'm in perfect health," she promised him.

"I'm not blind, Anna. There are dark circles beneath your eyes as if you haven't slept a wink," he continued as he helped her inside. He helped the maid in too and then, to her shock, joined them.

"What are you doing?" she demanded. "Get out immediately."

"I really do need to speak to your father," he claimed as he made himself at home in Anna's carriage, taking up all the empty space around poor Jane.

She scowled at him. "Then take your own conveyance."

"I sent it away when I arrived. Besides, there's nothing improper here. It's an open carriage and you have your maid to act as chaperone," he remarked, glancing toward the grinning maid. "There couldn't be a safer place to be. Jane here is quite sure to keep you from throttling me for any offense I might give."

The maid stifled a laugh. "It's no secret at home that Miss Anna would rather die than be alone with you, Lord Carmichael. I'll protect you."

Carmichael smirked at the maid's remark and then glanced at Anna with one brow raised. "You find me *that* repulsive?"

Anna smiled serenely and ignored the question. "What do you want with my father?"

"I was going to ask if he might like to spend Christmas at Edenmere this year. The place has become a tomb in recent years. You could come, and Jane, too, of course. I'm sure she would like to escape London and continue to protect me from your wrath."

"What makes you think your loneliness is reason enough to visit you?"

"I never said I was lonely," Carmichael said very slowly. "I was thinking it was time to open the house again to friends, now the renovations are done."

Anna and Carmichael were not friends. She wouldn't visit him unless Father insisted she had to. "You haven't hosted a holiday party since your parents died."

"No. Obviously not." He crossed his arms over his chest. "You may invite your friend, Miss Hayes, too, if you feel the need for added protection."

Anna shook her head. "Father and I have already discussed what we will do this winter. Lord Windermere is very keen for us to join them for Christmas at the Duke of Exeter's estate."

"Exeter, eh? Well, I cannot compete with that sort of invitation. I'm sure you'd rather go there." He told the driver to pull out of the traffic so he could exit the carriage. "I'll speak to your father another time about Christmas. Or perhaps he'll be interested in coming to stay next year after he's married you off. I'll see you at the Windermere ball."

Anna grabbed his arm before he could climb down from the

carriage. "Do not even think of asking your friend to dance with me again," she hissed.

He smiled widely. "As he said, I never did ask him to dance with you. He did that all on his own. I suspect you might have found a real admirer in him, Anna," he suggested. "Just remember, if you ignore the somber vicar's guise he chooses to don still, Sorenson is cut from the same cloth as every lord in London. We all want the same thing from a pretty woman," he said, including Jane in his warning look. "Be cautious of anyone who would lure you off alone."

Anna could only stare after Carmichael as he strode away. Despite the years of discord between them, and the warnings he'd uttered today, Carmichael had actually said something nice about her—thought she was *pretty* and had said so out loud!

She looked at Jane but she was staring after Carmichael, too. "He must be feeling ill or something," Anna murmured after she'd asked the coachman to continue driving them home.

"Or something," Jane agreed with a final shake of her head.

CHAPTER 7

Gilbert waved away the White's waiter impatiently when he lingered too long beside their table. "I said that will be all."

Carmichael raised a brow at his abrupt manner. "You seem out of sorts today."

Gilbert scowled and looked away. It burned that this killer remained undetected.

There hadn't been any reason for Miss Goldwell's death. None he could determine that did not involve the ridiculous idea she'd been killed because Carmichael had kissed her once. She'd been a bubbly and bright young woman. She'd had an easy manner, and was accomplished at music and art. She'd been loyal and well-liked by her friends and acquaintances. In short, she had great potential to make a good match this season. There were no dark skeletons in her closet. Her family were all upstanding members of society without a hint of scandal about them. "I cannot determine the reason the killer singled her out," he confessed.

Carmichael smiled tightly. "You know my thoughts on this so I will not repeat them again. If another reason exists, you will find it."

Gilbert glanced about White's but saw only strangers. He'd been a member of White's since shortly after his birth. Father had arranged his membership, though, as a vicar, he'd seldom had an excuse to come here. They were seated in the Morning Room, far enough away from their fellow members to keep an eye on them but not close enough to be overheard or encourage anyone to join them. He had a view of the ground floor hall to see who came and went and a view of the famous bay window, where Beau Brummell was currently holding court. Gilbert hadn't an acquaintance with him yet, nor did he wish to foster one in the future with such a ridiculous dandy.

"I wish I had your faith right now." He rubbed a hand over his face. He'd barely slept for the past few nights. He'd been prowling about society in Carmichael's shadow, pretending to enjoy himself. But every conversation he'd participated in frustrated him more. As much as he disliked the notion, heiresses *were* dying left and right. Further investigation had uncovered three other deaths last season, and all remained unexplained still. Gilbert had been given all the information to study and had been appalled that no one else had seen what Carmichael had stumbled upon by chance.

"What has you so concerned? I mean, you seem more perturbed than when you began."

"The violence is escalating. Miss Berry's death was quick and clean. Miss Goldwell's demise was carried out with brutal and very obvious intent."

"Do you think they suffered?" Carmichael asked.

"I hope not. Miss Goldwell was surprised perhaps, attacked when her back was turned. Lady Berry's conservatory was not lit well on the night of the ball." He licked his lips. "Our killer seems to lack the honor to look his victims in the eye."

Carmichael sat forward. "A weakness?"

"A hint of his true nature perhaps. A cowardly act."

"So, what you are saying is, we are not looking for a forward, outspoken person but someone no one considers in any way dangerous at first glance, or even second and third. Someone skilled at moving through society largely undetected."

"Exactly." He snapped his fingers and sat back. But that knowledge didn't help them one whit. Cowards did not wear a sign upon their backs, and they were very good at hiding their flaws.

"The Duke of Exeter has arrived," Carmichael murmured quietly, dropping his chin as if trying to hide. "Damn it all."

Gilbert turned his head slightly, noting the older man had come with his nephew, the Marquess of Ettington. The duke stared in his direction, frowned and then nodded, acknowledging him. They might speak, but then again, they might not. Exeter and his father had held opposing political views—often quite heatedly exchanged views across the floor of parliament and here, he'd heard.

As the duke finished his conversation with his nephew, he turned and came to meet Gilbert.

"My condolences," Exeter said as he extended his hand.

"Thank you, your grace," he murmured.

The duke looked about the room a moment. "What brings you to London, Sorenson?"

Taking the duke into his confidence was not part of his plan. In the future his connections might be useful to the investigation. But he needed more than suspicions to bring to the duke. He shrugged away the question and smiled. "The usual."

The duke smirked. "Hunting a bride already?"

Gilbert nearly choked, but noted many gentlemen appeared to be listening in now and nodding sagely. "Why would you think that?"

"You both attended Almack's. A first, I believe. It is all anyone is talking about."

He glanced at Carmichael. Gossip about them was expected but not quite so far reaching as to fill the duke's ears.

"We went for the amusement of the experience," Carmichael added glibly, finally looking up. "You'll be pleased to know the vaulted ceilings did not tremble to have men such as us attend those hallowed halls."

"The place could use a good scandal now and then." The duke chuckled without warmth. "But there's plenty of excitement and ladies to be found everywhere else, I hear."

Gilbert gestured to Carmichael. "Carmichael is all I require in a companion for now."

"Indeed. He is quite a character." The duke shrugged but then glared at Carmichael. "You stole my French chef from me."

Carmichael sighed, appearing pained. "I assure you, I tried to send him back but he won't go. He claims he'd rather cook for one than sit in a cold kitchen."

"What?" Gilbert frowned, not understanding the banter.

Carmichael smiled his way. "The duke has been traveling with family for most of the year."

The duke's eyes narrowed with displeasure. "I adore my family, but they do not visit London enough to appreciate my former cook's culinary efforts."

"And that is the only reason Monsieur Laffitte answered my advertisement," Carmichael promised him. "He felt he was unneeded."

The duke snorted. "Yes, well. White's will do for dinners for the present moment. It is so hard to keep good help these days. Do excuse me."

"Of course."

Exeter turned away, joining a pair of older gentlemen Gilbert did not recognize, who seemed very happy to meet him. He looked to Carmichael for information.

"The Duke of Staines and his younger brother, Lord Lynton Manning."

"I don't remember meeting them before."

"Not surprising. Staines hosts a good dinner now and then, though he's been keeping to himself this past year or so. The brother was once a vicar like you. Sermonized from the pulpit of St. George's until his marriage."

"Oh?" He looked at the gentleman closely. He seemed not at all familiar.

"Gave the church up for love. Estella Ryall, once Viscountess Carrington."

Now that title was familiar. "She has a son and daughter? Oscar, I think his first name was. Cannot remember the girl."

Carmichael nodded. "Both married with a dozen brats between them now. Not all of them are Carrington's, I hasten to add, but wards or some such nonsense. Bit of a scandal with his marriage. Breach of promise suit turned quite nasty. He too keeps to himself these days."

Gilbert nodded. "We were at school together with him."

"Were we?" Carmichael brushed lint from his sleeve. "And yet I don't remember Carrington at all."

"Why would you remember anyone? You hardly attended school." Gilbert laughed. "Your outside activities kept you quite busy."

"I'll have you know my education was first rate," Carmichael promised.

"Brothels do not count. Yet somehow you achieved an education most would envy, skipping lectures and still ranking as one of the smartest men I know."

"Not smart enough," Carmichael slouched a little, revealing his discontent.

Keeping Carmichael's spirits up was almost a full-time occupation for a friend. "Billiards or cards?"

"The betting book first then billiards. I feel the need to hit something."

They made their way to the betting book and scanned the latest wagers.

Carmichael sucked in a sharp breath. "Lord W bet Lord E that Miss B will marry Lord S before the season is out. That wouldn't be about you, would it?"

Gilbert shoved Carmichael aside and scanned the page. "Where does it say that?"

Carmichael laughed softly. "Just checking your reaction."

Gilbert scowled at his friend and then stalked toward the rear of White's without him. Now he too needed to hit something rather than his friend.

At the main stairs they were joined by Lord Wade, who seemed to have had the same idea as them about playing billiards. "Lord Wade."

"My lords." Wade allowed them to enter the Billiard Room first but turned toward an empty table and began to set up shots to play against himself.

Gilbert set up the balls and allowed Carmichael to break. Carmichael's shot cracked through the room and he sank two balls straight away.

"Beginners luck," Gilbert grumbled.

"Years more practice in low places than you, I expect, my friend."

Gilbert hid a smile and waited until it was his turn. Then he destroyed Carmichael's advantage by sinking every ball including the black.

He stood back finally, noting they'd drawn a crowd. "You deserved that for your earlier remark."

Carmichael stared at him in apparent shock. "Where did you learn to do that?"

He shrugged. "Between sermons. What else was there to do?"

Carmichael slung an arm around Gilbert's shoulders and shook him. "Remind me not to tease you about Miss B again."

"You really shouldn't tease her, either."

"You seem to have made an impression on her. She spoke very highly of you to my godmother earlier today."

"You finally spoke to her?" Gilbert asked, concerned for the woman. He'd been considering calling on her but wasn't sure how he'd be able to find out how she fared with a chaperone or her father in the room, too. "How is she?"

Carmichael winced. "She did not say much, there was a maid

present the whole time I was with her, but I know Anna well. She's very upset."

A throat cleared behind Gilbert suddenly, and he spun about. "Yes?"

"Can I challenge either one of you to a game?"

Carmichael smiled quickly. "Certainly, Wade. I'd be happy to play against you, for I shall never dare play against Lord Sorenson again."

Gilbert just laughed. He found a spot against a wall and pushed Miss Beasley's distress from his mind to watch the game unfold.

"You may break," Lord Wade told Carmichael, which was only fair, given he'd been the one to challenge Gilbert's friend.

Carmichael broke, exhibiting the same decisive precision as before. This time he sank three balls before ceding to Wade. The crowd of onlookers wandered away and Gilbert was grateful to be more or less alone. Watching every word around others was difficult.

Lord Wade took a moment to assess the placement of the balls on the table. "What are you pair up to?"

"Hoping not to lose again," Carmichael promised.

Wade glanced Gilbert's way. "I am aware of your other rather unusual set of skills, my lord. Vicars who solve murders are quite rare."

Gilbert's senses tingled but he made himself appear relaxed. "Former vicar."

"I misspoke. My apologies." Lord Wade performed his shot, sinking his color. "Do you know, I have heard that the Sorenson estates are in a rather bad way and were in dire need for attention before you inherited?"

Gilbert straightened, affronted. "The Sorenson estates are in good order. Whoever said they were not?"

"Well, everyone. Gossip about you is rife." Lord Wade sank another ball quickly. "Another rumor circulating is that you are here to find a wealthy bride, although I have trouble believing that tale. Even with Exeter's assumption just now."

Gilbert stared at the fellow, puzzled by his demeanor. "Do you always listen to private conversations?"

"Only when something juicy is being spoken of. Most often of late, that is you. But in this case today, the duke raised his voice as I was passing so of course I heard his question, along with everyone else in the Morning Room." Lord Wade frowned at the table. "If you want people to wonder about you, by all means keep everyone guessing which rumor is true."

"What other stories are circulating?"

Wade beamed. "My absolute favorite is that you've come to London to sow your oats after a boring few years as a vicar."

"That's a lie."

"I think so, too. Your attention swings from one pretty young thing to another too quickly. Are all of the rumors fabrications? I think they must be." Lord Wade sank another shot. When he straightened, he looked directly at Carmichael. "What has become of Miss Angela Berry?"

Carmichael grew pale.

"She was most often seen in your company until recently. Everyone knows a match was to be made between you both. But her family removed from London without warning and Miss Berry informed no one when she would return. In fact, none of her closest friends have heard from her since her mother's ball. They are becoming distressed about her absence from society."

Gilbert glanced about discreetly when Carmichael remained silent. They were alone for now. "What interest do you have in Miss Berry?"

"None. But watching the lengths she took to slip away from her chaperones to meet Carmichael here for kisses was the most amusement I've had at some *ton* events. I cannot believe she just gave up the hope that you'd offer for her. She seemed most ardently willing to be in love with you."

Carmichael froze. "She was."

Lord Wade tilted his head slightly. "She *was*. Are you?"

"Yes," Carmichael whispered. "I was in love with her, too."

Lord Wade set the cue back in its place on the wall bracket without another word. He stepped up to Lord Carmichael's side.

"Was? My condolences then," Lord Wade whispered. "She's not the only one, is she?"

"No." Gilbert moved closer, wondering what else Lord Wade had figured out on his own. "But no one can know."

Lord Wade's lips twitched. "I'm no one then."

Gilbert was about to say more when Lord Wade bowed. "I shouldn't detain you a moment longer. Do excuse me. I'll see you at the next ball."

Lord Wade strode off.

"Sorenson?"

"He's not the killer," Gilbert promised Carmichael.

"Then what is he about to ask so many questions about Angela?"

Gilbert wasn't sure. "I think we may have just recruited another set of eyes for the hunt."

Carmichael raked his hand through his hair. "But none of the ladies seem to like him very much. How can he help?"

"That could be useful." Gilbert smiled, feeling optimistic again. "They won't be watching him watching *them*. Everyone will be looking at you and the young ladies you single out, including the killer, I suspect, if your theory is correct. I think we can make good use of him."

CHAPTER 8

Anna applied her fan to cool her hot face and glanced with longing toward the open ballroom doors of Lord Windermere's residence. "Goodness, it is warm tonight."

Her companion was again Lord Wade, who seemed to be everywhere she'd been in the ballroom tonight. He'd asked her to take a turn about the room, since the dance floor was smaller than most and the numbers attempting to dance too great. It was safer this way, he claimed, and Anna had grudgingly agreed with him.

"It is indeed, even with the doors open," he remarked, glancing toward them, too.

They sidestepped a couple from the dance floor who had lost their way, and smiled at each other as they resumed their promenade.

Lord Wade was being very nice to her. Perhaps it was time to see if he sought her out because he was interested in romancing her. "Wouldn't it be wonderful to simply step outside together for a breath of fresh air?"

He looked at her, eyebrows raised high. "By all means, ask

your father to escort you if you need a respite from the ball," he offered. "I'd be happy to take you back to him if you prefer."

Anna was disappointed in his reply. If Lord Wade was interested, he should have leapt at the chance to stay at her side. Since he seemed indifferent, did that mean he found her uninteresting?

Lord Wade caught her eye, and then laughed softly. "Trust me, it's for the best," he promised.

"Of course." She glanced at the chaos of the dance floor, rather than think about her lack of suitors. "Lord and Lady Windermere's ball has proved immensely popular, don't you think? And while I dearly love to dance, this was very pleasant, too."

"Safer. Thank you for not dancing with me tonight," he replied as her father came into view at the far end of the room.

She nodded toward their hosts across the room—and stared in shock. Lady Windermere was caught in her husband's embrace yet again. "They look so happy together."

"Besotted indeed, as all newly married couples should be," Wade advised sagely.

She looked up at him in surprise. "They act so differently from other married couples I know."

"Openly combative one moment and yet still obviously smitten with each other the next. It's early days yet for their marriage." Lord Wade smirked. "There's nothing like a good argument between lovers to fire the blood."

Anna's face heated, but then she sighed with longing as her cousin placed a tender kiss to his wife's palm, smiling devilishly before he sauntered off into the crowd. Lady Windermere watched him go with a happy smile playing over her lips.

The pair were rather plainly in love, which was nice to see in a couple their age, but they made her envious, too. She wanted that for herself. She wanted to marry a man who wanted nothing more than to be with her. "Do you believe in love, Lord Wade?"

"Indeed I do. That's why I'm yet to marry."

She glanced at him, curiosity stirred. "I thought you might not have married because you haven't met the right woman."

"I've met her, but we're unfortunately stuck at the denial stage—before any of the lovely intimate pleasantries can commence."

She thought she knew what he meant and struggled not to blush in response. Had he not even kissed the object of his affections yet? Since Anna clearly wasn't the one to catch his eye, she felt instant sympathy for his situation. She hadn't met the right man yet either, she supposed.

"Poor Lord Wade." Anna laughed softly. "I wish you well in the end but with that naughty tongue of yours, you will probably have to wait a good long while yet."

Anna slapped a hand over her mouth but instead of being offended, Lord Wade burst out laughing.

"At last!" he cried.

"I am so sorry. I should never have said anything of the sort," she promised him. Why had she said that out loud?

"Nonsense. Your honesty is so refreshing. I have been waiting for you to say exactly what you think for so long. I never thought this day would come," he chortled again. "I'm impressed."

"Shh," she warned, glancing around her anxiously. "Be silent."

Instead, Lord Wade laughed even harder. He wiped at his eyes with his thumb. "I knew I liked you. We're friends, yes?"

Friends wasn't so bad, she supposed. At least Lord Wade could always be counted on to stand up with her at a ball when she lacked a dance partner. "Yes."

Anna and Wade had to pause their stroll when the path became congested. She looked around, seeking a way forward, and fell straight into Lord Sorenson's gaze. She became vaguely aware of Lord Carmichael standing at his side, but she couldn't look away from Lord Sorenson. He was very handsome, and there had been that brief, delicious moment when he'd held her in his arms.

Of course, she'd been too upset to enjoy the moment fully. But she did remember how comforting he had been, and the scent of him, his aftershave and warmth, was very nice, too.

They nodded to each other, and then Lord Wade drew her onward. After a moment, he cleared his throat. "Now, confess: who do you fancy yourself in love with?"

"I'm not in love with anyone," she said quickly, praying he'd not noticed her staring at Lord Sorenson.

"Oh, I think you are. Is it Lord Carmichael who now causes you to blush, or is it someone else entirely who has caught your eye and imagination?"

"A friend wouldn't ask me such a blunt question," she said, doing little to hide her discomfort.

"So, it's someone new. Not a bad choice, I suspect." A sly smile curved his lips. "It is hard not to notice your attention is divided tonight," he said quietly.

She glanced at him swiftly. "No, it is not. I would never be so rude to you."

"I think the fellow has utterly turned your head, and in so short a time, too. It might even be love at first sight." He nudged her shoulder with his in a companionable manner. "You needn't be embarrassed. I've known from the start how the wind blew with you. You hadn't yet met the one who caused your lady parts to quiver."

She gaped and then snapped her mouth shut. He couldn't have said that out loud? He couldn't know the effect Lord Sorenson had on her?

She didn't dare meet his gaze, and her face grew very hot as she tried not to think of Lord Sorenson and her lady parts. She wanted to flee from her embarrassment, especially when she realized her nipples seemed to have grown unusually sensitive beneath her gown. She had to get away from everyone until the sensation passed.

Unfortunately, Lord Wade took her arm and hooked it through his before she could take one step away from him. Anna kept her lips tightly shut. She would pretend everything was normal. It was the only thing she could think to do.

"It's a perfectly natural sensation. I'm happy for you. We're going to remain good friends, Miss Beasley, no matter what happens next. You're still the second-most interesting woman in the room."

Anna stared at him. "Second-most?"

"I knew you were still listening to me." He chuckled as she remembered what he'd confessed to before. What a goose she was. Of course, she would come second to the lady he admired. "Friends help each other see the truth, especially when it's to their advantage, and give their friend a chance to make someone see what they are missing out on."

Anna shivered, suddenly chilled. Lord Wade had no idea what he was talking about. She had no chance of keeping Lord Sorenson's attention. Her chances were less than hopeless. "He'd rather look at other women than me," she confessed quietly.

"Such an imbecile. Sorenson will come around eventually."

She looked at Lord Wade, startled. "I wasn't talking about him."

"I was." Lord Wade laughed again. "All men are devils until the right woman tames them. Sorenson watches you even now."

Anna glowered at Lord Wade. "He watches everyone."

"He's watching *you* now. *Again*. Look to your left and see."

Anna did—and her gaze fell on Lord Sorenson immediately. Carmichael was no longer with him, but Lord Sorenson was staring at her and Lord Wade, a frown line growing between his brows.

Hadn't he been farther up the room, closer to her father, a moment ago?

Anna turned away from him quickly, determined to put the earl from her mind. Lord Sorenson's interest was purely about how long she could hold her tongue about the murder she'd stumbled upon.

She looked around the room, resuming her search for an

agreeable husband. "As I said, he looks at everyone a great deal. Do you see Lord Carmichael anywhere about?"

"Carmichael? Why would you want him?"

She pulled a face. "So I might avoid him."

Lord Wade smiled slightly. "Yes, I'd heard you've been enemies since childhood. Surely he's not so bad."

"Indeed he is that bad." She dredged her memory for an example of Carmichael's real nature. "I have many good reasons not to like him. For instance, one day, just after he and his parents came to stay for a visit, Carmichael took my new parasol without my permission into a neighbor's dovecote so he might observe the birds without getting their leavings splattered over his coat. The parasol was a rare gift from his mother. It was beautiful and dear to me."

"That sounds a reasonable precaution but..." Lord Wade began, but then frowned. "How long was he inside the dovecote?"

"An hour and more. When I saw him, he just passed me the ruined parasol and thanked me for the loan of it."

Lord Wade scowled. "I think you're very wise to keep your distance from that one then."

"I wish I could, however, my father is his godfather, and he holds Lord Carmichael in great affection. Avoiding him is not always possible but I do my best."

Lord Wade smiled again. "You cannot hold his friend accountable for the childish behavior of a mutual acquaintance?"

Anna's cheeks heated. "Which friend?"

"You know the one: tall, red-haired, handsome, and with a fondness for following you about this ballroom."

"He is not."

"You two make quite the pair." Lord Wade laughed. "You've been sneaking peeks at him since the night you met him at Almack's, and he's doing the same now."

"I certainly do not look at him more than anyone else," she declared hotly, not enjoying Lord Wade's insistence.

"Not a bad choice, if you ask me."

Anna bristled, unhappy that Lord Wade was becoming overly familiar. No wonder Miss Hayes did her best to avoid him. She might have to withdraw her friendship if he kept this up. "I did not ask your opinion."

"No one ever does. Usually to their detriment." He smiled serenely. "I can spot an ill-fated match from twenty paces. And a better one in less time than that."

"If you are so skilled at matchmaking, perhaps you should consider stop being cowardly and face the facts. You are never going to win yourself a wife unless you take action. You should worry more about making a marriage yourself." She gasped quickly, shocked again by her own boldness at suggesting such a plan. "But not to me, of course."

"No, not you. We'd never suit for marriage."

Despite being cross, Anna felt bad suddenly for how she'd spoken. "I'm sure the lady would be happy to marry you if you are sincere in declaring your affections."

"Matchmaking is not a skill you possess, Miss Beasley, or our association would have borne better results by now." He sighed. "Your father is beckoning us to him."

Anna glanced ahead. Her father did appear anxious to have her return. He was craning his neck in a way he usually had no need to. Had he heard of last week's murder at last? Anna's stomach pitched and roiled in worry that he might learn what she had stumbled upon. "Thank you for your company, Lord Wade."

"As ever, it has been an enlightening experience talking with you," he promised.

They joined her father and Lord Wade quickly excused himself. She watched him flee toward the card room and then looked up at her beloved father. "Is something wrong?"

"No, no." He glanced around them, smiling broadly. "But I have news. Good news indeed to share."

Anna tried to smile too—to feign excitement she didn't feel at his words.

"Lord Carmichael has asked to stand up with you tonight," he whispered. "I promised him that you were free and very willing to dance with him at short notice."

Anna groaned under her breath. Lord Carmichael was a pain in her backside. She'd hoped to fill her dance card only with potential suitors.

She thought quickly of a way to avoid the dance for as long as possible. "If you will excuse me, I need a moment to myself."

"You are lovely already," her father promised. "But by all means, seek the retiring room to improve upon perfection."

He brushed her chin with his knuckles, beaming at her until she had to flee his presence. If only Papa wasn't so determined to have Carmichael squire her about the dance floor. He would be disappointed when Carmichael eventually married, most likely to Miss Angela Berry, and very soon, too.

Anna knew which rooms had been set aside for the ladies and followed a pair of chattering women in that direction. However, as soon as those ladies slipped inside the retiring room, Anna sidestepped into the very first chamber she came to and shut the door firmly behind her.

She pressed her hand to her chest, excited by her daring escape. She would be scolded if she were discovered here alone but there was no choice.

She would have to speak to Father about her intense dislike of Lord Carmichael. She had to stop him from making arrangements for them to dance together behind her back, and soon.

The air suddenly stirred beside her. "What are you doing here alone, Miss Beasley?"

CHAPTER 9

Miss Beasley yelped and turned to face the dark corner where Gilbert had hidden when she'd suddenly stepped into the room.

"Goodness!" she cried. "You scared me."

Gilbert moved toward her, lifting his gloved fingers to her lips. He pressed them firmly against her to silence her. "You must be quiet," he whispered.

"Why?" she mumbled around his fingers.

He was still a long moment, studying her in the moonlight cast by the open drapes. Miss Beasley intrigued him as no other lady he'd met so far had. A pity he'd not the time to explore the attraction building in him, and what he sensed of hers even now. "So no one learns we are alone together."

He brushed his fingers gently across her lips, wishing he'd taken the time to remove his gloves first. Miss Beasley had pretty lips. He found them fascinating to watch.

Unmindful of the potential scandal, she drew closer. "Did you discover who killed Miss Goldwell?"

"Not yet." But he had come to this room to lie in wait for a candidate. Carmichael had gone to another likely location where an attack might be made, the library on the other side of the house. Together, they hoped to thwart the killer if he was here tonight.

Gilbert's heart had stopped when someone had slipped into the room, and when he'd recognized Miss Beasley by the color of her gown and the curves of her body, his heart had raced with dread.

For a moment, a very brief one, he had wondered if he'd been so very wrong about her.

However, he felt the killer would have reacted very differently to his presence, had they come here with murder on their mind.

"I cannot forget what happened to her." Scared eyes met his. "Can you?"

He returned his fingers to her lips as women passed the door, laughing loudly as they went. He listened until they were gone. "I'm sorry you had to see her like that."

Miss Beasley shivered. "It is not right that no one knows about it."

"No, it is not right, but it is how it must be for now if the killer is to be captured."

Her eyes searched his face again. "Are there any clues at all?"

"Very few." Confiding in Miss Beasley hadn't been a consideration but he felt he owed her an explanation and hope. "We suspect the person responsible is someone frequently overlooked by society. Someone who stands at the fringes."

Miss Beasley swallowed. "Is that why you're hiding here? Are you trying to catch them in the act of attacking someone else?"

"Yes," he confessed. He smiled quickly, lest she thought he considered her a suspect. "But I seem to have caught a pretty lady instead."

"I'm not the killer," she said, fingers rising to her throat. "I simply needed a moment to myself before I return to the ball."

He noted she ignored the compliment but touching her throat revealed his words had indeed affected her. If it wasn't so dark in here, he thought she might be blushing. "What has upset you tonight?"

She frowned at him. "Why do you think I'm upset?"

"I saw your expression change as you spoke with Lord Wade."

She shrugged. "He unsettles me occasionally, but it is not him I flee."

Gilbert stood straighter, more than a little worried by that remark. "What are you afraid of?"

"I am not afraid. I am annoyed. Father has promised I will dance with Carmichael soon."

Carmichael was supposed to be patrolling the library by now. Had he intended to disappoint Miss Beasley tonight by not arriving to dance with her? That seemed unnecessarily cruel. "What if he didn't come?"

"Then he would finally do something to make me happy," she said, and then sighed. "No doubt my father pressured him to dance with me tonight. I'd rather not be a duty, all things considered. I just wish he'd go away or say no to Father with a hint of finality."

"I'll talk to him," Gilbert promised, silently vowing to keep them as far apart as he reasonably could.

"You will? Why?" Her hand moved to her cheek and yes, he was certain she was blushing furiously now.

"He's my friend and he's being manipulated."

"He has a spine made of jelly. He's forever promising Father one thing or another, and his godmother, too, for that matter. It is not possible to please everyone. I learned that long ago, and I wish he would, too," Miss Beasley declared, chin rising proudly.

Clearly Miss Beasley did not want to be around Carmichael, but she always seemed to be talking with Lord Wade, a man whose character seemed quite devious. She deserved better. "Is there something more than friendship between yourself and Lord Wade?"

She laughed bitterly. "I like him, but not the way you suggest. Not romantically."

Someone cackled with laughter directly beside them, outside

in the hall. He placed his hand over her mouth again, hoping whoever it was would quickly go away. He and Miss Beasley had been alone for too long. He had to let her go as soon as silence returned to the adjacent hall and send her on her way.

He bent close to whisper in her ear, "You should go."

"You keep saying that to me," she whispered back.

"I've no wish to harm your reputation."

She considered that a moment, and then sighed. "No one will notice I'm missing yet," she promised. "Do you need help looking for Miss Goldwell's killer? I should like to offer any assistance I can."

"Bow Street has the matter well in hand. I have Carmichael, too."

She rolled her eyes. "You need someone better equipped to ask intelligent questions than Carmichael."

Gilbert muffled a laugh. "I think Carmichael did too well turning you against him. You do know he's something of a genius, don't you?"

"Price Wagstaff is an imbecile and a scoundrel," she said flatly. "His friend would know that about him by now. All he is interested in is chasing the nearest skirt."

Gilbert was amused by her hostility toward Carmichael. "Carmichael may never have attended classes when we were in school together, but he passed every test with time to spare. He is smarter than most men, myself included."

"What? That cannot be right. You're…"

Gilbert touched her arms lightly. "I'm what."

Miss Beasley wet her lips. "Well, you're obviously very intelligent and…"

Gilbert cursed under his breath as his body reacted to the flick of her tongue across her lips, and the praise. He desired her, though he couldn't pursue her until the murderer had been captured.

Still, there was no reason why he couldn't reveal his interest and see what happens. "And?"

"What else is there to say?"

He leaned close. Recklessly close, and he heard her breath hitch. "I think you're very attractive, too. I notice you," he whispered. "When you arrive, when you leave. Who you talk to. Who you dance with."

Miss Beasley trembled when he set his hand to her shoulder. "You do?"

"Oh, yes. You are quite lovely to watch. So graceful and always smiling." He moved his hand so his fingers brushed against her throat and slid them up to cup her face. "If I had time to spare, I might do nothing else but watch you."

Miss Beasley collapsed back against the wall behind her. "You're too kind."

"I'm really not." Had she no idea of how appealing he found her? He'd have to fix her lack of understanding on the matter of her desirability. He moved closer, crowding her against the wall. His blood was pumping fast through his veins. Desire was robbing him of his manners, and he knew it. He didn't care. He lowered his head until their lips were very close. "If I was kind, I'd not want to do this."

He sealed his lips over hers and kissed her thoroughly for several long minutes. It was obvious Miss Beasley was inexperienced. He had to coax her to part her lips and when she did, he flicked out his tongue to taste her.

She tasted of the punch she'd sipped earlier and smelled of heaven, too.

He pulled her into his arms, setting aside what he'd originally come to this room for. All he could think of was showing Miss Beasley how much he admired her. She wound her arms about his shoulders and he moaned against her mouth, closing his eyes to savor the moment of their surrender to passion.

The next moment, Miss Beasley was wrenched out of his arms.

He opened his eyes in a daze and found Lord Wade's

scowling face before him. "Sorry to interrupt," Wade murmured. "But you should know better."

Miss Beasley blinked several times and then covered her lips. Her cheeks were definitely turning a fiery pink now, and her eyes were wide with shock.

Only then did he see their hostess, Lady Windermere, standing just inside the room, too. She did not look pleased with them.

Lady Windermere addressed Miss Beasley first. "My dear, unmarried ladies prowling the halls without chaperones in tow must always remember to lock the door when they sneak away for stolen kisses."

"She did not sneak anywhere," he protested, affronted on Miss Beasley's behalf.

"What else could this be but an assignation?" Lady Windermere studied him carefully. "Or have I stumbled upon the acceptance of a marriage proposal from you? If so, I couldn't be happier for Miss Beasley—my husband's cousin."

Anna Beasley was Lord Windermere's cousin? He had not known that about her, and really, he did know very little about the Beasley family and their connections.

There was utter silence for a full minute as the ramifications of Lady Windermere's second question filled him. There had been no talk of marriage or a future, only Miss Goldwell's murder and one stolen kiss. Actually, several stolen kisses, but he couldn't remember how many now. It wouldn't be fair for them to marry under those circumstances and yet, as family, Lady Windermere would expect him to do his duty and hush up any scandal.

Devil take it! He'd have to offer for Miss Beasley.

Gilbert reached for Miss Beasley's hand and cradled it tenderly against his chest. "We are found out, my love."

Panic flared in Miss Beasley's eyes as their gazes collided. She clearly hadn't expected him to offer endearments, but after that kiss, and being caught in his embrace, he had no choice but to play the part of a smitten suitor. He would do the honorable thing and lie that he had intended this from the start.

He hoped Miss Beasley could pretend happiness well enough to fool Lady Windermere and Lord Wade that she had been with him for this outcome.

Thankfully, Miss Beasley squeezed his fingers, but a question formed in her eyes just the same. "Indeed."

He covered her hand with his and held it tightly. They could talk about this later, after he'd spoken to her father and averted a potential scandal. The actual marriage could wait until the murderer was brought to justice.

Although…he couldn't say he disliked the idea of marrying Miss Beasley, even if it was a bit sudden. He hadn't come to London to find a bride, although he would need to marry in the next year or so if he wanted to see his sons grow to reach their majority. Miss Beasley was certainly a woman he would have considered, given time for a longer study of the marriage mart. He'd certainly enjoyed holding her in his arms tonight and kissing her witless. He could easily do so again. What might have happened if they'd not been interrupted? His pulse raced at the idea.

"I had hoped to speak to your father before anyone knew my intentions for us."

A pretty blush flooded her cheeks. "I am sure my father will be very happy to meet with you tomorrow, my lord."

"Why not speak to him tonight?" Lady Windermere asked with a bright smile. "He can announce the engagement before all our friends. My ball will become the talk of the season."

Gilbert thought it would be already, given the number of guests who'd come. Society seemed stunned that Lord and Lady Windermere had set aside their differences and married in the first place. There'd been a lot of gawking done tonight at the couple—mostly due to Lady Windermere's expanding waistline and this second pregnancy since the marriage began.

Miss Beasley released his fingers slowly. "I would not like to announce any engagement tonight."

"Oh?" Lady Windermere said, one brow rising in surprise. "Why ever not, my dear cousin?"

"My father dislikes being put on the spot, and he hasn't yet realized the depths of Lord Sorenson's interest in me. Tomorrow is soon enough for him and Lord Sorenson to discuss the future," she said firmly.

Gilbert suppressed a grin. Miss Beasley might seem quiet and prone to blushes but she wasn't about to be pushed around by her relation. Bravo! Now he was really looking forward to getting to know Miss Beasley better.

Lady Windermere took Miss Beasley's measure, and then nodded slowly. "As you wish, my dear. I will have to content myself with merely being the first to know of the engagement. If you need any assistance in planning the wedding or your trousseau, I'd be more than happy to help."

"Thank you for understanding, and for your kind offer," Miss Beasley murmured before looking at Lord Wade. "And you, my lord? I trust you are willing to hold your tongue, too?"

Lord Wade seemed vastly amused by Miss Beasley's question. "As long as I hear Lord Sorenson has called on your father tomorrow, I will say nothing."

"Thank you."

Lady Windermere beamed. "Well, then, now that is settled, Miss Beasley will accompany me to the retiring room, and then return to her father with me. He will be wondering what is keeping her."

Miss Beasley swayed a little, no doubt imagining the worst of how her father might take the news of her behavior tonight. Gilbert reached for her hand again, determined that her father would never learn of their interrupted kiss. "A moment."

"I should go," Miss Beasley begged.

"Very well," he reluctantly agreed. They should discuss the mess he'd placed them in, in private, before he spoke to her father tomorrow, if possible. Although he wanted her to linger with him, there was sense in pretending they had not already kissed. He nodded. "We will speak tomorrow then."

"I look forward to receiving you," she promised, before joining Lady Windermere at the door. With one last look, she swept out the door and out of his reach.

Gilbert let out a heavy sigh when the door closed behind her. He turned to Lord Wade. "Thank you for not raising an alarm."

Lord Wade raised a brow, all trace of amusement gone. "I trust my faith in you is not misplaced."

"I will call on her father tomorrow," he promised.

"Good." A little of his amusement returned. "Miss Beasley is a rare one, isn't she? Outwardly shy, but I detected no hint of that when she was kissing you back so ardently just now."

"Consider your next words very carefully, Lord Wade," he growled.

"So should you." Lord Wade glowered right back. "I would not be happy if my friend was disappointed in any way."

Gilbert frowned at the man. Anna Beasley had claimed no deep affection for Lord Wade existed. But with threats still tainting the air, he wondered if he hadn't come between a romance in the making. "You care about her?"

"No surprise there." Lord Wade shrugged. "She's one of the few ladies in society worth speaking to. Platonically, of course. Miss Beasley is entirely too trusting, so I do what I can to educate her about scoundrels. Myself included. Once she's happily settled in marriage, I'll turn my attention elsewhere."

Gilbert grunted in surprise. He'd never have pegged Lord Wade as anyone's guardian angel but the fellow seemed to have his heart in the right place. "Thank you, I think."

The man beamed. "I'll be rejoining the ball now, and listening for news of an engagement announcement tomorrow."

He sauntered from the room with a cheery wave.

Gilbert shook his head and returned the way he'd come, via

the terrace window as the clocks of Windermere House struck midnight.

He quickened his steps. By all the reports he'd cobbled together, the time had come and gone for the killer to act. There had been no cry of alarm. However, he would still like to search for an undiscovered body just to be sure nothing had happened.

He met a few older couples outside on the terrace, but no one he considered a potential murderer as he skirted the house. He recognized few so he kept moving. Checking out-of-the-way places for bodies, discreetly conferring with the Bow Street men who had slipped into the crowd to act as extra eyes, and receiving the all clear from them.

He breathed a sigh of relief—until he stumbled upon Albert Meriwether, leaning against a garden wall in dark everyday clothes.

"What are you doing out here?"

"You took my case from me." Meriwether's expression soured. "But the magistrate also hinted that there seems to be a pattern developing. I'm here in my own free time to see you in action and step in when needed."

"The killer did not strike down anyone tonight."

The fellow brushed himself off. "That is disappointing to hear. But I'll take my leave before I am seen. Expect to see more of me about."

He wasn't pleased by Meriwether's intentions. He'd been told he had the lead in the investigation. He didn't need the man under his feet. Gilbert drew near him. "If you beat another suspect to gain a confession on this case, I'll do the same to you."

Meriwether bowed coldly and then vanished into the night.

Having Meriwether around meant he could never fully trust any information he was given if it went through his hands first. Davis would not be pleased by the development, either. They'd worked well together without a third wheel. Davis was angling for a promotion, too, which Meriwether might not support.

On returning to the ballroom, he noticed Miss Beasley

immediately. *Anna.* She and Miss Hayes were together again and talking with great animation. Lord Wade was some distance behind them—keeping watch yet again. The fellow caught his eye, but then wandered off into the crowd just as Carmichael came into the room.

Gilbert wasn't sure what to do next about the killer, but he was absolutely sure of one thing—he really did want a chance to be alone again with Anna.

CHAPTER 10

Waiting was torture. Anna paced the little parlor on the first floor of her father's London home, nerves jumping at every sound. The panic she'd experienced at Miss Goldwell's murder had been eclipsed by even greater fears—what if Lord Sorenson did not come at all? What if he did?

She covered her face, glad that her father had gone to his study to read the newssheet and couldn't see her in this wretched, uncertain state. She'd barely been able to eat anything at breakfast, but somehow she'd hidden that fact from her father. His only comment that morning was that she was unusually pale and tired looking.

That was no surprise. She hadn't slept well in days.

The murder and now a suitor expected to call had both put her thoroughly on edge.

The knocker sounded on the front door, and she yelped out loud. Footsteps rushed down the hall and Anna strained to hear what was spoken. The next thing she heard was a woman's voice, and then the butler appeared in the doorway. "Are you at home to Miss Hayes this morning, Miss Beasley?"

Anna let out a shaky breath. "Yes, of course I am. Always."

He nodded and went away. A few minutes later, Portia Hayes swept into the room. "I simply couldn't sleep a wink last night," she announced as she grasped Anna's hands tightly. "Could you?"

Anna gulped, wondering what Portia had already heard about her but too terrified to ask. "I was up very early," she admitted. "Do sit down."

"Thank you. It is all so distressing."

She looked at Portia sharply. She must know. "What is?"

"Not being able to call on friends."

Anna released the breath she discovered she'd been holding in. No one knew what she had been caught doing with Lord Sorenson. Her reputation was safe still. For the time being at least. "What other friends did you want to call on?"

"Well, you and I both know Angela Berry has disappeared from society. Her family has gone to the country without leaving a word if they were even coming back."

"Have they?"

"So it seems."

Portia tossed her head from side to side. "And now I find Miss Goldwell has fled the capital as well."

At the mention of Miss Goldwell, cold clamminess swept over Anna. She had promised Lord Sorenson she would say nothing about it to anyone. "I haven't seen her, either."

Portia scrunched up her face. "Well, it is a nuisance to have friends and acquaintances that keep disappearing without a word of goodbye. We may have no choice but to make new friends if this decline continues."

"Or be content with each other's company and not need anyone else," Anna added with a forced laugh.

Portia reached for her hand. "Don't you dare disappear on me."

"I won't." She smiled. "You will probably never be rid of my company."

Portia smiled. "If you don't find a suitable husband, you know you can come and live with me when I do."

Anna laughed softly. "And the reverse applies. You can come and live with me, should the worst happen."

"Oh, I would, too, but I must warn you, I do intend to bring one of my suitors up to scratch before the season is out."

Anna leaned forward. Portia was a determined young lady, and she felt a twinge of pity for the poor fellow she singled out. "Who is the lucky fellow?"

Her smile grew sly. "It is a secret. For now."

"Ah, so only you have decided. Does he know he's in the running yet?"

"He will soon. He most definitely will." She laughed heartily.

Anna wished she had half of Portia's confidence when it came to men. But as the clock struck twelve, she feared she'd been foolishly hopeful. Lord Sorenson had promised to call in the morning but the morning was now gone. All that was left was a slow afternoon of knowing he'd deceived her.

Rather than think of her disappointment, she smiled at Portia. "How is your mother today?"

"She says she has a megrim."

"Oh, I'm so sorry."

"Don't be." Miss Hayes shrugged. "It's her way of avoiding my father, I suspect. It's either that or she returns to Soho Square to sort through Uncle Oliver's cluttered townhouse."

Anna laughed. "I thought the house would be cleared out by now."

"Goodness, I should say not. It will take us years to sort through the rubble to find the house beneath. You must come with me next time I spend an afternoon there. My uncle's collection is diverse and quite unusual."

"I'd love to go with you," Anna promised. Running away for an hour or two seemed a very good idea. "When and what time?"

Portia paused, peering around her shoulders. "It's a bit of a secret that I go there, actually. Don't tell your father, or anyone else for that matter. It's become my escape. We'll say we're going shopping, take our maids, and go there instead if you're willing to be a little naughty with me."

Anna hesitated a moment before nodding. How bad could it be if there was no one else with them but their maids? "All right. We'll say nothing more for now."

Portia beamed. "Good. What are your engagements for the coming week?"

While they discussed the week ahead, Anna comforted herself that even if Lord Sorenson didn't keep his word, she still had Miss Hayes' company.

Portia agreed to stay for luncheon and they settled into the morning room to a small feast. Portia glanced at the other two empty chairs. "You know, this is almost exactly what happened to us last year. Do you remember us all sitting here together? You, me and Miss Berry, with her other friend, Miss Newell."

Anna did indeed remember Miss Newell. The girl had made fun of her blushes. For a time, Anna had felt very uncomfortable, but forgave her when word reached them that she had died suddenly. "Yes."

"We included her then she vanished without a trace, and then we discovered that she had been murdered, of all things. I mean, who would ever want to harm Miss Newell?"

"I thought she died of influenza?"

"No, no. That is simply not true. Carmichael told me all about it some time ago. She ran afoul of a villain on her way home from a ball, or at the ball. I forget the specifics now."

"I thought she died in the country."

Portia shrugged. "Well, anyway, she died and I feel very put out. We made room for her and Angela Berry in our circle, gave them the advantage of our companionship and advice, and ended up with nothing to show for it. I thought Miss Goldwell might grow our numbers, but if she isn't at home when I call or doesn't send a note to one of us that she's going away too, I don't know what to think of her."

Another knock boomed through the house, and Portia clapped silently, glancing toward the door expectantly.

Anna heard a male voice and shivered. Lord Sorenson. Since the door to the morning room had closed behind Portia, she could not see him but she imagined him standing in her hall, and her pulse raced.

Portia leaned close. "Who do you think that is?"

Anna did not really want Portia to be disappointed with her about last night and what she felt she must do today. Portia might not be at all understanding that she had stumbled upon Lord Sorenson alone last night. She might conclude her fast, or worse for having kissed him back.

"I suppose it is Carmichael come to call on my father again," she said quickly, deciding misdirection her best course of action for now.

If it was Lord Sorenson coming to ask for her hand, she already had her speech prepared.

"Well, then. I suppose I should be on my way. Observing you two glaring at each other and squabbling over nothing became tedious last year."

"We do not squabble."

"You've never agreed on even a single topic. If you mention a chill, he will curse the heat. If you claim to be comfortably seated, he'll suggest going out."

"He is very childish sometimes."

Portia nodded quickly. "Yes, and he's not the only one afflicted with that ailment. Well, I will see you for our shopping excursion, or Friday night if our schedules don't allow us to meet."

Anna walked Portia to the entrance hall. "I'm sure we will see each other sooner than Friday. Besides, there's always Almack's on Wednesday, too."

"True, but who can really talk there?" With a wave of her fingers, Portia swept out to the street and darted into her waiting carriage.

Anna watched her departure from the window then turned. Her father and Lord Sorenson stood behind her. Lord Sorenson was smiling, but her father appeared confused.

She did like Lord Sorenson's smile and returned it. There was no reason to end today as enemies.

"Good afternoon, Miss Beasley," he said, coming forward.

"My lord," Anna murmured as she dipped a curtsy to him.

"Might I have a moment or two of conversation?"

"Yes, of course." She gestured him into the room, deciding where she'd sit. She chose a single straight-backed chair for herself, and Lord Sorenson took a place on the settee.

He beamed after the door shut. "You look lovely today," he told her.

Anna blushed at the compliment and turned to her father. However, Father wasn't beside her anymore. Her heart began to race.

"Your father will return after we have spoken," Lord Sorenson confided. "I asked if we might speak privately and he agreed."

Anna sank into her chair again and slowly lifted her gaze to the earl's.

Oh dear. Alone with the handsome devil yet again.

"You know why I have come," he murmured.

"Yes," she admitted. He'd come because she'd been very foolish. She'd compromised herself in his arms.

"Miss Beasley, I think you will agree with me that our encounter last night was serious enough to warrant this immediate course of action."

He had to ask. He had to say the words so that she had a chance to let him down gently and then they might never need speak of it again. Her heart began to race, and she fell back on empty pleasantries to buy time. "Did you enjoy the ball last night?"

"Indeed. I found the evening very exciting."

"Lady Windermere will be very pleased with the attendance at her first ball as Lord Windermere's wife."

His expression grew puzzled. "I wasn't speaking of the ball."

Anna pasted an innocent expression to her face. "I was."

His lips twitched. He rose from his seat, only to sink to one knee on the carpet before her. He caught her eye as he reached for her hand. "Miss Beasley, would you do me the honor of becoming my wife?"

For a moment, Anna's determination to reject him faltered. For a brief, glorious moment, Anna believed he really meant his offer. His haste in offering matrimony could be a sign of the most ardent affection.

And yet…as soon as his tongue darted out to wet his lips, she remembered last night all too clearly. He'd stolen a kiss (or two) and that was all there was between them. It was hardly enough to build a happy life upon.

She had no choice but to decline. "Lord Sorenson, your actions do you credit today but I am afraid I must refuse your kind offer."

She expected him to hear her words, mutter his acceptance of her refusal, and then excuse himself.

Lord Sorenson did not. He shifted till he was fully kneeling and shuffled closer. "Why *must* you refuse me?"

His words were low, intimate, and she felt each one as if his lips were against her skin.

"Last night was an aberration. We hardly know each other."

"That is what I thought you'd say, and you are correct. We have spent barely six hours at most under the same roof after we were introduced. Barely any time at all to know each other well enough for marriage."

"We danced but once."

"A lovely dance," he murmured.

"I cannot agree to marry a stranger based on so little information."

He grinned ruefully. "I imagine being counted as one of Lord

Carmichael's oldest friends isn't any recommendation of my character, is it?"

"I'm sure you are a better man than he is, but..."

"But you still couldn't consider marrying me under the circumstances," he finished for her.

"No." She tried to smile. "I am sorry."

He smiled though. "I thought I would have to convince you."

Anna waved away the effect of his smile and bravely pressed on, determined to convince him she was right. "I know Lord Wade and Lady Windermere expect news of an engagement, but all you really did promise was to call upon my father today. You have done that. If I refuse you, surely they will be satisfied."

"If only that were the case." He caressed her fingers, which she had utterly forgotten he held. "I think you should be allowed a chance to reconsider my offer."

Her eyebrows rose high. "My lord, you are not listening."

"I'm listening, but I fear you misunderstand my motivation for proposing."

She smiled sadly. "It is all very clear. You came to keep your word. To prevent my reputation from being ruined."

"I came to arrange to marry you. Your father was just as incredulous as you appear to be, but I must stress I am in earnest."

"But why?"

"Because of this." He leaned forward and brushed his lips across hers. It was a soft kiss, tender and full of gentle exploration.

Kissing him was what had gotten her into trouble in the first place. She pushed him back. "My lord!"

"My future bride," he said huskily, and then cleared his throat. "The memory of our kisses will keep me awake again tonight."

She drew back to look at his face, discovering her hand rested against his cheek now. She snatched her hand back. "You didn't sleep, either?"

He caught her hand and returned it to his face. Then he pushed his cheek against her palm. "I found myself reliving every moment of having you in my arms."

Anna blushed. "I shouldn't have allowed it."

"It will be our secret."

"Except for two witnesses."

"Who will say nothing because I kept my promise."

"You are honorable."

He ginned impishly. "What if we decide upon a secret understanding between us to appease Lord Wade and Lady Windermere while I woo you properly? We can set a date to marry when we know each other better."

That seemed fair to her, and yet—

Lord Sorenson kissed her again without warning. Anna grasped his shoulders as he swept her into a kiss unlike the others. She felt the tip of his tongue tickling her lips and when she parted them to protest, he deepened the kiss, and she forgot she meant to be good.

Anna wound her arms about his neck as he ate at her mouth like he was starving for her kisses. His arms closed around her firmly, and then he began to explore the curve of her waist and the length of her back. When his fingers caressed the back of her neck, she moaned a little against his lips.

She perhaps got a little too swept up in the kiss, because she didn't remember Lord Sorenson saying her father would return until she heard Father outside the door, clearing his throat very loudly before he rattled the handle.

"Well," Lord Sorenson whispered the moment he drew back. His face was flushed, and his eyes were wide and hot on hers. "Can you at least promise me you'll consider marrying me for the right reason after that kiss?"

He sat back on his heels, eyes fixed on Anna with one brow

raised, but then he returned to his chair as the door creaked open to admit her father.

Anna feared she was blushing as bright as the sun or her suitor's red hair, and glanced down at her hands while she decided what to do and say. That was a kiss she'd not soon forget. It was a kiss she would remember forever.

He was correct about one thing too, she wouldn't think of anything but him and his proposal now. It was a huge decision to make.

"Is everything all right, daughter?"

"It is, Papa. Lord Sorenson has asked me to marry him." Anna glanced up finally, looking toward her suitor with a new appreciation. She didn't want to refuse him but she also didn't want to be rushed. There was so much about him she couldn't know on so short an acquaintance.

Lord Sorenson's impressively wide shoulders sagged, and then he nodded. "She has—"

"Decided to consider his offer of marriage," she finished for him. "In my own time."

Lord Sorenson threw her a delighted grin.

Her father gaped. "Consider it? What is there to consider?"

"I am happy with her answer, sir. In her own good time, she will decide one way or the other," Lord Sorenson said, still smiling at her as if her hesitation was right and proper. "There's no reason for us to rush her until we know each other much better."

Anna was sure her father was about to curse but he pressed his lips together tightly and didn't argue with the earl. Anna had been on the marriage mart for two years and this was her very first offer. She'd known Lord Sorenson barely two weeks. She wanted time to become better acquainted with him…and his kisses.

When he continued to smile at her, Anna heart began to beat faster than ever. The Earl of Sorenson was actually a devil in disguise.

And right now, he appeared to be a very pleased devil indeed, judging by the appreciative glances he kept throwing her way as he reassured her father yet again that he was more than happy with the delay.

She could love him for his understanding alone.

But could she marry a stranger? She wasn't sure she knew the answer to that.

CHAPTER 11

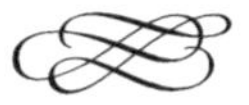

"No one died last night," Carmichael stated immediately as he stepped into Gilbert's Town carriage outside his home.

"That we know of so far," Gilbert warned, looking over Carmichael closely. The man appeared disheveled, as if he'd missed another night of sleep. Too much of that and he'd endanger the investigation and his health.

But he felt hope that they had passed the Friday without another loss. The question on his mind was, *why not last night*? Had the killer shed enough blood and quit the field entirely?

Despite the unending string of questions in his mind, Gilbert was a little distracted at the moment. He was bound for his club with the hope of running Lord Wade to ground, and then he would be calling on Lady Windermere. After receiving only a perhaps from Miss Beasley in terms of his offer of marriage, he was keen to inform Lord Wade and Lady Windermere that Anna Beasley and he had an understanding of sorts. He would court her properly, and she'd consider whether he might make an agreeable husband one day. The last thing Gilbert wanted was harmful gossip circulating about his reluctant future bride or for her to feel pressure to accept.

Carmichael stretched his legs out in the confined space. "Well, there was no screaming, or wilting debutants that I came across."

"Miss Beasley didn't scream." The thought of Anna made Gilbert unusually warm even now. She was quite delightful to kiss, but very determined to make a match for the right reason. He'd not meant to compromise her, but the kisses they'd shared and been discovered indulging in were all the reason he needed to make the most important decision of his life very quickly.

It was impossible to fake such innocent, ardent responses. Anna Beasley was the one. She surprised him at every turn, including her refusal to consider accepting his proposal straight away.

"Anna yelped," Carmichael told him. "She used to do that whenever I startled her."

"I can't say I blame her. By all I've heard, you've been beastly to her."

If he and Anna were to wed, Carmichael and Anna must become friends, he suddenly decided. This childish feud Carmichael had encouraged wouldn't be necessary once Anna was known to be betrothed to him and they eventually married. Mr. Beasley would stop looking at Lord Carmichael as a future son-in-law by then and accept she belonged to someone else. "You should be kinder."

Carmichael studied his fingernails. "I suppose I could. However, there's little reason to change my tactics now. Not after all the trouble I've taken to keep Anna from liking me. I don't want to give her father the hope of a match between us."

Gilbert grimaced. He wouldn't like that, either. It had taken quite a bit of negotiation for Mr. Beasley to agree to his request for a private conversation with Anna so he could propose. "I think you're in the clear."

The longer courtship suited him, although he was a little uncomfortable that he might have to continue to lie to Anna about the scale of his involvement with Bow Street. She'd seen enough of death, suffered enough of a shock over Miss Goldwell's demise. He'd shield her from anything else while the current investigation was underway and when they were married, he'd give up his pursuit of criminals for a settled and safe home life for good.

"I thought Anna seemed a little worried last night when we danced, but she would say nothing of her distress to me." Carmichael chewed his lower lip. "Have you by chance spoken with her?"

"We've spoken."

Spoken, and kissed again, too. Although he'd agreed to the delay, he was hopeful of more pleasant interludes like today's kisses. He'd been nervous as hell until he'd kissed her. After that, well…he'd done what seemed to come very naturally between them.

"And?"

"And what?"

Carmichael frowned. "Will she tell everyone that Miss Goldwell was murdered or not? We cannot have her informing society that there may well be a madman killing off debutants."

"She only knows about Miss Goldwell's death. She doesn't know about the rest," he promised.

"A mercy, that. Miss Hayes, another close friend of Angela's, asked me outright if I knew when Angela and her mother would return to London last night."

Gilbert winced. "What did you say?"

"I lied, of course. I told her I've no idea."

"Good. Good."

They fell silent for a bit, and Gilbert got his bearings. They were not far from the club, where he would begin to spread the word about his pursuit of Anna Beasley, but first he should probably inform Carmichael. Soften the blow, because the man had planned to marry Miss Berry this month and he was still grieving. He didn't like to keep secrets from his best friend.

"I lost you last night for a bit." Carmichael observed. "Where were you?"

"Why?"

"We should compare notes on whom we spoke to. Did you see anything suspicious?"

Carmichael was becoming obsessed with the chase.

"Not me. Davis reported nothing out of the ordinary last night. The only thing I noticed was Meriwether loitering outside in the garden."

"I know why." Carmichael chuckled darkly. "Meriwether was once known to be courting the new Lady Windermere, in the year before her marriage. Meriwether ended up marrying some silly country chit instead. A few months later, Windermere married his current wife and they will have nothing to do with him, or his reforms, now of course. I would say there is bad blood between them."

Gilbert grunted. "That explains his sour expression last night. What did you uncover? Anything?"

"Well, I did see something unusual but I'm not sure what to make of it." He leaned forward in his seat, resting one hand on a knee. "Lord Wade and Lady Windermere have suddenly become confidants. I noticed her husband didn't seem pleased at all by the private tête-à-tête they shared last night. There's something going on there. Do you think her already bored by married life?"

Gilbert blinked at Carmichael. "It's not what you think between them."

Carmichael frowned. "Lady Windermere had quite the reputation before she wed. She was rumored to keep a number of lovers dangling after her, including Meriwether. Since tying the knot, she's devoted her attention to her husband and new son exclusively. But she's no stranger to rumor or innuendo when it involves men younger than herself."

Gilbert sighed and cleared his throat. He would have to explain: about witnesses and kissing Anna last night. "They had a good reason to be whispering."

"Oh?" Carmichael asked.

"I asked Miss Beasley to marry me today."

Carmichael reached across the carriage suddenly and grabbed Gilbert by the cravat. He was shaken, and quite roughly, too. "What did you do last night to make such a sudden proposal necessary?"

Gilbert shook off Carmichael. "A kiss. Nothing more serious than that, I swear."

"I knew it. You like her! I said you were staring at her."

Gilbert straightened his coat and cravat, fighting a wave of shame. He'd behaved quite poorly last night, and maybe again today, too. But as much as it pained him, he'd sworn to deal honestly with his best friend some time ago. He couldn't lie to Carmichael and expect the same consideration in return. "Yes, well, try not to look so bloody smug about it. I admit, you were right. I haven't stopped thinking of her since I saw her."

Carmichael cackled. "Betrothed, and to *Anna*, within two weeks of coming to London. I knew it! I knew what I saw between you."

Gilbert allowed his friend his amusement. It was the first time Carmichael had seemed genuinely happy all week. "You'll stand up with me of course when the time comes."

"I would be very pleased to. When is the wedding to be carried out?"

"Not soon, I suspect. Anna feels we don't know each other well enough to actually accept my proposal, so a date has not been agreed to."

Carmichael squinted at him, his astonishment obvious. "Did she refuse you outright?"

"No." Gilbert shook his head. "When we were caught together last night, I blurted out a promise to visit her father today to Lord Wade and Lady Windermere, who found us together, to allay any gossip or announcement. Anna particularly did not wish to upset her father, and they agreed to say nothing as long as I called upon him today."

"So that explains them whispering." Carmichael glanced away. "And Anna's odd behavior."

"She wasn't upset about being kissed really." He nodded. "But it wasn't the way a gentleman with intentions should have behaved. Being found alone together sped up the business of offering for her."

"Once you know, you know," Carmichael mused, wiping at his eyes with his thumb suddenly. "Nothing can stop it…except murder."

"I'm sorry."

"At least Anna will be happy. I imagine her father will regale me with the tale of your appearance in his study in the near future."

"He seemed quite surprised by my presence."

Carmichael shook his head. "Why *was* there no death last night?"

Gilbert sighed. So much for a pleasant diversion by talk of the living and the future. "Perhaps the murderer was distracted."

"Perhaps they were not even invited," Carmichael mused. "We should ask Lady Windermere for her guest list and compare it to the others we've collected so far."

"I do have to call on her."

"To assure her you and Anna are bound for the altar eventually?"

"Exactly," he promised. "Or at least, I hope so. Lady Windermere wanted the honor of making the announcement last night but Anna begged her not to put her father on the spot."

"He hates surprises."

"So Anna mentioned last night."

"She's not wrong," Carmichael murmured. "He likes to think he sees all but he's often wrong. I hadn't the heart to tell him about Angela yet. I was hoping Anna would make a match before me so the discussion wasn't necessary."

"She was waiting for me to come to London," Gilbert

quipped, throwing a sly smile toward Carmichael in the hope he'd laugh again.

Carmichael rubbed his jaw instead, brow furrowed. "You know, once word spreads about your engagement, there will at least be one less young lady to worry about. The murderer has only attacked unattached females, haven't they?"

"I had noticed that." And the realization made him anxious, now, too. Despite his promise to give her time, he felt it might be in Anna's best interests to spread the word that she would be promised in marriage to him as soon as possible. "Where are you bound tonight?"

"A dinner with Lord and Lady Thwaite. I'm hoping to get a sneak peek at the guest list for the next ball they host. I had also better make a duty call to my godmother first, though. Lady Scott must be reassured that I've not lost my fortune gambling the nights away this week with you."

"You're not coming to the club with me?"

"You already beat me at billiards this week. I'll wait a month before suffering further humiliation."

Gilbert smiled innocently. "Would you like me to let you win?"

Carmichael glowered back. "I'd shoot you if you even tried."

Gilbert chuckled. "Continue on with my carriage from the club then and have them return for me in an hour. I'll visit you at home, or would you care to join me for drinks after dinner at my home?"

Carmichael considered it a moment. "I'll come to you after the dinner. Exeter has deeper pockets and lured Monsieur Laffitte back to his employ last night. We can discuss what I learn of the next Friday night ball over a nightcap."

"That would be very helpful." The carriage began to slow as the club came into view. "I'm sorry about your chef. Wish me luck today."

"Good luck today, and all the days after," Carmichael said as the carriage rolled to a complete stop and a groom jumped down to open the door. "I'll see you tonight."

Gilbert collected his hat. He'd convince Carmichael to spend the night again. The man needed to sleep more than a night of overindulgence.

But for now, Gilbert was going to have to talk fast. Lord Wade might expect a wedding announcement he couldn't give yet. "See you then."

He strolled into the club, scanning the Morning Room's few occupants. He smiled. Lord Wade was reading the paper all alone and there were very few who might hear their conversation.

"Good morning, Lord Wade. Might I join you?"

The fellow lowered the paper, inspecting him from head to toe. "She said no."

Gilbert sat, quite stunned. "How could you possibly know that?"

"If she'd said yes, you'd have strutted into the club. As it is, you've got a worry on your shoulder."

"She said she needed time."

Lord Wade folded the paper and tossed it aside on a chair. "Use it wisely."

Gilbert stared at Wade. "Are you sure you're not in love with her?"

"Patience is its own reward, my lord." He smiled smugly. "I suppose you're after a boon from me."

"I would like not to rush her into any decision."

"Anna Beasley couldn't be rushed unless her house was on fire." Wade pursed his lips. "Agreed. There's nothing to speak of again about the matter."

"Thank you," Gilbert said with considerable relief. Now Anna's continued good reputation was assured, he felt infinitely better.

"Shouldn't you be running along to Windermere House already?"

Gilbert nodded. "I suppose I should."

"I wouldn't waste time. Lady Windermere isn't a stickler for propriety but she is very protective of friends and family," Wade warned. "You would be wise to keep her informed of the progress of your courtship, too. She may even have some advice on how to win the fair maiden's heart."

Gilbert took the hint and hurried toward Windermere House without waiting for his carriage to be returned. Having Lady Windermere for an ally was a good idea, and he did need to acquire her guest list somehow, too.

CHAPTER 12

Being a woman with an ardent suitor at her side provoked numerous unexpected reactions in Anna. Although her father appeared confused over Lord Sorenson's proposal, and her delay in answering him, she felt justified in holding out for a proper courtship.

Her beau sent a different bunch of flowers each morning, came to call in the afternoons, and had promised to attend any event Anna was invited to if given notice of where she went.

All Anna could think about, dream about too, was when she might next have a chance to kiss him again. He did it very well, but it had been days since an opportunity to be alone with him had presented itself.

She stood at the side of the dance floor of Lord and Lady Thwaite's townhouse, watching Miss Hayes twirl about with the latest object of her fascination: Lord Grindlewood.

Grindlewood was rumored to have finally recovered his fortune. His ship had come in, quite literally returned to port after becoming lost at sea, with its hold bursting with a fortune in valuable goods. She and Portia had discussed his appeal and connections at length when they'd slipped away to visit Portia's uncle's cluttered former residence.

"Still admiring the pretty ones?" Lord Wade asked as he stopped at her side.

She laughed a little. "There are many pretty things in London, my lord. I recall you are partial to looking at them yourself."

Lord Wade smiled. "I thought the right man would bring you all the way out of your shell."

"My shell?"

He nodded slowly. "I constantly hear that ladies are not supposed to speak their minds in order to be considered good. You slip up on occasion, which is why I bother to speak to you so often."

"Oh," she laughed softly. "I thought you only spoke to me so Miss Hayes would have to acknowledge you."

He scowled. "Point."

"I didn't know we could keep score of our conversations," she said, fluttering her lashes innocently.

He scowled again. "Better not do that again. I have a feeling your suitor is a jealous sort."

Anna glanced around for her beau, hoping he had arrived. "Have you seen him?"

"Card room. Carmichael is there too, dazzling the new flock of squires fresh from the country out of their pin money."

Anna sighed. She was not permitted in the card room. Father insisted she not venture there without him, but after her marriage, she fully intended to go whenever she liked. Not to gamble, she had no skill at cards. But watching had been amusing the few times her father had taken her in. "It is not very nice to call country gentlemen sheep."

"I was talking about the ladies as well. A fair number are keen to wager away their allowances against him, and probably offer up their virtue, too."

"Don't say that," she warned, glancing around discreetly. "You don't know them. There is nothing improper about ladies wagering a small sum when they have a suitable chaperone advising them."

Anna glanced toward her father with longing. He did not agree with her about making small wagers on anything, even the outcome of a horserace between friends. He disapproved of gambling altogether and was constantly chiding Carmichael for his reckless behavior at the tables. That Lord Sorenson might gamble had never occurred to Anna. She really did not know her intended very well, but she wanted to rectify that. "Would you excuse me?"

"Of course." He smirked. "Do run along and protect your suitor from any unwanted advances. Until you actually accept his proposal, and the connection is widely known, the other ladies can have no idea he's off the marriage mart and might have already made a play for his affections in your absence."

Anna had already considered she might have made a tactical mistake in her delay when it came to her competition on the marriage mart. Her betrothed was quite the catch in her opinion. An earl. Wealthy. New to Town and easy to talk to. Handsome. He might grow bored with waiting if she took too long to decide about him.

She scowled at Lord Wade when she saw he was laughing at her. "Are you going to ask Miss Hayes to dance tonight?"

"No," he muttered with a firm shake of his head.

The last time Lord Wade had asked Portia to dance, she'd refused him outright by uttering the biggest fib she'd ever told. Portia had excused herself immediately, saying she felt suddenly ill. Anna thought her reaction unnecessarily cruel. There were kinder ways to dissuade gentlemen you didn't like.

Lord Wade rarely asked Portia to dance now, and his manner had become very cold and critical of the young woman's behavior in recent days, though Anna thought it was out of worry rather than any meanness. She couldn't blame him for caring.

Anna returned to her father. He was alone for a moment and

she leaned toward him to whisper, "Might we venture to the card room tonight?"

"I've no interest in gambling."

"Neither do I but…I should like to speak with Lord Sorenson again. I just learned he and Carmichael are there."

Father looked at her a long moment. "Very well. We will go and speak to Carmichael."

They made their way there, and Anna's heart beat fast when she sighted her suitor. He was seated at a table with three other gentlemen, a tumbler of spirits at his elbow and his winnings piled up before him. He seemed to be having a very successful night.

Carmichael waved them toward him as the group of men around Lord Sorenson started to stand and gather up their much smaller winnings. The game must have only just ended.

"I tell you, sir, he had the devil's luck tonight," Lord Carmichael enthused to her father, grinning from ear to ear.

Anna stared at Carmichael. He seemed very excited. More so than normal. "He won?"

"Every hand. He just emptied Lord Abercrombie's pockets too, and that old miser never loses against newcomers, don't you know?"

Anna knew little of gambling, especially the gentlemen who were good at it, but tried to appear impressed. "Good evening, Lord Sorenson."

"Good evening, Miss Beasley. I won, Carmichael, because Abercrombie played with one eye on the next table of players," her suitor countered. "He was too busy watching the action over there to notice what I threw out. It was almost a crime to pick up my winnings."

Carmichael beamed. "A few more weeks in London hitting the tables and we could become very rich men."

"I doubt gambling can hold my interest for very long," Lord Sorenson warned, moving to Anna's side. "You look lovely tonight," he whispered very quietly.

"Thank you."

Carmichael raised his glass, catching Anna's eye. His amusement was obvious. "A toast is called for I think."

Lord Sorenson's chest expanded as he took a large breath and let it out slowly. "Is that so?"

"Oh yes, this is absolutely the right moment," Carmichael promised, grinning from ear to ear.

Sorenson laughed softly and called over a footman holding a tray of drinks. He handed Anna champagne and her father took one, too. "Very well. What are we toasting to tonight?"

"To new beginnings and future happiness."

Anna stared at Carmichael, wondering what he was talking about, and saw him sneak a peek at Lord Sorenson and then look at her again. Carmichael inclined his head slightly and then took a sip of his whiskey, eyes brimming with amusement as he held her stare over the glass.

He *knew* Lord Sorenson was courting her! He likely knew Sorenson had proposed, too, and had been not exactly rebuffed but certainly delayed.

Anna wanted the ground to open up beneath her feet and swallow her whole. Carmichael would tease her about this without mercy for as long as she lived.

Aware she was taking longer than everyone else to join the toast, she buried her nose in her champagne glass and took a tiny sip. She didn't particularly care for champagne, preferring sherry if given a choice. If Carmichael hinted at anything that would embarrass her tonight, she'd stomp his foot and throw the horrid champagne at his face.

Lord Sorenson took the glass from her hand suddenly, a smile lifting his lips. "I think it's safer all round if I take that from you, now the toast is over, before you hurl the contents at him for teasing." He glanced toward Carmichael slyly. "Were you not to dance with Miss Lacy soon?"

Carmichael snorted. "Oh, yes. Mustn't forget Miss Lacy expects me." Carmichael looked about, wearing that silly false grin again. "Ah, there she is, crossing the hall and beseeching me with her eyes to follow. Do excuse me, Anna. Sorenson. Mr. Beasley."

"Yes, hurry to catch up with her, Carmichael."

"Don't come back anytime soon," Anna muttered quietly under her breath.

Lord Sorenson choked on a laugh. "Might I have the honor of the next dance, Miss Beasley?"

Her card was still empty of dance partners, but that wasn't the reason she nodded her acceptance. "I'd be delighted."

"Mr. Beasley, will you join us in the ballroom?"

Father hurried to finish his champagne. "Indeed I will."

When both Father and Lord Sorenson extended their arms, Anna chose her dance partner with an apologetic smile to her father. "The quadrille is about to begin, Papa."

He gestured her out of the room impatiently. "Off you go then."

Lord Sorenson wasted no time going directly to the dance floor. "Perfectly timed."

"So it seems." She turned to face him as other dancers lined up around them. "Did you dance very much in the countryside?"

"Country dances once a month at a local lord's home. Nothing compared to this."

Anna saw Carmichael speaking with one of the musicians and then smirking their way. The man was insufferable. "You were right to take my glass from me earlier."

He laughed, a sound that heated her whole body. "He only teases because he likes you," Sorenson promised.

"Likes to torment me," Anna grumbled.

He laughed again. "And I in turn tormented him."

The musician played a small introduction to the next tune. She was expecting a quadrille like everyone else, the order of the dances had been announced earlier, but the melody was wrong for it. It sounded like it would be a second waltz played instead.

Lord Sorenson shook his head, smiling. "Carmichael has been busy."

"Doing what?"

The earl held out his hand. "New beginnings."

Anna wasn't certain what to make of that remark but she was happy to be held close in Lord Sorenson's arms again, even if it was just to dance. He was so very tall and comforting to be around. She hoped not to blush the whole way through the set. "Were you truly horrible to him or just trying to make me feel better?"

Lord Sorenson drew closer. "Carmichael has always come to stay with me during the summer. At Kent, and also when I had the vicar's living, he liked to strut about the village, charming all the local lads and ladies with tales of his exploits in London."

"He does that in the winter too," she grumbled.

"Not much of the tales were even half true so, well, every now and then, when Carmichael was getting too full of himself, heavily embellishing his tales, I'd suggest we all take a walk outside together."

Anna leaned in closer. "Pray continue. What did you do to him outside?"

"*I* did nothing." Lord Sorenson pulled her tighter as the dance began. He was silent a few moments as they spun about the room. "I've kept dogs since I was a boy. Nearly a dozen spaniels at one time, but one in particular was very obedient. Because that one liked water so much, I trained him to shake off the excess water on my command so he wouldn't do it indoors."

"A clever precaution."

"Well, there are some lovely views in Kent, a winding river with many shallow backwaters for the dogs to swim in, and most of the pack would run off for a dip whenever we went out walking. They always came back muddy and, depending on how annoyed I was with Carmichael, I'd signal my dog to shake the moment he was close enough to wet him."

Anna struggled not to laugh. "That must be why he avoids dogs and taking country walks in the winter months."

"He prefers London and the safety of carriages to keep his coat clean." Lord Sorenson winked. "He still hasn't caught on that it was never random chance."

Anna sighed, enjoying the feel of Lord Sorenson's large hand shifting around on her back a little. She could become used to having all of his attention. "I wish I could have seen him covered in mud just once. He is so particular about his appearance. He must have been mortified."

"Truly. Yet he still visits every summer despite the unruly beasts I keep about." Her suitor grinned. "I am expecting him to visit us in June. I'll have to teach you the trick to command the dogs yourself before he comes."

Anna grinned, glad to have a conspirator against Lord Carmichael at last. Perhaps it wouldn't be all bad marrying a man she hardly knew. He made her laugh, didn't he?

But there was the matter of his gambling to learn about. Carmichael's words had suggested he was as adept as anyone in London, or perhaps even better.

"Miss Beasley?" Lord Sorenson murmured.

"Oh, sorry. I was wool-gathering a little." She blushed and paid more attention to the man holding her. Marrying a man with a strong desire to gamble didn't appeal. She had her future to consider, their children's future depended on how their father managed their eventual inheritance.

"What's on your mind now?"

"It's nothing."

He smiled wryly. "As a vicar, I drew from my own experiences in society when preparing my sermons. I preached thrift, sobriety, and kindness to others. A week in London cannot overset the habits of the past years so quickly. I might wager with the best of them but prefer not to."

Anna blushed, astonished he'd guessed the direction of her thoughts so easily. "I never thought you did."

He frowned as the music drew to a close. They stopped and exchanged a smile before clapping along with everyone else. Lord Sorenson moved to take her arm. "In London," he whispered, "a gentleman must be seen to have an understanding of the most common of pastimes, an aptitude for games of chance, drinking too, to fit in. I will do so without ruining myself. Carmichael has no chance of corrupting me if that is what makes you frown."

Although startled that he could read her mind so easily, she smiled up at him. "You're very wise."

He covered her hand resting on his sleeve. "And you, my dear lady, have nothing to worry about when it comes to the future, should you choose me. The Sorenson estates thrive, despite any rumors you might hear to the contrary. I am in fact a rather serious man with few vices."

"I think you're very amusing."

"The only vice I currently crave is a chance to kiss you again," he whispered.

Anna's face flamed with heat. "How do you know what I'm thinking?"

"You bite your lip whenever you have a question you're not sure how to ask."

"I had no idea I did. No wonder Lord Wade can read me like a book, too. I will have to learn to be inscrutable."

He looked down on her, suddenly serious again. The heat in his gaze made Anna shiver all the way to her toes. "I think you are perfect as you are, sweet and kind," he promised in a husky tone. "And entirely kissable," he whispered.

Anna had to drop her gaze quickly before she burst into flames under the heat of his. She wanted more of his kisses too before she decided one way or another. "Thank you."

His arm slipped around her back briefly and she felt the warmth of his embrace to the depths of her soul. They navigated a large group and then walked on side by side to rejoin her father, who was watching them closely.

Lord Sorenson seemed entirely wonderful—considerate and

very interested in her thoughts—but she still did not wish to make a mistake she might later regret.

There was always tomorrow to decide about his proposal. Tonight, she wanted to be courted with sweet words and perhaps share a third stolen kiss with him.

She lifted her gaze to her suitor, seeking reassurance that despite the necessity of his proposal, they were both falling in love with the idea of being with each other forever.

Lord Sorenson's jaw was set, his gaze fixed over her head again. He didn't miss a word of conversation with her father for the next several minutes, but she was sure they had none of his attention.

CHAPTER 13

Gilbert ran up the steps of the Beasley residence full of anticipation for seeing Anna again after a tense meeting to complain about Albert Meriwether shadowing him. Meriwether was definitely acting without orders. He would be reprimanded and threatened with dismissal from the ranks of Bow Street in disgrace if he did not mind his own damn business.

The Beasleys' modest townhouse was very pleasing to visit after the chaos of the Bow Street offices. The Beasleys themselves were kind and well-liked by society. He felt comfortable with Anna, not so much with her father as yet though. It was to be expected the man wouldn't want to give up his only daughter to a near stranger, even if he was an earl, without revealing some doubts about the match.

He knocked on the blue-painted door and was let in immediately.

The butler looked at him expectantly.

"I am invited," he promised, flourishing Anna's note asking him to come to call.

"Indeed," the man muttered.

Gilbert unbuttoned his great coat and handed it and his hat to the Beasleys' butler, and then pocketed Anna's note again so he would always have it as a keepsake.

"This way," was all the butler said as he was led deep into the house.

He was brought to a small intimate chamber, a cozy sitting room decorated in shades of blue and gold. Anna was alone in the room.

When the butler began to withdraw, Gilbert spoke up. "A chaperone."

"That will be all, thank you," Anna announced firmly.

"Very good, Miss," the man replied but his expression was disapproving.

Gilbert turned to Anna immediately. She did not smile at him, and his happiness at the unexpected summons diminished to concern. "What is going on?"

"Please sit down."

Gilbert did but he was uncomfortable all of a sudden. "Where is your father?"

"I think the time has come for us to have a frank talk, my lord."

That did not sound good. Not at all. "I thought we had already been doing that these past days."

"Yes, of a fashion." She took a deep breath and then seemed to square her shoulders before she spoke. "I cannot help but feel your proposal, whilst made with the best of intentions, was an ill-timed decision on your part."

Was Anna Beasley about to refuse him? "Why do you say that?"

"Let me be honest. Despite the kisses we have shared, your interest seems to lie elsewhere."

"My interest is with you," he promised immediately. Entirely with Anna, in fact. He was already dreaming of bedding her, but he couldn't confess that yet. She'd be embarrassed and blush again. He wanted her to be comfortable around him if they had any chance of being happy together. "What have I done to make you feel my attentions are insincere?"

"Surely you will not make me come out and say it."

He sat forward. "I am doing all I can to convince you to marry me."

She pulled a face and looked away. She sighed heavily before she spoke. "Whenever we are together, dancing and such, you're often looking at everyone else in the room. Particularly at attractive young women."

Damn, she was observant, but it wasn't what she thought. He considered everyone he met a suspect and worried that any young, unmarried woman might be at risk of attack at a later date.

"It is you I'm interested in, I swear," he promised. "I don't mean to seem distracted and I'm sorry that you have misunderstood."

"I don't believe I've misunderstood anything, and I do know there are women more beautiful than I. You are new to your title, finding much in society to interest a bachelor after years buried in the country. It is perfectly natural for you to indulge your senses on the prettier sights to be found in Town. But I cannot compete, and I don't want to." She looked at him with a pained expression that tore at his heart. "The best thing to do is to end this here and now before hearts are broken."

Gilbert's stomach pitted. He might have blundered into offering marriage but that did not mean he didn't want Anna. She was beautiful to him.

He cleared his throat. She was completely wrong about him —and her own appeal. "Before I accept your decision, I would have you know a little of why I am in London in the first place. I came because Carmichael begged me to come."

"Begged?" She frowned. "I thought you were here on business."

"That is what I needed everyone to think." He'd come for the pleasure of Carmichael's nuptials, but only found death. "I came to meet Carmichael, and I have stayed to solve a puzzle for him."

"A puzzle?"

"It is complicated." He raked a hand through his hair. "I cannot reveal very much to you about the matter. It is something he cannot do, but I have the requisite experience for the task, so here I am. I am looking for someone on his behalf."

"Who?"

"I really don't know yet. Carmichael does not know, either. That is why it seems to you that I might be interested in other people, particularly women."

Her eyes narrowed with suspicion. "Is Carmichael being blackmailed by some poor girl he led on?"

"What makes you ask that?"

Her eyes widened in alarm. "I know him, and I've noticed a change in him. He has become wary when questioned."

"Then you know him very well indeed. He's not being blackmailed, but he certainly feels threatened. I had asked him to do his best to keep the problem to himself but it seems those closest to him were not fooled."

"Will you tell me what is happening?"

He couldn't. Anna would worry unnecessarily, not for Carmichael but for herself and for her friends' continued good health. She'd already alluded to having bad dreams after Miss Goldwell's grizzly death. He didn't want her to know of the other murders he'd connected to Miss Berry's killer. "I don't want to."

She sat back, delicate jaw clenching and unclenching. Her eyes narrowed with suspicion. "Now I am worried."

Gilbert sighed and sat forward. She needed to believe him. He needed her not to worry. He and Carmichael and Lord Wade and Bow Street's Runners were investigating. "There is nothing for you to worry about. It is a matter for Carmichael and I and others to sort out."

"I do still think—"

"That I rushed my proposal." Her eyes widened. "I believe so, too. If I had waited until you knew me better, you might not feel so uncertain about your future as my wife. I should have taken more care of your reputation but what is done is done, and I cannot and would not change one thing." When she frowned, he rushed to add, "I noticed you even before we were introduced at Almack's."

She looked astounded by his confession. "You did?"

"Carmichael saw my interest, if you don't believe me. That's why he introduced us. I couldn't stop looking at you…even if I told him later that I was only impressed by how you managed to gracefully carry your long bow."

"Carmichael and I do not share confidences," she muttered. "If you were so interested in me, why did you not ask me to dance that night?"

"It was late, and I imagined I would have no chance of securing a dance with you. I also thought the timing of a romantic pursuit wrong. I still do, I'm afraid, which is why I am happy with your desire to take your time. A long engagement would suit me, too. I'm a stranger to society. To help Carmichael, I must make the acquaintance of a great many people I should have known all my life. I might not, I'm ashamed to say, be the most attentive suitor in London in the next week, two at most."

She shook her head, scowling. "This is beginning to sound very far-fetched."

He took up her hand. "What I do is very important but secrecy is vital at this delicate juncture. I cannot have anyone else know the other reason I linger in London. Not yet."

She frowned. "But you said you are helping Bow Street in the hunt for Miss Goldwell's killer too, didn't you?"

"Yes, of course I am helping with that as well," he promised. The two situations were certainly entwined. He couldn't tell her of the other deaths, all young women robbed of their lives before they'd truly had a chance to live and love.

Anna's fingers curled around his suddenly. "Am I in any danger?"

"No. Quite the opposite, we think, if you were to accept my proposal."

"We?"

"Carmichael and me. I don't keep secrets from him, nor him from me, so he knows I am courting you, and that I compromised you." He loosened his neckcloth, remembering the altercation in the carriage. "Just about strangled me for kissing you."

"Carmichael has no right to interfere in my life," Anna exclaimed.

Carmichael would interfere regardless. "You may not seem to get along, but to him you are family, and you should be protected from scoundrels. You have other defenders, too. Apparently, Lord Wade feels protective of you, although he swears to a purely platonic interest."

She shrugged. "He says I'm interesting to talk to."

"And he is right. You are very interesting. I noticed that right away."

"People usually notice my blush first."

He sighed. "Give me a chance, Anna. We've only just started to become acquainted, but I swear I will reveal all my secrets as soon as I am at liberty to do so."

When she stared at him, he saw uncertainty in her eyes, and skepticism, too. She might continue to think they would not do well together if he remained completely untruthful though. She might not think she could even love someone she'd only just met. He wasn't yet willing to admit he might be halfway in love with her already. He needed time to convince her to place her trust in him. He was determined to earn it.

For now, all he could do was nurture and encourage the attraction blossoming between them. There was one way to deepen their acquaintance here and now...if she wasn't against the idea or the risk. "Kiss me."

Her gaze darted toward the door but it was still closed against intruders.

When she turned back slowly, he could see he'd said the one thing that interested her most. She was attracted to him. He could press that advantage and offer himself up without any expectations of acceptance. "Kiss me, and stop when you've had enough of me."

She frowned and lowered her voice to a whisper. "Would you use such a lapse to ensure we married?"

"No. Not if it remains our secret. I've no wish to trick you into matrimony."

She considered that and then her eyes flew to his. "You have too many secrets, Lord Sorenson. I happen to have none."

He smiled quickly. "I'd hope if you had any, you would feel comfortable telling me of them one day. I will not keep secrets from you for long. I need a little time to help Carmichael then my life will be an open book. Do you believe you can trust me?"

"I… Yes, I think that might be possible."

"I trust you, and I'm willing to wait for you." He drew breath. "If we were to marry, we could live a long life together. It is important that we know each other inside and out. The good and the bad. I will tell you anything you want to know about my life. I will keep nothing back from my wife, and I hope she will do the same."

A hot color had filled her cheeks and he smiled quickly, glad to see that reaction.

"Marriage where there is a lack of feeling, of desire, is something I would like to avoid. I want my wife to desire me, and I think you might…though, of course, those emotions can take time to feel natural."

"I agree with all you say," she said, eyes softening.

He moved to sit on the settee where there was more space for kissing and whatnot.

He patted the spot beside him and then set his arms wide—

one hand on the armrest and the other arm draped along the back of the settee. "I'm all yours for the next twenty minutes. My hands will remain right where they are now so you may examine me, and your own desires, at your leisure, with my promise your virtue is perfectly safe for the duration of the experiment."

CHAPTER 14

Anna bit her lip. Very tempted by his offer. Father was away from the house for at least the next half hour and the servants would not interrupt them unless they were called. Father had gone to his club, a usual habit of his, and wouldn't need to know. Anna had promised her father she wouldn't go out or receive callers while he was away.

Lord Sorenson wasn't an ordinary caller. He was an earl determined to marry her. And he'd already been granted permission to speak to her privately on a previous occasion.

Although she shouldn't even consider Lord Sorenson's suggestion, she would like to kiss him again, without the romance of moonlight or surprise to cloud her judgment. A planned kiss, with no expectation of interruption, would decide her one way or another about him, she hoped. A conscious choice rather than a momentary lapse of reason was a sensible course of action to take.

She moved to sit beside him. "This is very unexpected of you," she murmured.

"If you had the faintest inkling of your own appeal, you wouldn't be surprised by my offer at all."

She turned to look at him properly. The Earl of Sorenson was a very handsome man. Stunning green eyes, wavy dark red hair; his closely shaven cheeks and high cheekbones suggested he kept himself to a healthy weight. He cared about his appearance but wore his clothes with ease. Unlike Lord Carmichael, her tormentor, he presented himself as a prosperous country gentleman despite his title.

But he was a scoundrel beneath it all. A man who spoke of desire when he should not.

A gentleman who had offered himself for her exploration without expectations or threat of ruin. The Earl of Sorenson wanted her to explore *him* intimately, and she wanted to do it, too.

She placed her hand on his thigh, felt hard flesh and warmth beneath her fingertips. She had admired many a man as they danced, legs encased in breeches molded tightly to their skin. The mysteries of Lord Sorenson's body sparked her curiosity.

Lord Sorenson's lips parted slightly as her fingers crept up his thigh. His breath became louder the higher her hand traveled up his leg. "Are you sure you want to explore that part of me first?"

She looked down at her hand and noticed her fingertips were trailing along the inside of his limb, nearing the junction of his thighs where the male anatomy differed from hers. She slid her hand back into her lap. "My pardon."

His eyes glowed with amusement. "Perhaps that exploration should come later in our acquaintance but please, don't stop touching me."

Reassured, she moved her hand to his chest and felt him inhale a deep breath as she explored the upper parts of his body. His chest was quite wide and felt hard, muscled. His arms strong but tense where they rested. "You seem quite fit and healthy."

"I did everything I could to avoid becoming a pudgy country vicar. The volume of food the parish wives delivered to my housekeeper for the poor lonely bachelor was quite staggering."

"What did you do with it all?"

"Invited those with less to dine with me most nights," he whispered.

Anna's fingers had reached his throat, and then she touched the point of his chin, high above the collar of his crisp white shirt. "That was good of you," she told him in a voice she almost didn't recognize. She licked her lips. "You're a good man."

"I certainly try to be," he promised. "But being good is a struggle right now."

He dipped his chin and her fingers came to rest on his lips. She brushed them, remembering how often he'd touched her lips the night of their first kiss. She felt a quiver of sensation between her legs as his tongue darted out to lick her. He looked at her sharply then smiled and did it again.

That same strange sensation caused her to shift to a more comfortable position. She rested against his thigh, bracing herself against him. She laughed suddenly. "I don't normally behave like this."

"I believe you," he promised, lips curving into a smile. "Please continue to misbehave with me," he whispered. "Come closer. Touch me some more, Anna."

Boldly, Anna swept her hand over his cheek and tangled her fingers into his hair. The color fascinated her, as did the texture. Coarser than hers but still very soft and clean. She'd never actually caressed a man's head before, not even her father's when he was unwell.

Lord Sorenson leaned into her touch, turning his face so that his lips brushed across her exposed inner wrist. He kissed her there, a playful smile hovering on his lips.

"I thought I was supposed to be exploring *you*," she complained.

"My hands haven't moved," he promised with a wink. "Come and kneel beside me," he begged.

"Why?"

"I'd like to be beneath you, at your mercy some more."

Anna laughed softly. She didn't think he could ever be at her mercy, but she liked the idea. She moved to her knees on the sofa, and as promised, Lord Sorenson kept his hands to the sides. He rested his head back on the cushion and smiled up at her. "You are so lovely. Come and claim your kisses."

Slowly, suddenly unsure of herself, she hesitated. She'd never kissed a man. Lord Sorenson had started both prior kisses. How did one begin exactly?

"Anna?"

Lord Sorenson stretched up suddenly and stole a quick kiss before she could decide how to take her own.

He lay back again, grinning hugely. "Couldn't wait another moment."

She laughed at his antics, bending closer to him as she did, then turned her lips to his grinning ones and kissed him.

Sorenson groaned darkly, parting his lips to capture her in a deeper kiss than she'd first thought to share with him straight away.

Anna drew back. "Was that all right?"

"Very right, actually." He made a show of reestablishing his grip on the furniture, knuckles white as he held himself to the rosewood. "I'm ready for more kisses, please," he said.

Anna put a bit more effort into the next kiss and felt the soft brush of Lord Sorenson's tongue against hers. Her lady parts quivered and she drew back. "You did that before. Why?"

"Did you like it?"

"Yes." *Very much.* She bit her lip. She liked the feelings he stirred in her body.

"Then do it to me, too," he asked. "Let me taste you again."

Anna dropped her lips to his but kept her eyes open, watching his face. His dark lashes closed slowly as the kiss intensified—as if he relished each moment with her. She did her best to mimic his kisses and they seemed to please him, given the little noises he made.

Kissing Lord Sorenson was wonderful, even when he was doing nothing to seduce her. Her body felt strange, restless.

Thinking of how much better it would feel, Anna found his right hand, pulled it from the armrest and brought it to her waist.

His fingers slid around her as he dragged her sideways onto his lap. Half lying atop him, Anna searched for his other hand. She tugged at his arm until she was fully in his embrace. Sorenson moaned softly against her lips again, and then completely swept her under his pleasurable spell as he kissed her witless once more.

True to his word, he made no move to exploit her weakness and growing excitement. He simply held her and kissed her thoroughly and slowly.

Anna wound her arms about his shoulders, holding herself to him as she accepted that her response to him felt right and more. She threaded her fingers into his hair and traced the shape of his ear.

But she was very restless against him. Sharing every breath and soft exhalation with him.

"It's become very heated between us," he whispered in her ear when their lips finally parted. "We should not let this go too far."

Anna whimpered. "But…"

"I know exactly how you feel, sweetheart." He drew back and caught her eye. "If this continues apace, I fear I won't be able to keep my promise to you."

"What promise?"

"You deserve better than to be tumbled on your father's settee the first time we make love. I don't want to ruin you but your kisses are driving me wild."

Anna drew back, smiling at that admission. "They are?"

"You have every right to gloat. I did say I wanted a wife who would share my desires, and we do. I want to continue. I absolutely do. But further intimacies should not be rushed." When he brushed her hair back from her cheek, Anna gave him another kiss. She did not really want to stop. She felt so very wonderful but strange, too.

Anna pressed her legs together firmly and moaned softly at

the pleasurable tenderness pulsing at the apex of her thighs. She was feeling very warm now. Gilbert's kisses had awoken her body in a way she'd never experienced before or expected. She ached for…something more from him. Something a wife would have.

Something she could have every day of her life if she accepted his proposal.

Anna drew back, struggling to catch her breath.

"You're biting your lip again. What is it?"

"Hmm, you might be right."

"About which matter?"

To feel this way again, to discover the rest of what pleasure means, she might be wise to marry Lord Sorenson sooner rather than later. Marrying this man had a greater appeal, now she knew the power of his kisses and her own. He'd kept his word. Allowed her to make love to his lips without rushing her or attempting to lift her skirts to take what might be his one day soon.

But could she live with him keeping secrets? If they did not affect her, as he'd promised, she'd only be depriving herself of a future she'd always hoped for. To marry well, to have a home. To have a husband who was comfortable to be around.

She took in her current position perched on his knees. Lord Sorenson was quite nice about allowing her to sit there still. His arm was loosely wrapped around her and she could flee at any time.

She stayed exactly where she was because she felt safe…and perhaps a little loved.

Her friends had always aspired to capture the attention of a titled gentleman for a husband, though Anna hadn't really believed she could do the same. But she had Lord Sorenson at her mercy now, an earl with a great estate in far off Kent, and he might just be the most appealing fellow she'd ever met, too.

Marriage was always a delicate meeting of two lives. She did not expect perfection. So far, aside from not knowing what Lord Sorenson was up to with Carmichael, he seemed an open book about everything else. He liked her, was curious about her interests, and desired her. He was waiting very patiently for her to explain her last remark, too. That meant a great deal to her—and she decided it worth the risk to accept him now.

"I would be honored to marry you, my lord."

She kissed him quickly to seal their bargain.

His grin when released was immediate and genuine. "It is I who is honored, Anna. Thank you."

Anna bit her lower lip, staring down into his eyes. She teased his ear again and he turned his lips to kiss her wrist once more. "Now what do we do, my lord?"

"To begin with, my name is Gilbert when we are alone."

"Gilbert."

He brushed her lips with his fingertip until she flicked out her tongue to touch him. Gilbert's eyes darkened further. "I'll need to speak to your father again now. For some reason, he didn't seem to believe I really meant to offer for you last time."

"He was only looking out for me," she conceded. "We hardly know each other."

"Trust me, Anna. You will know me better than anyone ever could." The pitch of his voice dropped, low enough to excite Anna, as it had the first night they'd met.

He set his hand to her hip and slowly skimmed down her leg and back up. Anna was nearly breathless by the time he stopped.

He chuckled softly at her response. "After the events of the past twenty minutes, I believe we'll be very happy living as man and wife."

"Twenty minutes have passed?"

He nodded. "Yes. Why?"

"Oh, dear. My father could be back at any moment."

"Good. I'd like to speak to him today and have the matter of our betrothal settled." His eyes twinkled with excitement but he lifted her up from his lap, stood and, after pulling her to the nearest looking glass, helped her straighten her gown and hair into some semblance of neatness. His lips strayed to her throat and when he kissed her there, Anna's legs nearly buckled under the onslaught of sensation that tore through her body. She may have even moaned out loud a little.

Then Gilbert suddenly stepped back and, staring into the mirror, raked his fingers through his own hair. He straightened his coat and waistcoat so it looked as if they had not just almost made love on the settee. That would be their secret forever.

He led her by the hand to a nearby grouping of chairs. "Now, tell me more about you. Have you ever visited Kent?"

"No," she confessed. "I was to go to Gloucestershire for Christmas with my father this year. That of course will change, now we are to marry, so tell me about your home and the families who live nearest to you."

When her father returned, they were laughing together, discussing the delights of his home in Kent and Anna's preferences for keeping dogs and cats as pets.

To say Father was surprised by Lord Sorenson's presence was an understatement. They were unchaperoned, and that fact utterly compromised her in her father's eyes. Anna did not feel she had been ruined by their private interlude, but she felt enlightened and excited. Her suitor was an equally honorable and wicked man.

And all hers now.

Father became instantly agreeable to a marriage between them when Lord Sorenson asked for her hand a second time.

CHAPTER 15

Gilbert struggled to hide his amusement. Gentlemen seemed surprised by the news of his betrothal to Anna, and there was consternation among even her acquaintances that Gilbert had proposed so quickly. Was everyone in London half-witted when it came to Anna's appeal?

She was delightful, soft and warm and very, very kissable. She was remarkably eager and that pleased him immensely. He leaned down to whisper in her ear. "Our dance is about to be called."

Her smile slipped a little. "We don't have to dance tonight."

"Of course we do. I intend to dance with you twice, too."

He wanted the killer to hear, see, that Anna Beasley was a woman off the market, even if she was not married yet.

A frown grew over her face at hearing his intentions, though. That Anna did not appear enthusiastic for a second dance with him meant he still had some ways to go in reassuring her, despite her acceptance of his proposal. He would repair the damage he'd unwittingly inflicted on her confidence if it was the last thing he ever did in his life.

Gilbert held his hand out to Anna, and with her father's permission, led her across the dance floor.

Anna fit perfectly in his arms and as the musicians began, he smiled upon her upturned face. "You look lovely tonight," he promised. "I think I might be the luckiest man alive to have won you."

"If you'll forgive me, I must confess there wasn't much competition," she told him in a whisper with apparent discomfort.

"And are they not idiots to have not seen your appeal?" he whispered. "They'll never know the thrill of holding you in their arms like I do."

"Now you are determined to make me blush," she chided.

"Just reminding you of how pleasant the occasion of your acceptance of my offer was for me."

She looked up then, shy, eyes sparkling with desire. "And for me."

He spun her about the room, fascinated by the light flaring in her eyes. She'd felt desire when they'd kissed. He'd noticed her little moans and how she had drawn her thighs together tightly.

Other men might have taken advantage but Gilbert was playing the long game, a game he needed to win for her sake. He wanted Anna to want to make love to him after they wed. Preferably on their wedding night but if not, sometime soon after, he hoped. Once she felt secure of her place in his affections, he saw no reason why they couldn't have a very satisfying marriage.

He was so swept up in Anna's expression, he nearly missed Carmichael slipping from the ballroom alone and out onto the terrace. He frowned when he didn't immediately return. There were Bow Street men outside, keeping watch over the house in case a stranger tried to slip in or out.

He glanced down at Anna, noticed her attention fixed over his shoulder, too. "May I escort you into supper tonight?"

"Isn't Carmichael expecting you to help him find this person he seeks?"

"He can wait. I'd rather be with you."

She glanced up, her lips lifted into a smile once more. "He hates waiting for anyone."

"He'll have to become used to coming second to you in my affections from now on," he promised.

She bit her lip and Gilbert laughed softly. "He can pout all he wants. I won't change my mind."

When the dance concluded, he was disappointed to have to let go of Anna. But he consoled himself that as an engaged couple, he could linger in her presence most of the night and, in due time, he could dance every dance with her after they married. People might be scandalized but what could they do about the behavior of a married couple?

When they were married, he'd be very happy to create any sort of scandal to prove to Anna she was dearest to him.

He curled her arm about his possessively and slowly strolled with her back to her father. The older man hadn't quite accepted their future marriage as fact and may never do so, Gilbert had already concluded. Mr. Beasley was much too fond of the idea of Anna and Carmichael marrying one day to consider anyone else might suit her better.

"How did I do?"

"You danced very well."

"But did you feel you had all of my attention?"

"I did." She looked up at him shyly. "I loved dancing with you."

He beamed at her, glad to know she was satisfied. "May I claim the honor of escorting you and your father home tonight?"

"You don't have to do that."

He didn't have to but he wanted to. "I think your father and I need to become better acquainted, too, and I wanted to show him the new carriage I've purchased for your use."

A look of wonder crossed her face. "You purchased me my own carriage?"

"I would buy you anything you might require for your comfort."

"I need very little."

"I'm sure that is not entirely true." He smiled again. "A second carriage will ensure you may visit anyone, should I be out in the other."

After a moment, Anna leaned into him. "I'm sorry about father. He just thinks he knows what is best for me."

"He wants Carmichael to be in my current place. That is not possible now."

"His dream was *never* possible." She shivered. "I'm so sorry if you feel slighted."

"Over Carmichael, never. Carmichael would not have agreed to marry you anyway."

"Do you say that because of the problem you are solving together?"

"Because Carmichael fell in love with someone else," he confessed.

She looked at him sharply. "Carmichael? In love?"

"I cannot say more," he confessed.

Anna frowned. "Is that part of the secret you share?"

"It is."

She bit her lip and then smiled up at him suddenly. "My father will come around eventually but…I don't suppose you fish, my lord?"

"I do. Why?"

Her smile widened. "Are you any good at it?"

"Fair."

"Then you should tell my father about the river that runs through the Kent estate and ask him if he fishes. My father loves nothing more than speaking to other anglers. I'm sure that will help him see the benefits of our marriage very soon afterward."

He beamed at her. "Very clever. I will do as you suggest and see if that does not improve my appeal."

Gilbert and Anna joined her father, and Gilbert remained at Anna's side. He resisted the urge to watch young women slipping away from the gathering, even though it was again Friday evening. Bow Street had hired more men than ever for tonight and Carmichael was somewhere outside, too. He was sure his absence from the patrol for one Friday would not hinder the investigation one little bit. After all, he had a betrothal to celebrate with Anna.

He posed Anna's question to her father and soon they were discussing the best fishing grounds they'd each tried, the size of their catches, and the delights of the Kent estate's nearly private river to fish on. Mr. Beasley was an avid angler, far better than him, too. At least they had a love of fishing in common, so he made sure to invite the man to come visit them in Kent as often as he liked so he could fish to his heart's content.

Just as he was beginning to really enjoy the discussion, a terrified scream rent the air.

The sound seemed to come from all directions at once. He looked around, just as everyone else was doing, too.

The orchestra fell silent, as did the entire room.

Anna clutched his arm as a second anguished scream broke the silence of the room and was abruptly cut off.

He looked up to where the sound seemed to originate. A dome ceiling loomed over them.

Carmichael barreled into the room, a look of panic in his eyes. "What has happened?"

Gilbert peered into the shadowed upper reaches—and saw a white gloved hand stretching lifelessly through the balustrade above them. "There," he said as he pointed up.

"Come on," Carmichael urged as he sprinted away toward the main staircase.

Gilbert hesitated, glancing at Anna. "Will you promise to remain with your father and never leave his side?"

Her grip tightened. "What about you?"

"I need to see what might be done."

"All right."

Gilbert ran after Carmichael, dodging slower guests intent on climbing the stairs. At the top, he found his host, Lord

Thwaite, standing over the body of a fallen woman. Lord Thwaite was pale and shaking. His grip on an unknown lady at his side, protective.

"She's dead!" Thwaite said in a horrified voice.

"Who is it?"

The woman in Lord Thwaite's arms answered after a pause, "Miss Myra Lacy. We just left her father in the card room not ten minutes ago. He was winning."

"Have him sent for." Gilbert pushed forward as Carmichael gently closed Miss Lacy's eyes. "Who found her?"

"We did," Lord Thwaite admitted.

"And the screams?"

"Mine," the lady admitted with a little sob.

"We did not see her at first," he confessed, looking uncomfortable.

Gilbert assessed the pair, weighing the odds of them being truthful. Their clothing was disordered, as if they had dressed in a rush or had been undressing. A tryst interrupted most likely, but Thwaite and the lady—not his wife—would bear further scrutiny.

"Carmichael?"

"She's been slashed across the throat." He moved a little, and Gilbert saw a long blade remained in her chest. "Sliced across the throat first, and then stabbed in the heart?"

He peered at the blade more closely, noting the fine, almost delicate design of the thing. It was not a weapon he was familiar with. Bespoke most likely, but not in any way ornate. It would be difficult to locate the craftsman but he would let Bow Street narrow down a likely manufacturer.

He looked around the high balcony. The location of this murder was exposed to discovery by anyone who happened to stumble up here. However, the imperfect illumination must have hid the assailant, at least at first. Given the amount of blood around the fallen woman, the killer must have some upon them, too.

"We need to hurry," he told Lord Thwaite. "Detain everyone."

The earl rushed off, shouting orders to his servants to secure the house.

Gilbert gestured Carmichael close. "Follow him and make sure no one leaves. Also, send Davis up after he sends for the magistrate."

As he spoke, he caught Anna gaping from the crowd near the top of the staircase. She was with her father, but her eyes were locked on the corpse.

"I just spoke to her tonight," she whispered to herself. Tears slipped down her cheeks in unending streams. "She congratulated me on my betrothal. She was happy for me."

Anna lifted her gaze to his and she sobbed.

Since her father could do nothing but stare in shock at poor Miss Lacy, Gilbert hurried to her and drew Anna into his arms to let her sob against his coat. She'd witnessed violence twice now, and he felt bad about that. He set his hand to the back of her head while he fumbled for a handkerchief in his pocket. "Here," he whispered.

She clutched the handkerchief to her face and continued to sob quietly against him.

"Someone had to see something tonight. Someone will have Miss Lacy's blood on their hands or clothing."

"I'm going to be sick," Anna whispered urgently, pushing out of Gilbert's arms and fleeing down the hall. He considered following but as she neared a room where two maids lingered, he hesitated.

"Is there a retiring room up here, too?" he asked of no one in particular. "I thought it was downstairs nearer the ballroom."

"Lady Thwaite always has an extra room set aside upstairs for the ladies with more delicate constitutions and sensitivity to crowds," Mrs. Hayes advised, growing pale with concern.

"I'll make sure Miss Beasley is all right." With one last

darting glance at the victim, Mrs. Hayes turned away, saying, "How terrible to die like that."

Mr. Beasley finally came out of his stupor and glanced around. "Anna?"

"Anna felt ill, sir," he advised Mr. Beasley.

Gilbert glanced down the hall, anxious for Anna to reappear. Anything could happen in that room, and she'd be defenseless.

Carmichael returned. "Davis was already at the door when I went down. The Runners have secured the house and begun inspecting every guest and servant they see for blood. Perhaps this time we will have the upper hand."

Mr. Beasley sucked in a sharp breath. "This time? Don't tell me this has happened before?"

"Shh," Carmichael urged quickly, pulling Mr. Beasley aside. "Best not to increase the panic of the guests any further."

Worry gnawed at Gilbert. There might still be other deaths if they didn't catch this killer soon. In the meantime, he was determined to ensure Anna remained safe. He couldn't bear the thought of losing her now. "Sir, might we both talk to you later in greater detail?"

The older man nodded as he spotted Anna returning. "I'm taking my daughter home now."

He'd been with Mr. Beasley and Anna all night, so he could vouch for them personally. "Neither of you are suspects."

Gilbert smiled at Anna as she returned. She was pale and trembling still. "I will see you to your carriage but Carmichael and I must stay. We will call on you both as soon as possible."

She nodded but leaned heavily upon her father as they made their way down the stairs. Gilbert followed them to the carriage door and waved them off. Then he returned upstairs to view the body of poor Miss Lacy.

"Another young life ended all too soon." He turned away from the body after making notes on how she'd fallen. "Damnation! Who is this attacker?"

"Miss Lacy's dowry had been five thousand pounds,"

Carmichael informed him. "She'd had many suitors, but none so far had won her hand that I've heard of. She was popular, and outrage will grow over her death."

Gilbert appreciated the information but he had a delicate question for Carmichael to answer. "Ah, I have to ask...did you kiss her too?"

"Not this lady. I had decided on Angela by the time we met." Carmichael's voice broke on his last words.

Gilbert set his hand to his friend's shoulder and squeezed. "We will have to reveal the loss of the rest of them now. Especially Angela."

Carmichael paled. "What will the killer do next, once everyone knows there's been a string of deaths—retreat or become even more unpredictable?"

"I don't know, Carmichael. I just don't know."

CHAPTER 16

Gilbert and Lord Carmichael arrived just before full dawn. Both were still wearing their evening clothes as they stepped into Anna's front parlor. Both appeared exhausted by their long night.

Only her betrothed smiled at her, and she rushed to meet him. Last night had been a grisly scene, so much worse than the last one. Anna couldn't close her eyes without seeing that horrible, sharp blade run through Miss Lacy's pretty pink striped muslin gown.

Gilbert took her hand in his and begged to know how she fared as he sank down at her side on the nearest settee meant for two.

"Better now that you have come," she promised him. "And you?"

"No worse for wear I expect." He kissed the back of her hand gently. "I'm sorry you had to see that again," he whispered in a voice that wouldn't carry far.

"The second time was worse because I knew Miss Lacy better than I did Miss Goldwell. She was nice to me, even if I wasn't brave the way she was about finding a husband."

He kissed the back of her hand again and squeezed her fingers firmly. "You're brave in the ways that count to me."

She looked across the room, where Carmichael and Father were talking amongst themselves in low tones. Father made a grab for Carmichael's shoulder, but Carmichael shook off the touch. "I'm all right, sir. Let us sit and I will start from the beginning, so that Anna might hear what we say, too."

Her father took a chair. "Yes, that would be appreciated. It seems you have been keeping secrets from me, young man."

Gilbert gripped her hand a little more firmly and then laced their fingers together. She stared at their hands and smiled slightly. She felt infinitely better when he was near.

Carmichael cleared his throat, drawing Anna's attention from Gilbert, and he winced. "I am sorry to have not been honest with you both, but you will see the situation is far worse than I ever wanted you to know. Angela Berry is dead, Anna. She died the night of her mother's ball," he told her with tears in his eyes.

"What? How?"

"She was murdered, in a kinder fashion than Miss Goldwell, and Miss Lacy last night."

"I say! Is Miss Goldwell dead, too?" her father cut in, sounding very shocked.

"Yes, Father. Two weeks ago now it was," Anna confirmed to spare Carmichael the confession. She'd never seen her tormentor so pale before or more upset. "I am so sorry about Angela, Carmichael. I know you were very fond of her."

"I loved her," he said simply. "We were to be married. I had already proposed, and we would have announced our intentions to our friends and family the night she died. She would be my wife today if someone had not struck her down."

"Have you hidden the truth all this time?"

He nodded. "For good reason. I was at first suspected of killing her. I found her lying on the conservatory floor and rushed to lift her up. Her blood stained my clothes, and without proof I'd just found her, the initial investigator detained me for questioning. If not for Sorenson's intervention, cool head and greater knowledge of investigation techniques, I might still be under a cloud of suspicion."

"No!" she cried. Carmichael might be many unpleasant things, but killer could never be one of them. Anna knew the Berry conservatory well. It was out of the way. Angela had suggested it was the most romantic place she knew. Anna had spent many a happy afternoon there sipping tea and trying to talk Angela out of falling in love with Carmichael. She could imagine Carmichael rushing to pick her up had she fallen, too. "It wasn't like her to leave her mother or her friends during an entertainment they were hosting."

Angela had loved the noise and chaos of society just as much as Carmichael did. She had thrived on entertaining. It was Anna who slipped away to find a quiet corner when the crowd became too overwhelming.

"No, she was very good," Carmichael said, voice cracking with the most dreadful pain, "but I have a terrible feeling she was lured away under the pretext of meeting someone."

"She would only have slipped away to meet you," Anna suggested. "She said once that she'd do anything if you would but ask. After all, your continued interest had pleased her mother to no end and made her life bearable at home at last."

Carmichael licked his lips. "Our arrangement was her idea in the beginning. I grew to enjoy our time together very much. Our conspiracy against her mother's matchmaking efforts was great fun. I wished to make it more." Carmichael bowed his head, and then shook it. "Angela was too good to be stolen away like this," he exclaimed suddenly. "So were the others. I will find who killed her, and them."

Gilbert brushed his free hand over his eyes. Neither one must have slept, but she kept her attention trained on Carmichael.

"You hinted there were other deaths last night," Father asked.

"Yes, sir. After Angela died, I recalled there had been other unexplained deaths. Sorenson looked into my suspicions, and now he and Bow Street believe they were victims of the very same killer."

She looked at Gilbert in surprise. "How did you do that?"

"I have worked for Bow Street for a number of years." He gestured to Carmichael. "I knew he was innocent of course, having been the recipient of his written confidences about his affection for Miss Berry for some time. His connection to the other victims is flimsy at best but it is the only lead we had to begin with."

"What connection?"

"I had kissed them," Carmichael confessed.

Anna gasped but Father did not seem shock by that admission. "You thought you were responsible?"

Carmichael looked away.

"Miss Lacy's death breaks the connection to Carmichael," Gilbert murmured. "He did not kiss her and so her death lacks that similarity to the other murders."

"I see." She looked at her betrothed more closely. He exuded confidence and familiarity in the detection of crime. He was far and away more secretive than she'd imagined. "This was the secret you kept from me?"

"I did not want you to be afraid." He nodded. "All the deaths we've connected to this murderer have occurred on Fridays during a popular ball," Gilbert murmured as he reclaimed Anna's hand. "There are enough deaths spanning two seasons to justify a full investigation by Bow Street."

She stared at Carmichael. No wonder he'd been so odd of late. "There has to be a reason the people around us are dying. These are my friends," she cried.

"Do you think I don't know that?" Carmichael snapped, raking his hand through his hair frantically. "Do you think I would not try to stop it if I knew how?"

"That's why I must remain in London," Gilbert said with deadly seriousness, drawing her attention. "I've had enough experience investigating crimes that Bow Street has put me in charge of the investigation."

"They call him the Almighty's bloodhound in his parish," Carmichael remarked, moving to stand behind a single armchair. He gripped the back so tightly, Anna feared the wood would crack.

Gilbert grimaced. "London is a more complicated situation."

Her father stood and poured himself a drink. Anna noticed his hands trembled as he set the decanter down. "So do you have any leads yet?"

"We are interviewing all parties involved with the victims," Gilbert replied. "We've been at this for weeks now, and still have nothing but more bodies."

Anna squeezed his hand tighter. "You'll figure it out. I have faith in you. In both of you," she said, including Lord Carmichael in her comment. He seemed quite upset over Angela, and she felt she owed him her compassion and support. "We were talking only last week about where Angela had disappeared to."

"We?" both Gilbert and Lord Carmichael demanded.

"Myself and Portia Hayes are friends and confidants. We could not understand why Angela was not in London when you were obviously attending every *ton* event."

Lord Carmichael pinched the bridge of his nose.

"Steady, Carmichael," Gilbert cautioned. "Tears won't bring her back."

Lord Carmichael looked their way. "We're going to need a wedding."

"A wedding?" Anna asked.

Carmichael strolled close, staring at Gilbert. "She needs to be protected."

Gilbert sighed.

Anna glanced between them. "Who does?"

"You," Carmichael stated. "I want you and Sorenson to marry immediately. I need certainty that you are safe."

Anna blushed and extracted her hand from her betrothed's. "Carmichael, that is none of your business."

"It *is* my business. You are my oldest friend, and I need Sorenson in his right mind. I can't do this alone. Sorenson is always hovering over you as it is. Until Miss Lacy, the deaths have only been unmarried women in want of a husband that I have kissed."

"You still worry you're to blame?" She stared at Carmichael. "You kissed *me* once. I suppose that's why you think I might be next."

Anna's father spluttered at her remark. She hadn't blabbed to Father about Carmichael's shocking behavior some years ago. She couldn't look at her father now, or her betrothed.

Carmichael shrugged apologetically. "There *was* mistletoe hanging over your head and everyone else was doing it."

When she risked a peek, Gilbert did not seem pleased by the news. He seemed to swell in place and become threatening. "When was this?"

"Many years ago," Carmichael promised. "A peck on the lips."

"I was fourteen, and Carmichael a pretentious eighteen years of age. I hated him for it. He only did it to spoil my memory of my first kiss, which should have been my future husband's."

Carmichael appeared abashed and mumbled out an apology. "Regardless of that, marrying Sorenson will put you firmly out of harm's way."

"*Could* put her out of harm's way," her betrothed cut in, correcting Carmichael. "There are no guarantees the killer has even considered her a target. I won't coerce her to marry me. There are a few days left to make any decision about advancing the date precipitously. The killer only ever strikes on a Friday, usually at a well-attended ball or route. As long as Anna remains around people day and night, she should be quite safe."

"And what about the others who slip away while your attention is fixed on Anna next Friday?"

Gilbert shifted a little. "Anna will always claim my attention. Marriage will not change that."

Anna felt a burst of pleasure at his words. It was one thing to have him reveal his interest in private but quite another to hear it openly declared before her father and oldest...well, what exactly should she call Carmichael now? He'd been truly horrible to her as a child, but that was then.

"As a married woman, she could also keep an eye on her friends with us," Carmichael suggested. "She would be a chaperone to them."

"That could very well put her in danger," Gilbert protested, voice rising.

He shook his head, seemingly unconvinced that she could help. But Anna decided there and then that she would help by removing herself from any danger. "We could marry, my lord, if it would free your time to catch Angela's killer."

"Anna," Father cut in. "I think we gentlemen should talk in private now. Go to your room while we discuss what to do next."

"No, Father. I will not cower and hide from this." Anna smiled at her father, hoping he would one day understand. "I am marrying Gilbert, Papa.

"You said yourself that you needed time to get to know him."

"But I know *myself*."

Gilbert's fingers tightened on hers but he was smiling now. "You don't have to decide this today."

Anna held his gaze, feeling the desire between them stir. A rushed wedding wouldn't ordinarily be her first choice but she suspected she wouldn't regret doing so. He made her feel things she'd never experienced before. He would make her feel more on her wedding night. "I do want to marry you, my lord."

"You could get a special license," Carmichael suggested.

"I could do that, yes."

Anna studied her betrothed. Did he look a little pale all of a sudden? Marriage was a big step, for both of them. He had always sounded so certain about marrying her that for a moment, she worried he was the one now having doubts. Yet the way he continued to caress her hand spoke of affection. Perhaps he simply disliked the suggestion that they rush to the altar.

"We could certainly decide the details of the wedding," she suggested.

"That should be enough for now."

"I agree," Anna said. "My friends will be surprised by the rush but they will help me."

"Surprise them. Surprise everyone," Carmichael declared suddenly. "Other people don't matter when you love each other."

Anna nearly choked over the mention of love but Carmichael wasn't finished.

He squatted down before her and stole her hand from Gilbert. "I want your promise that you will remain at home with your father until the wedding day."

The warmth she'd begun to feel for Carmichael diminished. "Despite everything that has happened, you have no right to tell me what I must do or not do," she reminded him.

"You'll do as I say and be sensible. I won't have Sorenson fretting over your safety. There are other ladies in danger who need our help. Women like Angela Berry and Miss Lacy, who never deserved such deaths. I won't have yours on my conscience, too."

Anna's irritation drained away in the face of his words. Carmichael was right about the marriage being a distraction, and he so obviously blamed himself about Angela and the other poor victims.

She didn't want to die. She didn't want anyone to worry over her, either. If Gilbert had come to care for her as much as Carmichael suggested, he would worry and not have his mind on the business of chasing down this horrible murderer. "I'll stay at home," she said meekly.

"Thank you, Anna," Carmichael murmured. He stretched forward and pressed a kiss to her forehead. "I couldn't bear to lose you, too. You're almost a sister to me."

Anna scowled. "I hate to think how you'd behave toward a

real sister when you were a boy. How you've convinced Lady Scott you're an angel rather than a devil is one of life's great mysteries."

"My godmother knows that not all I say is strictly true. Some of my scandals are made up just to amuse her." Carmichael barked out a laugh and drew back. "I should be going. I need sleep and there is still so much to do."

"And I must go too, unfortunately," Gilbert added as he gained his feet. "I may not be able to see you very much in the next few days."

Anna chuckled softly and stood, too. "I think I can survive a little time apart from you without feeling abandoned." Anna walked him to the door. "I will see you when I see you."

"If I cannot come, I will send round a note before bedtime." He kissed the back of her hand tenderly again, a habit Anna thought very sweet. "I'll be back to see you as soon as I can, and we'll talk again about setting a wedding date and everything else."

Anna's stomach flipped. She would be his wife soon...and all the duties and delights that entailed would begin sooner than she'd ever dreamed. She wet her lips and looked at his. Kisses and more to share with her handsome suitor. She wasn't a fool to be afraid of marriage. She was looking forward to being alone with him again. "I'll be waiting right here," she told him. "I promise."

CHAPTER 17

Gilbert pulled Carmichael close on the footpath outside the home of Mr. and Mrs. Lacy, parents of the latest victim. "I hardly think now is the time to be grinning."

"I would stop if you would cease looking at your pocket watch." He assumed an innocent expression. "Eager to get back to your sweetheart, are you?"

Davis made an odd sound, abruptly cut off.

Gilbert simply stared at his friend and the Bow Street Runner and shook his head. Carmichael had been teasing him mercilessly about Anna, much to Davis' amusement. But Gilbert also understood why his oldest friend was making a fuss over his new status as a soon-to-be-married man. It *was* sudden, the last decision he'd ever wanted to rush into. It was yet another way Carmichael hoped to distract himself from missing Angela Berry and what might have been if she'd lived. It was easy to forgive Carmichael his little digs. "The Lacys are expecting us, yes?"

"Yes." Carmichael smiled tightly. "The mother will weep."

"All mothers do."

"Do they? I wouldn't know from my own experience."

Perhaps not. The late Lady Carmichael had been a cold one,

more interested in status and appearances than offering her only son any sort of affection. That was why Carmichael had so often visited him in Kent. The late Lady Carmichael had never been at home and had flitted about society, seeking attention and amusement at the expense of her relationship with her son. She had ignored her husband, too, and the late Lord Carmichael had lived his own separate life to the full in London.

Gilbert rapped the knocker and they were shown into a drawing room shrouded in black crepe already; with the drapes almost fully closed against the outside world, he shivered. The family, father Percy and mother Beatrice, were flanked by their oldest son and younger daughter, John and Rhea. The victim had been the middle child, and he could see her features in each person before him.

"Thank you for agreeing to see us, Mr. Lacy. Mrs. Lacy. Please accept our sincere condolences for the loss you have suffered. You know Lord Carmichael of course, and this is my associate, Mr. Davis of Bow Street."

Mr. Lacy nodded, a sharp dip of his chin, and bade them sit.

"Carmichael here has likely explained why I wished to speak with you today. Your daughter's death must be solved of course, but I am afraid to say there are other deaths that might be connected to this killer's actions. Every little detail could be important. Would you repeat again what you remember of the evening?"

The father seemed to shake himself awake. "Yes, well. Our carriage arrived to take us there after nine and we drove directly to the ball."

"We arrived before ten," the mother murmured. "I heard Lord Thwaite's clocks chiming the hour not long after Myra took to the dance floor the first time." Mrs. Lacy sniffed back her emotions. "She danced with her father first, and then was claimed by Lord Carmichael."

Gilbert consulted his notes, as Davis looked on over his shoulder.

"Her later dance partners were Lord Grindlewood, Lord Bellows and Lord Wade," Davis murmured, and all present nodded to confirm.

"Between sets, do you recall who she spoke to?" Gilbert asked Mrs. Lacy.

"Oh, everyone we knew most likely," the grieving mother promised. "My daughter was well liked by all."

Gilbert wet his lips. "Did she go off without one of you, other than to dance?"

"Just the once." Her mother lowered her chin. "She never came back."

Young Mr. Lacy shook his head, and Gilbert watched him a moment before speaking. "Whatever you tell me will not be spread about to harm her memory. I swear it."

The brother drew in a shuddering breath. "She was alone and unchaperoned for a few moments an hour before she disappeared," her brother confirmed.

The family turned as one to stare at young Mr. Lacy until he spoke again. "She walked the ballroom with me for a time and then begged to cry off," he said.

"Cry off?" Davis asked.

Mr. Lacy squirmed. "Yes, she withdrew," he muttered.

Gilbert glanced at Davis. "To the ladies' retiring room."

"That is where she said she wished to go. I don't know if that was true or not now." Mr. John Lacy nodded, glancing a little guiltily at his mother, who was staring at her son in horror. "I didn't consider it dangerous to let her walk there alone," he promised. "It was just the retiring room. She must have drunk too much punch earlier."

"And it may not be important at all," Gilbert said quickly to allay John Lacy's fear that he'd let his sister down.

He thought a moment. A quick trip to the retiring room was common, unless she wasn't really going to that room but met with someone instead. "What was her mood upon her return?"

"Happy, buoyant, in fact," Mr. Lacy answered. "She seemed as if she'd received good news or amusing gossip."

So she did meet with someone—a suitor perhaps. "Did she mention what was the cause of her improved spirits?"

"No, and I did not think to ask. I had a dance next and went to find my partner as soon as she returned to Mother. I did not speak to or see Myra alive again that night."

Gilbert glanced around at the victim's remaining family. Her parents had been at the ball, not the youngest daughter, so he looked to them first. "Did she mention anything to either of you that might be worth repeating? Gossip, running into a friend? A suitor?"

"No, I was by then in the card room," Mr. Lacy informed him, face crumpling as if he was about to cry. "I won a thousand pounds as my darling girl lost her life!"

He stood abruptly and departed the room in a rush, which Gilbert understood and did not seek to prevent. Carmichael, however, hurried after him. Gilbert could hear them talking in the hall but nothing of the meaning.

Gilbert turned back to Mrs. Lacy. "And you?"

"I was talking with my friends." She burst into tears and, like her husband, fled the drawing room.

Gilbert knew abrupt emotional responses were common during an interview with the families of victims. Still, he had so many questions about Miss Lacy's nature to uncover. He faced the Lacy siblings, who had drawn closer to each other on the settee.

"We are sorry to ask such distressing questions," Davis began. "But it is important that we learn everything we can about your sister."

"We understand, sir. We want our sister's killer brought to justice. It is very good of you all to come," Rhea promised Davis, sounding much older than her fifteen years and quite sure of herself. He remembered Miss Lacy had spoken to him in a similar way.

Davis smiled warmly and the younger girl smiled back shyly.

Gilbert cleared his throat and brought her attention back to him. "What sort of sister was Myra?"

The girl's face lit up. "She was wonderful. She gave me some of her nicest gowns, and a gold chain, even though she could still wear them. She told me all about the *ton* and the important friends she'd made during the last two seasons."

"I have only recently returned to London but I hear she was very popular," he suggested, eager to judge the siblings' reactions to that description. "Particularly with the gentlemen in want of a wife."

"My sister was admired by many potential suitors," Miss Lacy claimed proudly. "Her dance card was always full."

The young John Lacy, however, had folded his arms across his chest and scowled at him.

Gilbert focused on the younger girl. He did not want to tarnish the younger sister's memory of the recently departed by suggesting something that might not be true but he needed to know who she liked best. The sisters might have shared secrets. "Did she favor one gentleman over another?"

Miss Lacy glanced around him toward the door, looking worried.

"It's all right to say she did," Gilbert promised. "I will not spread it about."

"Well…" She glanced sideways at her brother.

"Tell us," Davis begged of her. "It could be very important."

She winced. "She fancied Lord Carmichael quite a bit."

"I see." No surprises there. Gilbert was fairly sure his friend featured in any number of young women's fantasies. "How exactly do you know she favored him?"

"She wrote a poem about him once."

Davis sat forward eagerly. "Did she send the poem to him or show anyone?"

"No. Never." The sister shook her head quickly. "I took it

from her room after she died so Mother and Father would not know how silly she was about him."

Davis' eyes narrowed. "But you read it?"

The young girl nodded quickly.

"Rhea!" John Lacy exclaimed in shock. "How dare you go through her personal correspondence?"

"It was dreadful, John." Rhea scrunched up her face in disgust. "I knew she had hidden it in her room. She wouldn't want Mother or Father to read it. They would have thought less of Myra for writing such fanciful imaginings," the sister whispered to her brother.

Gilbert brought his finger to his nose, indicating he'd keep the secret forever. He did not believe the knowledge that the recently deceased Miss Lacy was writing love poetry about Carmichael would make his friend feel any less at fault.

A servant appeared at the door. "Your mother asks for you, Miss Rhea."

Miss Lacy offered him a quick smile and excused herself to answer the summons.

Gilbert turned back to the brother. He was on his feet, staring down at him. Gilbert quickly gained his own, sensing without the need for words that this interview was almost over.

"We are returning to the country to bury my sister tomorrow," John Lacy announced.

"I would attend if it were not so vital to remain in London and continue the hunt for her killer."

"Thank you," he murmured. He stepped closer, one eye on the door where Carmichael and Mr. Lacy still spoke together. "My sister was a good woman, or would have been, if she hadn't been so foolish sometimes."

Gilbert inhaled sharply, scenting information he sorely needed. "Foolish?"

"She had it in mind to decide her own fate, choose her own husband, much to my parents' disapproval and mine."

"Many women want that," Davis remarked. "Doesn't make them any less foolish than the men who want the same."

Gilbert hushed Davis. Getting into a debate over freedom to choose was not what they were here for. "What sort of fellow was she chasing?"

"All of them, at first," the brother said with considerable embarrassment. "She would have caught one by fair means or foul."

"Would she have slipped away to meet one of her suitors if she believed she could bring him up to scratch?"

John Lacy nodded, lips pressed tight together.

"Was she as interested in Carmichael as your sister hinted she was?"

"I suspect so." He pulled a face. "I know Carmichael did not return the sentiment but Myra was definitely trying to catch his eye any way she could. I believe he wasn't involved in her death but still, he never managed to dissuade her to look elsewhere for a husband."

Gilbert did not like where this conversation was headed. Carmichael already blamed himself. "Carmichael may not have noticed her particular interest to pay it much thought. He grieves for Miss Angela Berry."

John Lacy's eyes widened with shock. "Is Miss Berry dead?"

"I am afraid so. Murdered, too. Carmichael was on the verge of announcing their marriage when she slipped away from a ball," he shared. "He found her, already gone. We feel almost certain the deaths must be connected in some way."

"So that's why Myra couldn't have him," Mr. Lacy said in a hushed tone as he rocked back on his heels.

"I beg your pardon?"

John Lacy frowned. "When we first came up to London, nearly two months ago now, someone suggested to my sister that a titled husband was beyond her reach, especially him."

"Who said that?"

"She never did tell me, but it was someone who must have

known the *ton* well to give advice so freely. Myra was infuriated by the advice and became quite determined to prove them wrong. She declared to anyone who would listen that her heart was fixed on bringing Lord Carmichael up to scratch. She planned to make him fall in love with her as soon as possible."

"I would have done the same thing if someone tried to deny me my heart's desire," Davis mused out loud.

John Lacy nodded, his eyes widening once more. "Do you think the killer disapproved of Angela Berry, too, and killed her to stop her marrying Carmichael?"

Gilbert nodded slowly as he considered the question. Every new bit of information led his enquiry straight back to Carmichael. "Yes."

"Dear God, my sister must have known her killer. *He* must, too." John Lacy sank into a chair as if he had no more strength.

Davis drew Gilbert aside to whisper, "I know he is your friend and innocent of the crimes, but we must look into Lord Carmichael's affairs again."

Gilbert glanced quickly over his shoulder. "Carmichael wouldn't have willingly colluded with a killer. He is too soft-hearted to wish anyone ill. The killer might hold a grudge against him or might even be in love with him."

"Agreed, my lord," Davis promised.

Gilbert pondered the two possibilities with concern. Whoever it was, they had stopped Carmichael from making a match with Angela Berry, someone they must have perceived as unsuitable. "We must keep this conversation between us. I don't want him knowing anything about this yet."

Davis pursed his lips. "Very well, my lord. I'll keep quiet. For now."

He found a new page in his book to write upon and returned to John Lacy. "Tell me the name of every person you recall your sister speaking to in the last two weeks. Everyone."

"That's a lot of names," Mr. Lacy warned.

"Don't leave anyone out. Everyone she might have contact

with is a suspect. I am at your complete disposal for as much time as you can spare," Gilbert promised. He needed to know precisely when Myra Lacy and Carmichael had met, and where also.

And then, despite the awkwardness he would feel, Gilbert would put his best friend's affairs under a microscope…and hope he never learned of it.

CHAPTER 18

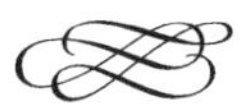

Anna sighed as she arranged roses in the morning room. She was feeling so happy today but decidedly sad, too. She was getting married soon but her friends had been murdered. Their killer remained at large somewhere, plotting to carry out unspeakable evil again most likely. Although she hadn't seen her suitor in days, he had written her sweet notes to let her know he was always thinking of her. He never mentioned much of his investigation but to say it continued.

She trimmed the stem of the last budding rose and popped it into the vase with all the rest. Gilbert sent flowers every morning. Today, a larger bunch than usual had arrived to brighten her day.

"There you are," her father said as he strode into the room.

"Good morning." She kissed his cheek and returned her attention to filling the vase with water from a jug. These were her favorite flowers of all those her betrothed had sent so far. "You're up early, Papa."

"I wanted to talk to you before you became busy." Her father reached for her hands as she moved a stem to a better position. "Anna."

Father wore yet another serious expression on his face. Had

he come to talk her out of this marriage again? "I won't change my mind."

"Marriage is forever."

"I agree." She smiled. "I know Lord Sorenson well enough to look forward to forever with him."

"He has not called on you in days," he said, eyeing the vase with a scowl.

"He said he might not find the time. He does write each evening. They are very sweet notes. We have no secrets anymore."

"A letter a day hardly counts as a proper courtship," he grumbled, handing her a flower she had missed, hiding under wrapping paper.

"Father, please," she complained, turning to face him. "What is it about Gilbert that displeases you? He is always a gentleman, an earl, serious in nature, and very pleasing to me."

"This is not what I imagined for you. He consorts with the criminal class."

"He *catches* criminals. There is a vast difference between the two," Anna reminded him. "I know you always wanted Carmichael as your son-in-law."

Her father fell silent, looking down.

"We don't like each other that way. I always hated visiting him when I was young," she reminded him. "Carmichael gave his heart to Angela, and I will give mine to my husband."

Her father sighed. "I think his words and actions have proved he cares very deeply for you."

"He cares for me enough to prove he doesn't want me to die," she said softly. "That is not the love I want from my husband."

Her father sighed again. "He kissed you."

"Not a very good kiss." She punched her hand on her hip, studying her arrangement one last time. She knew what a real kiss was like, not that Father could ever know that. The mere thought of kissing Carmichael the same way as she'd kissed her betrothed made her feel ill. "I kicked him in the shin for that."

Her father chuckled. "You always did complain about him.

Even when you were small, you would cry when he came too close. Your mother said you would come around."

"I'm sorry to say this, Papa, but Mama was very wrong. I think she would have liked Gilbert very much."

"Gilbert now, is it?"

"You'll like him if only you'd give him a chance. We have all sorts of amusements planned for you when you come to stay." She looked at her father curiously. "Are you worried you'll be all alone and forgotten when I marry?"

He shook himself. "I have my club."

She hugged her father. "You will still have me, and Carmichael will need you, too. He may not have married Angela Berry but he loved her very much, the way I think you loved Mama. We should keep an eye on him to make sure he does not become cast down and despondent."

Father nodded. "I asked him what I could do to help but he wouldn't hear of it."

"He is always stubborn."

She set her flowers on the wide mantel, longing for the return of her betrothed. Gilbert made her happy, excited and eager for marriage, and the marriage bed. It was a yearning she would keep to herself. Father was not aware of her scandalous behavior with Gilbert, but if known, he would be disappointed in her and might dislike Gilbert even more. Fast women were shunned by other women of the *ton*. She'd heard that many times in the last two seasons from her mentor.

A throat cleared. "Miss Hayes has arrived, Miss Beasley."

Anna smiled. "Do show her in," she exclaimed. They had so much to talk about, none of it involving unpleasantness.

Father slipped from the room, allowing them privacy.

Portia was helping her decide on items for her trousseau. Without a mother to guide her, she was a little uncertain of what she would need for her wedding night. Miss Hayes, who possessed a sweet if scatterbrained mother, had offered to look over her purchases and make a few suggestions if anything more might be needed.

Portia rushed into the room looking harried and embraced her. "My dear Anna. What a relief to finally be with a friend."

Ordinarily, she and Portia did not embrace each other with such affection. "Whatever has happened?"

She glanced around, no doubt making sure they were really alone. "I couldn't wait to escape my parents. They really have no idea how to behave."

Anna laughed softly. Portia was a dramatic one and her parents vastly amusing sometimes. "Tea?"

"Yes, please."

Anna rang the bell to summon a maid and turned back to her friend. "What have your parents done now to embarrass you?"

"Since the moment they heard about Miss Lacy's murder, they've become ridiculously concerned about my whereabouts, even at home. I swear they deliberately follow me all over from room to room."

"They love you."

Portia pulled a face. "I woke this morning to find my mother standing over my bed, waiting for me to wake up."

Anna did not remember her own mother at all. "How sweet."

"It was not sweet when she's never done that before." Portia shuddered. "It was downright unsettling. This morning, I was having a lovely dream just before I woke. You know, one of *those* dreams."

Anna blushed. Anna had those, too. She wouldn't want anyone observing her asleep when they happened, either. "Oh, dear."

Portia swooned back in her chair. "Quite ruined those lovely sensations, I promise you that."

Anna knew about those lovely sensations firsthand. They were better in real life than in her fleeting dreams. "Who was the lucky gentleman?"

"I will never reveal his name so do not ask."

Anna sat forward. Portia liked to talk about her fantasy lover but was always cagey when it came to revealing his identity. "Was it the same man as last time?"

"Perhaps," she murmured with a pleased grin.

"We need to get you a husband," Anna teased.

"Fantasies are all very nice while you are having them, but the reality of life tends to bring one back down to earth quick smart."

"What has happened? Did the man you like snub you?"

"Not at all," Miss Hayes promised. "But someone else thinks he has a chance of winning my hand by cozying up to my parents."

"Who?"

Portia screwed up her face and it seemed she was stewing over his identity.

"Portia?"

"Lord Wade keeps coming around. He had dinner with us last evening." She shook her head. "I fear my father likes him too much."

"Oh," Anna mumbled.

"He's rude and vulgar and my parents won't listen to my warnings. They think he's a gentleman just because he is a viscount, and they force me to join them when he calls."

"Did he call on you today, before you came here?"

"He did." Portia smirked though. "But I slipped out before I could be forced to drink another cup of tea with him. That'll teach him for not taking a hint. And on top of everything, one of my coachmen swore another carriage followed us here."

What was Lord Wade doing? He already knew Portia disliked him as a dance partner. Anna hadn't thought him so determined to pay her back for that, which befriending Portia's parents proved he was. She glanced at the small mantel clock. "He called on you very early."

"If he continues coming around, everyone will think he's a

real suitor. I swear I saw him standing outside my house last night before I went to bed. He's become insufferable."

Anna winced. Lord Wade was asking for trouble, following Portia around like that, if it really was him. People would talk, expecting a proposal. "I know he likes you, even though you've never once encouraged him to think you could feel the same way."

"Yes! I've done all I can but give him the cut direct. I fear I shall have to be that mean if I'm to have any peace. It is ridiculous the way my parents are giving him false hope. I have never encouraged that man. I've done all I can to repel him, but still he comes back for more of the same."

"Well, he's not here now so you may breathe easy."

"Thank heavens for that."

The tea came and they drank in silence. What Lord Wade was doing was unsettling. Unmarried heiresses were in danger.

She looked at Portia again as a sudden thought dawned—Lord Wade knew about Miss Lacy's death, and the others, too. Her betrothed had told her Lord Wade was helping with the investigation. Was Lord Wade trying to protect Portia, in his own clumsy way? She thought that might be a possibility, given her parents were such scatterbrained creatures. Everyone knew that about them. Portia had slipped away from them any number of times, and completely undetected, too.

Lord Wade had told Anna she was the second-most interesting woman in society, but he hadn't revealed whom he considered the first. He may not be trying to be one of Portia's suitors, but if he was following the woman, the killer would never catch her alone.

What was it Lord Carmichael had confessed? The killer had targeted young women who had kissed him, besides Miss Lacy.

She glanced at her friend suddenly. Lord Wade knew a lot about everyone. He might know that fact, too. Portia had allowed some of her admirers to kiss her in the past. She claimed it was the only way to tell if a gentleman was worth considering as a potential husband. Her parents probably had no idea their daughter might be considered a little fast by some.

"Portia?"

"Hmm," she replied.

She sat forward and dropped her voice low. "Have you ever been kissed by Lord Carmichael?"

Portia glanced her way and didn't answer at first, but her lack of expression and stillness suggested she had.

Her heart rate increased a little. Portia might be in danger and not know it. "Does anyone know?"

Portia frowned. "Yes."

"And..."

"Lord Wade saw us together." Portia wrinkled her nose. "Last season, before Carmichael and Angela became a pair. You're not going to tell Angela, are you? She will be so cross with me for not telling her about it first."

"Angela will never know." She bit her lip. "What did Lord Wade say?"

"Nothing. He turned his back and stalked off. A pity he didn't keep going." Portia smiled quickly. "What of you? Has Lord Carmichael ever tried to steal a kiss from you?"

Anna scowled. "When I was fourteen. Kisses at that age hardly rate a mention, but I told Angela all about Carmichael stealing my first ever kiss."

"The first kiss doesn't matter as much as the last one." Portia smiled. "Where is your earl this week?"

"He has a few business matters to deal with, but he sends me flowers each day and a pretty note each night."

"Love notes? Let me see one!"

Gilbert's notes were not exactly declarations of love, but she still would not share them for what they would reveal of his secret investigation. Occasionally he asked her questions, which she faithfully answered by messenger the same night. "They are very personal."

"But I tell you everything about my admirers," Portia

exclaimed. "How can you be so mean to me when I show you mine?"

Anna saw movement beside Portia and cried out, "Lady Scott! Lord Wade! Father!"

The butler hadn't announced any further callers, and she wished her father hadn't just waltzed his visitors into the morning room without any warning. Anna had never even heard the front door open and close or footsteps in the hall.

She jumped to her feet quickly and dipped Lady Scott a deep curtsey. Portia was wise enough to do the same, hiding her feelings about Lord Wade's arrival behind a wide smile for Lady Scott.

You did not fail to show respect to an elder lady of the *ton* or a member of the aristocracy when you were not one. Lady Scott had warned Anna that she would quickly be removed from guest lists if one whiff of improper behavior were linked to her name. The same would be true for Portia if she were not careful.

Anna quickly gestured to the vacant chairs. "Please, won't you all join us?"

She shot Portia a warning look when Lord Wade chose to sit beside her friend. Lady Scott took the chair nearest Anna and was watching them both through narrowed eyes. Father took his customary place beside the fire.

She saw worry in his eyes. Just how long had Lord Wade and Lady Scott been listening to her private conversation with Portia? Hopefully not long enough to overhear everything they'd spoken about. Especially not about kissing and receiving love notes.

"How lovely to see you both," she said, although for the first time she did not mean it.

"I've just been speaking with your father about this match you've made," Lady Scott began. "Quite unexpected."

"Is it?" She looked to Lord Wade when he made a sound.

He smiled quickly. "Not unexpected at all, my lady. Lord Sorenson is a lucky man to have quickly captured the attention of the woman he admired at first sight. I trust the wedding will not be far off."

"I am not certain," she confessed. "We have not as yet set a date for the marriage to take place."

"But he will procure a special license soon," Lord Wade told her, nodding as if he knew.

"He promised he could when the time came, and then we have a month to wed, I believe," she told him.

"That is correct." Lord Wade sat back, smiling broadly. "He'll go of course to see his former colleagues in the church to complete the ceremony."

"We hadn't discussed particulars of the service as yet."

Lord Wade nodded. "I am sure I am right that he will."

"Your father has been telling us about Lord Sorenson's involvement with Bow Street, to solve Miss Lacy's demise, Miss Beasley," Lady Scott told her. "I cannot say I like the idea of someone of his rank consorting with criminals."

"He has a long association with Bow Street, and is very determined to catch Miss Lacy's killer," she said with a quick glance toward her father. "There is nothing about the earl and his involvement with Bow Street that is in any way disagreeable to me."

Her father voiced his agreement, and Anna was relieved to finally hear him support her betrothed.

"Indeed. Have you fully considered the implications of marrying a gentleman involved in such a dangerous business? If your mother was here—"

"Well, she's not." Anna stared at her mentor hard. "Surely you could not object to a man pursuing such a noble cause. Never forget, he is titled—which had seemed to me to be everything that you required in my future spouse."

"Was a title really all that you cared about, Miss Beasley?" Lord Wade asked with a knowing smile.

"Don't be ridiculous. I really like him," she insisted. "He at least listens to me."

Lord Wade laughed then and rubbed his ear. "If you speak that loudly all the time, we all could hear your opinions and not have any doubts."

Anna, unaware that she'd shouted her praise, got her temper under control very quickly. "I won't change my mind."

"Anna's opinion is the only one that should matter when it comes to marriage," Portia declared, frowning at Lord Wade, as if perplexed they were on the same side of an argument. "If she likes him, that is good enough for me to call him my friend, too. Anyone can see they are smitten, bound to fall in love."

"It does seem that way." Lord Wade smirked slightly then. "You must have known quite a few brides since you came out three years ago, Miss Hayes. What does love look like on a woman's face?"

"Two years ago," Miss Hayes bit out.

Anna quickly slid her foot sideways and bumped Portia's before an argument could be started. Quarrelling with Lord Wade would not do her reputation any good. Lady Scott was absorbing every word and might just have Portia's name stricken from her friends' guest lists if she didn't like the response. She had to fix this, calm everyone down.

Anna pasted on a smile and looked at her guests. Lady Scott always told her that to recover from a disagreement brewing in her own home required a lady to set aside her feelings and act as a proper hostess at all times. "Would anyone care for tea?"

CHAPTER 19

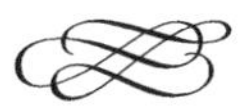

"We're ready," Gilbert murmured as they entered White's just before midday. There were a dozen of the wealthiest lords already seated in the Morning Room and a dozen or so coming and going on the stairs. The *Times* newsman had the official story from Bow Street. The printing presses should be running at full speed. Details of the killings would be in the papers that very afternoon. Soon enough, members of the club would have the afternoon paper spread out before them and the questions and suspicions would begin to circulate.

"I don't like this," Carmichael murmured, taking a seat and asking for a pair of whiskeys to be delivered to them. It was early to be drinking but Carmichael had taken to imbibing much earlier in the day than he used to since Angela Berry's death.

"Steady, man. This was inevitable. It will work." He certainly hoped so. Innocent lives depended on the word spreading as fast as possible. There was no way they could keep the other murders quiet any longer. The killer was too fast, too clever. Gilbert was about to unleash the wrath of the *ton* upon their heads.

Carmichael drowned the drink quickly and asked for a refill immediately.

Gilbert only sipped his. "There's nothing more we can do."

"Panic is sure to spread."

"Yes." Fathers would remove their unmarried daughters from London, shielding them from the threat. He wanted that.

Carmichael was collapsing under the weight of self-doubt and misplaced guilt. It was also time they had a little chat about his absence from the Thwaite ballroom the night Miss Lacy died, too.

"How are you sleeping these days?"

Carmichael shrugged, staring down at his drink. "Every time I close my eyes, I still see her face. So pale. So still," he whispered.

"You must try to turn your thoughts back to happier times you shared. I know you're finding it difficult to hide your feelings. She would not want you to suffer like this."

"How would you know what she would want? You never met her."

He nodded. "The woman you described to me loved life and loved to laugh. She loved her friends and amusements to be found in London. The little notes she added to your letters proved her bubbly character. You made her happy, you said, at a time when her mother's expectations were unbearable."

Carmichael looked down at his hands. "I didn't deserve her."

"She loved you and wanted to marry you without question. Remember that, and know you'd chosen well for yourself." He sighed. "I'm worried about you. I know you're slipping away alone at night without telling me where you're going. Drinking too much, too. You need to be with friends more, not watching life pass you by from the shadows. If you do not feel you can turn to me for comfort, then remember you have your godparents, too. One day, you'll find room in your heart to love life like you once did."

"Beasley said something similar, but you know neither he nor Lady Scott married a second time."

"I cannot speak about Beasley's situation, or your godmother's. You must know Beasley better than anyone, but he had a daughter to love, and that might have been enough for him. All I am saying is do not commit yourself to any decision yet. Give yourself time to heal."

Carmichael smiled quickly. "You are a good friend."

"The best," Gilbert promised, smirking a little to make Carmichael's smile widen. "Now, what do you say we spend a little time in the dining hall and get some food into you before you get drunk."

"Might be wise," Carmichael agreed.

An hour later, when Carmichael seemed to be dozing after they'd taken luncheon together, servants swept into the club carrying freshly pressed news-sheets.

"The news-sheets have been delivered early today," he warned Carmichael, who came fully awake immediately.

One by one, the news-sheets were passed about the room. Carmichael grabbed one for them and scanned the article. "Exactly as you wrote it, I think."

Gilbert read it too, pleased there had been no sensational embellishment added to the story before printing.

Within minutes, a deathly silence fell over everyone. The faster readers, especially those who must have female relations in London, were quick to find their feet.

Each cast a shocked glance toward Gilbert, because he was named in the article as an investigator working for Bow Street to catch this killer. His association with Bow Street had never been widely known before, and he had liked it that way. Some might consider him a spy in their midst and be put out with him, too. He'd danced with a lot of daughters in recent weeks. They might feel he'd been disingenuous with them all.

However, catching the murderer was more important than a few ruffled feathers. Each murder had been described in the paper with just enough detail that he hoped to tug at the memories of those who'd attended the events.

A reward for good information had been offered, mostly

funded by Carmichael's estate, and some from Gilbert's own pocket, too.

The men with daughters fled the club. The others merely stared at each other. Soon enough they began to talk amongst themselves, discussing the deaths and the locations mentioned.

Lord Wade rushed over. "This is how you chose to inform society?"

"We didn't want to create a panic borne from distorted fact," Gilbert explained.

"Guaranteed you'll have one now." Wade shook his head, jaw clenching, and then he left, too.

Gilbert frowned after him. "Wonder where he's off to in such a rush? Does Wade have an unmarried sister I don't know of?"

"No. He does have a younger brother though." Carmichael frowned as well, staring after him. "Were you sure he was innocent?"

"There's always a first time I could be wrong." And if he'd made a mistake in clearing him, some young lady would pay for it. "I'll follow him. See where he goes," Gilbert decided. He looked at Carmichael. The man was tired. "You better stay here a while and collect information from those who come looking for me. I will see you at my home later, all right?"

Carmichael agreed.

Gilbert rushed outside to the footpath and looked around.

He spotted Lord Wade nearly running away from the club and gave chase. Given Wade's haste without a known cause, Gilbert trailed behind at a discreet distance to see what he did next without alerting the man that he was followed. However, his caution was unnecessary. Lord Wade never looked back once. He went straight to his home, a modest dwelling on Hanover Square, and disappeared inside.

Gilbert stopped a distance away but kept an eye on the front door. After a few long minutes, he began to look about. He couldn't watch Lord Wade's home all day. This was a Runner's work. A gentleman in fine clothing loitering on the street was bound to draw attention if he did not have a reason for being there. He didn't know anyone who lived on this street, unfortunately, so he had to find someone to take his place.

Just as he spotted an urchin to watch the house, a carriage drew up before Lord Wade's dwelling. The viscount emerged a few minutes later. He carried a sack in one hand and a basket in the other. A pair of servants followed, carrying a trunk between them.

Lord Wade was leaving London—and in something of a hurry, by the way he barked at everyone who worked for him.

Alarmed, Gilbert started forward to intercept. Unfortunately, Wade dived into the carriage and it pulled away before he could reach the house. The carriage moved fast and was soon lost from sight in the thickening traffic. He looked about for an empty hack, or even a horse to commandeer, but there were none in the street to be had.

Gilbert swore under his breath and considered his chances of following Lord Wade on foot and catching him with his head start. The odds were not good.

However, there was a young man from Lord Wade's household standing on the pavement, watching him. The man could tell Gilbert what he needed to know, or be taken in for questioning.

"You there, where has Lord Wade gone?"

"He didn't say." The fellow looked him up and down. "But he said someone might come. Lord Carmichael…or is it Lord Sorenson?"

"Sorenson," Gilbert said uneasily. "What is he up to?"

"My brother does what he thinks is necessary. It isn't always appreciated by the recipient," he said, smirking. "Now if you will excuse me, I'm responsible for our aunt now. Never an easy task."

"Wait. I want to speak to her."

The fellow looked surprised. "Are you certain you want an interview with her? You won't like what she has to say. No one ever does."

Lord Wade's aunt, Mrs. Hesper Lenthall, was often with Lord Wade at society events. She may have her own suspicions to share about where Wade was going, and he needed that information now. "Yes, I need to speak to her."

"Very well, but don't say you were not warned." The fellow held out his hand. "Nigel Royce, my lord."

They shook hands, and he was led inside a very modest townhouse and into what must have once been a beautiful drawing room. The fabrics used to decorate the room were faded now, the colors dulled by age and exposure to light.

"Auntie," Nigel Royce called softly to wake the woman from her drowse.

The small woman, perched on a chaise lounge, blinked her eyes and peered across the room at them. "Is that you, Mouse?"

"Yes, Auntie," Nigel promised. "We have a visitor."

The old lady brought a lorgnette to her eye and studied first Nigel and then Gilbert. After a full minute of scrutiny, she set the lorgnette aside and popped a sweet into her mouth. Her eyes were bright, sharp, like a bird who sees a shiny new treat has landed at her feet. "Lord Sorenson. What an unexpected pleasure this is for me."

Gilbert swept into an elegant bow.

Lord Wade's brother dropped into a lounge and sprawled out. "Wade was right that someone would come," he told her.

"It is a mistake to underestimate him," she said, and then cackled with laughter. "That boy does provoke the worst suspicions in people."

Gilbert sat when gestured to a chair. He perched on the edge, aware he might be delivering terrible news to someone so old. "Do you know where Wade has gone?"

"Of course." The woman peered at him. "My nephew tells me everything."

"Then you know I'm investigating the murder of innocent young women?" Gilbert asked.

The lady and nephew looked at each other then burst out laughing.

"This is not a matter to laugh over," Gilbert told them, incensed for the victims.

"Well, it is if you suspect my nephew of such actions. Wade wouldn't harm a fly."

"Well, he frequently kills those," Nigel stated, giving the old lady a wink.

"Indeed he does. And I have no complaints about that habit of his." She reached for her wine glass and took a sip.

Gilbert cleared his throat. "I need to know where your nephew has gone, madam."

"Away with a clear conscience that he has done all he can for the little doves he admires," she promised. "Wade noticed the absences first. Even so, we can't help but lament that the boldest fillies have all disappeared from the race to the finish line. It's been a very dull season without them enlivening proceedings."

"The boldest ones are dead?"

"Why, yes. Don't you realize that yet? Well no, I suppose your attention is somewhat distracted by your own little dove." The old lady smirked. "The lasses bound for ruin have always been the most amusing during the season. I remember the year I married, there were three deaths that year. Harlots, every last one of them, too. Terribly popular they were. Such a shameful waste of future gossip."

Gilbert stared at her, thinking of the statements piled over his desk at home. Yes, the victims had all been outgoing young women, but could it be as simple as that? He'd looked for links to Carmichael and found none but kisses connected them. They had studied other rakish bachelors who may not be acceptable enough to make a match with the victims, as well as any debts the victims' parents may have held over others.

Was it really as simple as someone trying to get rid of women they considered a bad influence?

That would confirm that Anna was in no danger. She was an

innocent—or had been before they'd met. But if anyone found out what they'd done together before the engagement was announced, would she still be safe?

Sudden fear gripped him. Lord Wade and Lady Windermere had known all about Anna and him since that fateful Friday night. They had *found* them together, and knew Anna had been compromised. If the killer had learned of that meeting somehow, Anna might still be in danger.

"I have to go," he said. He needed to marry her and put her good reputation beyond any doubt. "Thank you for seeing me."

"Yes, you'd better rush off to that sweet little thing you're to marry. Wade wouldn't like anything bad to happen to her," she suggested. "She is such a naïve, trusting gel."

Anna had assured him she would not venture out without her father, but he had no idea who might have called on her in her own home over the past few days. The killer might change their tactics and strike out at any time.

Gilbert was out the door, arm raised to signal the first carriage that spotted him, and on his way to Anna's home, still too slow for his liking.

CHAPTER 20

Anna hurried to the drawing room to greet her unexpected visitor, her maid hard on her heels. Her betrothed had come to call at last. "My lord!"

"Anna," Gilbert said with a heavy sigh, and then came forward to take her hands. "It's very good to see you."

"And you." She looked up into his beautiful eyes but worried at the strain she saw in them. "Is everything all right? There hasn't been another death, has there?"

"No, it's not yet Friday, thank God."

She breathed a sigh of relief too and smiled up at him. She had been worrying for nothing, but after reading the afternoon paper over Father's shoulder, how could she be blamed? Her betrothed had told her only part of the scope of his investigation. "Can you stay awhile?"

"Yes, all afternoon in fact, if you will allow it."

She did her best not to crow with excitement at having him all to herself once more. It had been a difficult few days. She'd been looking for him all week and had made do with his letters. "I'd like that, too."

"And who is this?" he asked, looking behind her.

"This is Jane Lord, my maid and companion since I was a girl."

He smiled warmly at Jane. "A pleasure to meet you, Miss Lord."

"And you, my lord."

Gilbert turned his attention back to Anna, lifted her hands to his lips, and pressed a gentle kiss to her knuckles before lowering them again. "There is much I'd like to talk to you about."

"I feel the same, although now you're here, I've no idea how to start any sort of serious conversation. Come, sit down with me."

Jane scooted into the room ahead of them, finding a corner chair where she could sit unobserved and work on mending. After reading the paper today, Father now insisted Anna never be alone, even at home. Unfortunately, that meant she wouldn't be able to kiss her betrothed unless Jane turned away.

Gilbert hesitated to sit. "I should make my presence known to your father."

"Father is in the study with Lord Carmichael," she told him.

Her betrothed frowned, glancing toward the doorway in obvious surprise. "Carmichael's here?"

"Yes. He came not long ago actually, but I think they might be arguing now."

"Arguing? Over what?"

She shrugged, glancing at her maid, who nodded. "Father and Carmichael do not agree on every subject, even if Father loves him very much."

"What are they discussing today?"

"I've no idea. I gave up listening long ago. Jane, did you hear anything?"

Jane cleared her throat, looking a little guilty. "Begging your pardon, but Mr. Beasley is concerned about Lord Carmichael's association with Bow Street."

Anna was not surprised, given her father's concern over her betrothed's involvement with them, too. "Someone has to investigate, and it might as well be someone who has suffered a loss," she said. She looked at Gilbert curiously. "Was that how you became involved with them?"

"A death in my parish. The local magistrate recommended me to them afterward for another case."

"I see." She smiled brightly, determined to distract him. "Tell me about your day, since I don't imagine I'll receive a letter from you."

He smiled quickly. "You've read the afternoon paper, yes? Well, after seeing that handed out to the club patrons, I spent today chasing down a new lead in the investigation. That's actually why I came to see you, to ask for your advice."

Gilbert had been very curious about her life and her connections in his letters, so she nodded, eager to be of assistance yet again. Though she did wonder what more she could share with him that he didn't already know. "Oh, what would you like to know now?"

He glanced in Jane's direction.

"She can be trusted completely, about everything, I promise," Anna whispered.

He nodded. "Tell me about Lord Wade."

"Lord Wade? But I've told you he's just a friend."

Gilbert gave her an odd look. "Pretend I'm your best friend in the world. Tell me what he is really like."

"But I have. We talk, because we attend many of the same balls. He calls on me the day after we have danced together, as expected." She sighed. "He is courteous but occasionally a little blunt when he speaks."

"Disrespectful?"

Was he disrespectful? Not really, but she wouldn't want him to speak his mind any louder around others. "Coarse, is perhaps a better term. I've come to think he does it on purpose to ruffle our feathers."

"Yours and...?"

"Oh, myself and my friends." Anna smiled quickly. "I think

he says a lot of things in order to draw attention to himself. He seems intent on upsetting Miss Hayes most of the time, and that would be because she dislikes him."

"Really? I hadn't sensed that."

"Portia goes out of her way to avoid Lord Wade. She is always complaining about him watching her. Just the other day they were both here in this room. The air was so thick with tension it was a relief to have them gone."

Her betrothed considered her remark a moment. "He disapproves of her?"

"I suspect he likes her, actually, but Portia will have none of him, though he has never confirmed his interest other than a vague mention of 'being at the denial stage' with the object of his affections. Unfortunately, her parents remain oblivious, and have forced them together by inviting him to dinner and tea of late. Which reminds me, would you care for tea?"

"Yes, thank you. That would be lovely."

Anna turned to Jane. "Would you mind asking Cook for a tea tray to be sent up soon? For yourself too, Jane."

"Thank you, Miss. I'll be back in a moment." Jane slipped from the room with a soft laugh.

"There," Anna said as she faced her betrothed. "Alone at last. I'm sure you did not come to visit me just to pass the whole time in idle gossip."

His smile was immediate. "Well, perhaps not only to gossip."

Anna threw herself into his arms as soon as he finished speaking. The investigation was important, but so too were the feelings he stirred in her. She needed to be kissed. Yearned for his arms to be wrapped around her body again.

She found his lips and kissed him. Gilbert was quick to respond, cupping the back of her head with one hand to hold her near. Yet he drew back too soon, resting his head against hers in a way that melted her heart. "We'll get in trouble for this if caught," he whispered. "If Jane were to tattle…"

"Then we'd better not get caught," she said before kissing him again. "Jane will say nothing."

"Still," he said, drawing back farther. "Should your Father come in, he would not be pleased with me."

He was probably right that she ought to restrain herself a little. Fighting her desires, she sat back and straightened her gown. "My father and mother had an affectionate courtship. He used to say that she made him feel wonderful just by stepping into the room. You do that for me, too."

"Your mother died when you were very young?"

"Youngish. I remember a few things about her still. Her hands cupping my face, wrapping a blanket around me a little tighter on a cold night." Anna smiled. "She liked bluebells best of all. Father still keeps pots of them about the house at all times even now."

"That is a sweet gesture." His frown returned. "They had so little time together."

Her mother had died when she was four. They'd never had another child, and the loss of her had nearly broken her father's heart into little pieces, he claimed. "A few years really. Father never considered remarriage, although I'm sure he had admirers."

Gilbert looked down on her. "I begin to understand only now why he wouldn't want to marry again."

Jane returned while Anna fought another blush. Such a sweet thing to say but also sad, too.

She poured him a cup of strong black tea, the way he liked it, and then offered him cake. She'd already gleaned some of his preferences. A discreet enquiry by Jane to his household staff had yielded surprisingly useful information. He was a man of simple tastes and habits, some of which mirrored her own. He would be easy to manage, to live with, if he was always honest with her.

She felt he wasn't being completely forthright today. "Something is wrong. I can feel it."

"Yes." He smiled. "I am worried, Anna, about the delay we agreed to with our marriage."

"How so?"

He moved closer, perching on the edge of his chair. "You and I have begun to know one another very well. But if certain aspects of our private rendezvous were known…"

"I would be ruined."

"Considered ruined, yes," he said. "I have begun to worry that the killer is someone you might know."

"I have thought of that, too. The victims were my friends, and my friends introduced me to theirs many times."

"You are not much different than the young ladies who met a grisly end. Young, unmarried, well dowered, pursued by scoundrels." He winced. "You allowed me to capture you."

He felt guilty about what they had done together. "We are an engaged couple and you're not a scoundrel."

"Without a date set for the wedding to occur, I fear you now stand out for closer scrutiny. We have been alone together several times now," he murmured. "Even today."

"You want to announce our wedding date?"

"I want to marry you and ensure your safety," he told her.

Anna stood, disturbed by his sudden haste. A few days ago, he'd been content to wait for as long as she needed. She had enjoyed getting to know him. She had enjoyed kissing him and touching. But now waiting, allowing her further time to explore this man and the depths of their feelings for each other, was something that made him concerned. "What has happened that makes you wish to rush?"

He swallowed. "In speaking to others, now the truth is out in the open, it has been brought to my attention that the victims of this particular killer may have been considered to be *too* friendly when it came to the gentlemen courting them."

She spun about, offended by what he said of her friends even if there might be some truth to it. "They are my friends. Carmichael must deny such allegations."

"Not just with Carmichael, whose offenses I consider harmless."

She gaped. "You believe they were killed because they were considered fast."

"I am afraid it is a distinct possibility, whether they were or not."

The time she had spent alone with her betrothed would certainly damage her reputation if known or gossiped about. If anyone discovered she'd kissed him several times, perched boldly on his lap and allowed him liberty to touch her body, nay encouraged him to do so, while she touched *him*, she might as well paint a target over her heart, too.

"What have I done?" she whispered.

He stood and captured her hands in his. "Don't be afraid, but do you understand why we must keep to a very proper courtship from now on? We should never be alone again, and you must never hint that we have been before."

A proper courtship would mean no more stolen kisses. She would see him, chaperoned at all times. They would dance together and talk in a crowd but never while alone together. Now she knew her own needs, she did not want to be proper anymore. "What you suggest is unacceptable."

"Anna," he chided. "I only want to protect you."

"And you will." She bit her lip. Now was not the time to grow timid again. "Did you by chance secure that special license you spoke of?"

"I have one, but there are weeks left to use it."

Anna grinned. She did not want to wait weeks to kiss Gilbert again. She knew her own mind. "We will marry tomorrow."

"Tomorrow?"

She smiled at his surprise and brought his hands to her lips. She kissed them the way he kissed hers. "I don't want to wait. I don't want to miss another moment with you."

She didn't want to die a virgin.

Across the room, Jane quietly clapped with considerable excitement, bouncing in her chair. "At last, a wedding!"

Gilbert threw a grin at Jane before turning back to Anna. "Your father may not like the rush."

"Everything is already decided. The housekeeper, Jane and I, and Portia Hayes have already planned what must be done on our wedding day. The wedding breakfast is already decided, guest list prepared, though it will take Jane and I most of today to be ready to leave for your home by tomorrow afternoon."

Gilbert lowered himself to the arm of a chair and drew her close. He smiled up at her shyly. "You wouldn't set a date for our marriage, but you meticulously planned for it anyway?"

"I like to be prepared for anything." She shrugged. "Tomorrow will go very smoothly, I'm sure. We will be married before the killer has a chance to strike and you will be free to catch them without worrying about my safety. Do you have someone in mind who might marry us that quickly?"

"Yes, an old friend from the church has already said he would be happy to preside over our nuptials. I'll visit him after I leave and make the necessary arrangement."

"Good. Eleven would suit for the ceremony, if you don't mind."

Her betrothed smiled, holding her hands firmly. "All we need to do now is inform your father of our decision."

"We should see him together."

"That might be a fine idea." Yet Gilbert made no move. He sat smiling up at her, a ridiculously happy grin on his face.

Anna leaned down and kissed his lips quickly. "There."

"That will just hold me over until tomorrow," he promised.

"Me too." She pulled him to his feet but he spun her around until she was leaning into him.

"I'm ready, and my household is ready, for our marriage, too," he confessed, dropping a kiss to her cheek.

"I cannot wait to see my new home." She looked across the room. "Neither can Jane. She will be coming with me, of course, to act as my lady's maid."

"Excellent idea," he agreed. "Let's find your father and give him our happy news, shall we?"

They trouped from the room arm in arm. Tomorrow she'd be a bride, a wife, a lover to the man who made her feel things she'd never dreamed of.

Jane trailed after them, being the dutiful chaperone Father demanded. She promised to wait outside while they consulted with her father.

Father's study door was shut.

They knocked at the same time and then grinned at each other.

Father jerked the door open, scowling fiercely. "I said I wasn't to be disturbed."

Anna faltered in the face of his expression. "Even by me? We have news, Papa."

She looked behind him to Carmichael, who was sitting before Papa's desk, face ashen. Anna rushed across the room to him. "What is it?"

"It is nothing, Anna."

"It does not look like nothing." She turned on her father, putting herself in front of Carmichael. "What have you said to upset him? He has every right to consort with Bow Street to catch Angela's killer if he wants to."

She felt a tug on her gown and turned. Carmichael was grinning up at her. "Are you attempting to protect me, Anna?"

She frowned at him. "I approve of what you're doing. Angela would too."

"We were just talking about her," he promised, tears forming in his eyes again. "And how one day I would not feel such pain over her loss. I cannot imagine that."

"You're young yet," Father murmured. "The pain never goes away but we grow used to carrying it with us."

Carmichael nodded. "I loved Angela, and she's gone, and there is nothing that can change that," he murmured. "People depend on me at home. When the killer is brought to justice, hanged for their crimes, I intend to return to Edenmere and remain there for the rest of my life."

"You'll feel differently in a year's time," Father told him. "You'll long for friends to share new adventures with."

"Besides, we do expect you to visit us this summer in Kent," she told Carmichael. She moved to stand at Gilbert's side, curling her arm about his. "We have decided to marry tomorrow. Gilbert has a special license."

"Tomorrow?" Father and Carmichael said at once.

"With your blessing of course, Father," she murmured. "And yours too, Carmichael, since you will stand up with Gilbert. I would like to be safe and securely wed before Friday arrives. I know it could be dangerous but I want to help if I can, even if it is only to make sure my friends are never alone at the next ball."

"Congratulations," Carmichael said, striding forward to shake Gilbert's hand. "This is just the happy news I needed today."

Carmichael turned toward Anna. "May I?"

Anna wasn't sure what he meant, but when she stepped forward, Carmichael pulled her into his arms and hugged her tightly. "He's the best man I know. He'll make you so happy."

It felt strange to be embraced by Carmichael, but she did not resist. "Thank you."

"Do you think we could be friends now?" he asked.

"That depends on whether you intend to borrow my parasol ever again."

"No," he said, and then chuckled softly against her hair. "I've no reason to hide in dovecotes anymore if you're going to be married."

She felt a firm tug on her arm and looked around.

"That's enough of that," Gilbert complained as she was dragged from Carmichael's embrace to his. "She's mine now."

Carmichael laughed and turned to her father. "What do you say, sir, shall we drink another toast to the happy couple?"

"Yes, I think so. In a moment." Her father looked at her with his lips pressed together, but then he held out his arms. She rushed to him, and her father held her tightly. "I will miss you, daughter. I will miss you very much."

"I will miss you too," she whispered.

When her father drew back, his eyes were suspiciously moist.

Carmichael drew his attention immediately. "Now, sir, what are you doing for Christmas this year? Anna said you might have plans but if not, I'd be very pleased to have your company. My dear godmother may even join us if we are fortunate."

Carmichael clapped Father on the back and led him toward the whiskey, winking over his shoulder as he went. "Nothing needs to change between us, sir, when Anna marries old Sorenson here," he promised. "Except now we may both indulge in the contents of my wine cellar without Anna glaring at us all night."

CHAPTER 21

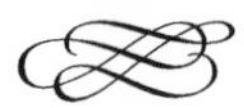

Gilbert was nervous as he mounted the steps to Anna's the next day. At his side, a vicar that would marry them, an old friend from his college days who had joined the church with him.

He rapped on the door and was let in. He'd sent a note last night to confirm all was well, and another when he first woke, to let Anna know he was thinking of her.

He was shown to the drawing room, where Anna sat waiting with her father. He sighed at the sight of her. She looked lovely, if a little pale. The rush of the marriage would be unsettling, so he would forgive her any awkwardness that might arise. He felt a little of that, too.

"Miss Beasley," he said as he stepped forward to kiss the back of the hand she held out to him. "May I introduce an old acquaintance of mine? This is Mr. Jackson Fielding, of St. Bartholomew the Less. He's graciously agreed to marry us today."

"Leave off the remarks about my age, Sorenson. I'm only a few days your senior." He held out his hand to Anna. "How do you do, Miss Beasley?"

"Very well, thank you," she said, smiling widely. "I am so glad you could be here today to marry us."

Fielding narrowed his eyes on her. "Are you sure you want to marry him?"

"Why wouldn't I?"

"Well, look at him. He's not aging well," Fielding warned, throwing Gilbert a cheeky smile.

"Pay no attention to the good vicar," Gilbert advised. "The man is nearly blind and in his dotage. I suspect he has only just enough strength in him to get us married."

Anna laughed softly. "My eyes are perfectly sound, and I think he is perfectly handsome."

Fielding laughed. "My word, you've definitely pulled the wool over her eyes."

He glanced at Mr. Beasley, noting he also looked a little pale. He made the introductions but wondered if his future papa-in-law might be ill. Although, Gilbert remembered, he had been still toasting the marriage with Carmichael when Gilbert had left the day before.

Gilbert introduced the vicar to her father.

"We need witnesses," Fielding murmured, looking around the empty Beasley drawing room with a frown.

"They will arrive shortly," he promised, smiling at Anna's maid, Jane Lord, as she slipped into the room to view the wedding ceremony from the corner.

Mr. Fielding glanced his way. "Who will they be?"

"Lords Carmichael and Windermere. I believe you will remember Carmichael from school. Lord Windermere is Miss Beasley's cousin, and his wife will be joining us too, as will Miss Hayes and her parents, along with Lord Carmichael's godmother, Lady Scott."

Anna came close and Gilbert took up her hand, wishing he could steal a taste of her lips before everyone else arrived. It was remarkable how often he thought of kissing Anna when he couldn't be with her. Soon, he'd never have to wait for the perfect moment for kisses ever again.

There was a kerfuffle at the door as the first of his witnesses arrived, full of excitement for the wedding.

After greetings were exchanged, Lord Carmichael pulled him aside. "Are you nervous?" he asked.

Gilbert snorted. "Not at all."

Carmichael nodded, glancing across the room to where Gilbert's future bride stood chatting with Miss Hayes. The pair seemed very excited.

"Have there been any developments?"

"Grindlewood has been cleared," Gilbert told him. "As has Miss Hayes and anyone related to her."

"At least after today, Anna will be safe," Carmichael added. He still looked worried but there was nothing Gilbert could say that wouldn't increase his anxiety. The investigation was now focused on Carmichael's life and connections, but he didn't know that yet. Bow Street Runners followed him everywhere, and everyone he spoke to, even in passing, fell under suspicion.

"We have a few days until Friday's ball." He patted Carmichael's shoulder. "Bow Street has committed even more men to the chase. Exeter is funding the venture."

"Good. I think—"

Mr. Beasley signaled to him impatiently, and they gathered everyone into the drawing room, with himself and Anna standing in the middle before Mr. Fielding.

Fielding smirked at him and then opened his hymn book.

Gilbert had performed a number of weddings before and knew the marriage service by heart. Instead of listening to the words, he watched his bride's expression as Fielding spoke. He'd never seen her so lovely as when she committed herself to him.

He took her hand, slipped a simple gold band upon her ring finger and sealed their lives together. His name to spare her life. He glanced at the guests, smiling, until he saw Lady Scott's cold expression. That was another connection of Anna's he had yet to win over. And he would, after the murderer was caught.

He squeezed Anna's fingers as the service concluded and kept hold of her hand as they were congratulated by their witnesses.

Anna kept sneaking peeks at him until Miss Hayes joined them. "I always thought I would marry first," Miss Hayes said immediately after kissing Anna's cheeks twice and hugging her tightly.

"So did I," Anna promised, brushing away a happy tear as she laughed.

Gilbert put his arm around his bride's waist. "I know I am one very lucky man."

Miss Hayes beamed at him and then returned her attention to Anna. "You will write to me, won't you, while you are away?" she begged.

"We're not leaving London," Anna said at the same time he did.

Miss Hayes appeared disappointed. "I thought you would have embarked on a wedding tour. Didn't you say you always wanted to visit Cornwall when you married?"

"We're not going yet." Actually, Gilbert hadn't considered a honeymoon trip at all, but now he knew where he would take Anna when the time came. "But we will tour Cornwall soon, I assure you."

Anna smiled happily at the news.

He looked away a moment to view the other guests. Carmichael appeared a little lost now the ceremony was over, and he was going to leave Anna to speak with him—until he caught Miss Hayes' next whispered words.

"Are you nervous about tonight?"

There was a telling silence from Anna. Of course she would be nervous about her wedding night, but she had nothing to fear. He turned back to his bride before her friend could put ridiculous ideas into her head to make her dread the coming evening. "Darling, we should circulate."

"Of course," Anna agreed. "Excuse me, Portia."

He looped her arm through his and kept her at his side for the next hour as they spoke to friends. He had to admit, facing Lady Scott felt just a little daunting. Apparently, she had only learned there would be a wedding service as Carmichael's carriage brought her here. The lady was a little frosty with him but when she spoke to Anna, her voice was full of warmth. "Your mother would have been so proud of the way you comported yourself today."

"Thank you," Anna murmured. "I like to think she was looking down on us today. As I was standing beside Father, I felt the strangest sensation across my skin, like a gust of happy breeze on a still day."

"I'm sure you did," Gilbert murmured. "My late mother would have loved you, too."

Then the time came to sit down to the wedding breakfast, a vast feast his bride had rushed to prepare. "This is wonderful," he whispered to her. "I can see I'll never starve."

"No, my lord. I aim to keep you very satisfied at home."

He raised a brow at that statement. Anna was a fast learner when it came to intimacy, but he did not think she'd meant her words as they had first sounded to him. "I look forward to that," he murmured, and then dug into what remained of the feast that left nothing to be desired, until it was time to leave.

Full and replete from the wedding breakfast, he said his goodbyes, and then waited for Anna to do the same. Parting from her father seemed the most difficult. He was glad to be away in the end, glad to at last bring Anna safely to his home just as night was falling.

Gilbert's staff were lined up in the front hall, and he introduced them perfunctorily, conscious they had returned late. The servants picked up on his mood and scattered as soon as he dismissed them, returning downstairs to partake of their own evening meal.

"Let me show you around your new home," he murmured, snatching up a brace of candles to light the way.

"I've been trying to picture you here, writing your letters to me," she told him.

"Those were written in the parlor. The servants' staircase is behind the staircase down here to your left. The door to your right leads to the dining room, farther back is the master bedchamber and a dressing room." He took her to the staircase and they ascended to the first floor, side by side. "On this floor is the drawing room and over there is the parlor. I spend most of my time in that room."

They stepped into the room and Anna looked about her eagerly. A fire was already burning and a selection of cold food and wine had been laid upon the table already in case they were hungry. Thanks to the sumptuous twelve-course wedding breakfast Anna had meticulously planned and served up, he would have to eat lightly for the next week.

Against every wall of the parlor, piled high on every surface except the chairs, were books he had acquired during his visits to London over the years. He'd never been here long enough to have more shelving installed but he probably should one day. "The library in Kent is just as crowded."

Anna nodded. "This is a lovely room."

He leaned close to her. "I'm willing to share," he promised.

She glanced up at him, eyes bright with excitement and anticipation. "I do hope so."

That expectant look could cause mischief if he had the time to spare. "Second floor next." He led her up the next flight by the hand. "I think you'll find this floor most useful to you."

"Oh?" she murmured. "Why is that?"

Gilbert opened the door to her new bedchamber. "My housekeeper spent the whole of yesterday in here straightening up so you would be very comfortable."

A fire burned in the hearth here too, the bed was newly made with fresh linen, and the space decorated with an abundance of sweet-smelling flowers and a dozen or so new pillows scattered about.

"Oh, how lovely and large. I'm sure I will be very happy here."

"There's a dressing room through there, a washroom

adjoining it, and another smaller bedchamber and closet farther down the hall for any guests we might have one day."

She nodded and then turned, bottom lip caught between her teeth. She released it to ask, "Where do you sleep?"

"I occupy the ground-floor master bedchamber. You won't be disturbed by my coming and going." A little frown line appeared between her eyes, so he hastened to add, "I've been keeping very odd hours. I should warn you that Carmichael often stays when he's feeling low, too. Falling asleep in the parlor if he drinks too much."

She looked at him with a deeper frown. "Carmichael really did love Angela."

"Indeed he did. I don't believe he's sleeping very much at all, which makes him more emotional than ever."

"He looked so sad today. At our wedding."

"Yes, he usually hides his pain better. I've been worried about him. The way he's been drinking isn't healthy."

Anna sighed and began to remove her gloves. Gilbert covered her hands. "I will leave you now."

She glanced at him in obvious shock. "So soon?"

"I thought you might like to be alone to settle in."

"But tonight is our wedding night," she protested.

He took her to the window seat and eased her down onto it. Gilbert sat at her side. "It's not that I want to leave you, but I feel I should."

"Because we rushed to marry?"

Gilbert nodded.

She appeared very surprised. "You would wait?"

"A week, a month, a year." Perhaps a year might be too long to wait to be her husband. He did find her very attractive, and he thoroughly enjoyed kissing her and being kissed. But the type of intimacy he wanted required her full and enthusiastic participation, and no doubts. "Whatever amount of time you need is yours."

A little smile appeared. "Thank you, my lord."

"Gilbert. Remember?"

She leaned close to him. "We married so I could be alone with you, Gilbert."

He had wanted to marry a lady who desired him, and apparently he had. "Well, in that case." He lowered his head a fraction more. "May I kiss you, Anna Bowen, Countess Sorenson?"

She blushed. "Yes, you can kiss me, Gilbert. Anytime you like."

He bent his head the rest of the way and captured her soft lips with his. Anna lifted and wound her arms around his neck as the kiss deepened. The passion of their first, second, and third kiss flared hot and immediate between them.

Gilbert drew back reluctantly before he could get carried away. "I should give you a few minutes alone."

Anna's lips brushed his cheek and then she laughed softly. "Why?"

Her lips were so close to his ear that he shivered. He pulled Anna against his body a little higher, exploring her back and tiny waist with his hands. Leaving his bride alone on their wedding night seemed to have been the most ridiculous notion he'd ever had.

He set her away from him firmly and struggled out of his coat.

A hurried bedding would not impress Anna, and he intended to impress her all night long.

CHAPTER 22

Anna set her fingers to Gilbert's waistcoat the moment he tossed his coat aside, and then slid her hands up to his wide shoulders. As much as she should appreciate his consideration for her feelings and the beautiful bedchamber around them, she would rather appreciate him at close range. "I'm glad we're finally alone together at last."

He pulled her hands down from his shoulders, squeezed them, and drew her across the room. "I want to see you naked."

Anna's stomach flipped. Without clothes. In front of him. She wanted to touch him everywhere she could reach, too.

They stopped in a patch of moonlight near another window and kissed again. Gilbert cupped her face, and then she felt his fingers pulling pins from her hair rapidly.

Her hair tumbled down her back, and Gilbert grasped the long strands while they kissed. She felt his fingers at the back of her gown, tugging at the buttons next. "Shall I turn around?"

"We couldn't kiss if you faced the other way," he murmured against her lips. Another kiss and his large warm hand slid inside her gown, over her stays. Clearly, he was adept at undressing ladies. She didn't care how he'd learned the skill so long as he only ever undid *her* buttons.

Anna shivered, not from cold but from desire. Soon he would touch her everywhere, and she could begin her exploration of him.

She searched for the buttons of his shirt, undid them and tried to push the garment aside. Unfortunately, she was less adept at men's fashions than he was with hers.

"We'll need to remove my waistcoat first," he suggested in a soft rumble of laughter. "And my cravat too."

Anna shivered again, closing her eyes momentarily. "Yes. Hurry."

His answer was a soft chuckle and the rustle of fabric. When he drew close again, her fingers met bare skin. Anna slid her hands up his torso, breathless again, discovering his skin soft and so very warm beneath her palms. She encountered patches of coarse hair in the center of his chest and lightly teased her fingers through them. Gilbert groaned as her wandering hand encountered a flat male nipple.

She looked up into his shadowed face quickly. "Did I do something wrong?"

"Never." He lowered his lips to her ear. "I happen to love how you touch me."

She ran her fingers over his skin again, brushing out along his strong arms until she met his fingers. He caught her hands in his. "Let's finish undressing and get into bed together," he suggested.

"That might be a good idea. I feel so very strange."

He turned her about, finished unbuttoning her gown and slid it down past her hips. "That means I'm doing something right, you know."

Anna stepped out of the gown quickly and turned to face him. Even though she was still wearing stays, chemise and stockings, she felt utterly exposed. "You are?"

"I want you so damn much," he told her. "I'm trembling, too."

Anna exhaled. That made her feel better. She tugged on the laces of her own stays and pulled them over her head, but became trapped when her shift lifted, too.

Gilbert helped free her, laughing softly. She met his gaze and then leaned in to kiss him, quite embarrassed to be the only one naked but for her stockings, and not in bed. Gilbert pulled her into his arms, lifted her from the floor and wrapped her legs about his waist. He kissed her and moved them to the bed, where he gently set her down on the edge while still kissing her.

When he stopped, she looked up into his shrouded face and smiled. "Now what?"

"Now I'd better get out of these damn breeches and boots so I can make love to you all night," he all but growled.

"All night?" she asked in surprise.

"Maybe," he teased.

He wasn't gone long enough for Anna to become cold or self-conscious. She eased down to lie on the bed as he turned toward her. She caught one quick peek at his nakedness before he moved over her, lying between her spread thighs.

He brushed her hair back from her face as he brought them closer together. He was hot against her side, exciting.

"My God, you are perfect," he whispered as he trailed his fingers from her shoulder to her hip.

"I'm not perfect but *you* might just be," she suggested, touching him in the same manner. She brought her hand back up and across his stomach. He sucked in a sharp breath as she slipped her hand downward. She smiled slightly. He was aroused and quite obviously so. "Did I do that?"

"Oh, yes." He nuzzled her neck. "Every time we kiss. You have very talented lips."

"I'll add that to my list of accomplishments," she told him, laughing along with him. She'd made the right choice in marrying Gilbert. He made her heart so happy.

He settled closer, wrapping her legs about his thighs until she felt his naked heat all over her front. Her face grew warm yet again and she was very grateful for the shadows that hid her blazing complexion. Propped up on one arm, he ran his fingers down her body from shoulder to hip again, a little more firmly.

Anna shifted restlessly beneath him. She could feel him, hard and burning hot between her thighs, and then he moved away.

He moved his hand toward her stomach and then down into the curls between her legs. Anna gasped aloud as he touched her there, gently at first but with growing firmness.

Slowly, she realized she was moaning to every stroke of his finger. She looked up into his face. "What are you doing to me?"

"Loving you," he promised.

He moved to kiss her neck just below her ear, where she discovered she was most sensitive, and her whole body quivered with need. She lifted her hips toward his brushing fingers but that only made him slow his movements until he stopped. Anna wanted to protest. She widened her legs a little more, hoping to entice him back to touch her.

Gilbert shifted over her again, one arm braced beside her head.

He slid his other hand beneath her hip and grasped her bottom firmly. He tilted her hips up.

A little adjustment and he was there, at her opening at last.

"I'm afraid this may hurt," he whispered.

"I know it will," she promised. "I'm innocent."

"Not for long." He pushed her thighs a little wider. She felt pressure at her sex, a sharp sting followed, and then there was a little more discomfort to be endured. He withdrew a little then pressed against her sex again.

"That's it," he whispered. "Just relax."

She was trying to. She blew out a breath as Gilbert settled fully over her, resting his weight on both arms.

She put her arms up around his neck, shifted her body a little against his invasion, seeking relief from the strange sensation of pain and pleasure.

But he was inside her. She was a wife now.

She flexed her hips again and discovered the pain had diminished.

"Anna?"

"I'm all right," she promised, a little amazed by that. For the last two seasons, she and her friends had heard whispered stories about the wedding night horrors. It wasn't as bad as everyone made out, if that was all the pain she'd suffer.

He kissed her gently. "I'm going to move again now."

She gaped at him. "There's more?"

"Yes, that was only the beginning." He moved again, and she felt the strangeness of him being inside her. There was no pain now but an odd fullness. She squirmed a little and found she liked the sensation better.

She moved her hands down to his chest, discovered him warmer than before and his skin slightly damp with perspiration.

He groaned as she brushed over his nipples accidentally. "Put your arms about me again," he begged.

Anna linked her arms about his neck and drew him down for kisses. Gilbert moved against her firmly, jolting her with each short thrust. She was beginning to feel warm all over, too.

Gilbert was so close, becoming so much a part of her, that she almost couldn't breathe. The intimacy between husband and wife was overwhelming.

He eased back to push his hand between her legs. When he touched her there again, an unladylike moan tumbled from her lips. She sealed them shut as her body trembled anew.

Everything he did to her just increased her restlessness.

"That's it," he whispered.

She looked up at him as he began to thrust slowly while he toyed with her sex. She lifted her hips, seeking more of that sensation.

He thrust harder, and she struggled for breath. She was so hot, so desperate for more of this feeling.

"Come for me, Anna," he whispered.

Anna had no idea how to do that.

But when Gilbert moved one of her hands to her own breast, closing her fingers over her nipple, she shuddered. She squeezed her own breast as Gilbert thrust again, much harder than ever before. His fingers moved quickly over her.

Anna arched under him and suddenly cried out.

Waves of heat and pleasure rolled through her body and she had to close her eyes as Gilbert thrust frantically within her. He came to a shuddering halt, buried deep inside, and groaned against her ear.

He hovered over her. Panting loudly against her ear still. His fingers slipped from her sex slowly and she flinched a little. Gilbert eased her legs open and then gently slipped from her body. Anna hissed in pain and drew her legs together tightly.

"I'm sorry. There will be a little pain for the next day or so, I hear," he whispered. "It won't always be that uncomfortable for you."

He eased to the bed beside her and after a moment, she rolled onto her side to look at him, naked in the moonlight. "I was told to expect some discomfort at first and afterward, but not how I would feel while you were making love to me. That was unexpectedly good."

"I'm glad to hear it." His fingers were gentle as he caressed her face. "Do you need anything?"

He sounded so concerned her heart melted a little. "Only a little rest now, I think."

"I'll go then?"

Anna reached for his hand before he could move. After that experience, she didn't want to be abandoned immediately. "No. Don't go yet."

Reassured, he settled at her side again. "I'll stay until you fall asleep."

Anna rolled close to him and inhaled the scent of her husband. This was her gentleman, the man who'd claimed her body and her innocence. She wasn't yet ready to be without him.

"Stay until morning?" she asked, knowing already that many

married couples only came together for pleasure and children. She hoped their marriage could be different. So far it had been.

He smoothed her hair back from her face. “You wouldn’t mind if I slept here, too, on occasion?”

“No. At least I don’t think I will. Ask me in the morning though.”

He kissed the top of her head. “I’d like to stay but do kick me out when you don’t want me sleeping here anymore.”

“I will,” she promised, but as she cuddled up to him, contentment filled her. She did not think she would send her husband away just yet. She thought she could easily get used to seeing him naked by moonlight every night, too. She couldn’t tell him of course. She didn’t want to seem too bold yet.

CHAPTER 23

Gilbert was just about to find a book to read to pass the time when Anna arrived in the parlor without warning. His wife looked lovely, if a little unsure of her surroundings as she paused at the doorway biting her bottom lip. He stood immediately and crossed the room to greet her, intent on claiming a midday kiss.

He'd considered doing that when he'd awoken beside her in her bed that morning. But hadn't wanted to wake her when she was most likely tired after the events of last night and yesterday. She'd looked so adorable lying on her side, one hand stretched toward him in sleep, her shoulders still bare from making love to him. They had slept together, entwined in each other's arms, for most of the night. But on waking, he'd stolen from the room like a thief, determined to leave her be.

But he hadn't stopped thinking about her for one moment all morning long. He no longer lived alone and he already liked it.

He could still remember her hands pulling him close as they had made love in her bed. Her legs twined with his. Her gasps and moans mingling with his as they'd found their release close together. Tonight or the next night they would share his bed, and back and forth forever, he hoped.

Damn but he was a lucky man to have won her hand in marriage. She had been everything he'd hoped for in a lover.

"Good morning, beautiful," he murmured before capturing her lips.

Anna leaned into him, allowing him to kiss her deeply. She kissed him back, her fingers rising to his hair as he devoured her mouth. He lifted her higher, until her feet no longer touched the floor, and then moved her to the velvet couch beneath the window, where he'd been when she'd first come in, and pulled her into his lap.

He cradled her face, allowing the kiss to continue.

Anna seemed to be enjoying herself on his lap, squirming around and holding him tight to her. He considered his chances of making love to her again but dismissed the idea. He recalled her hissing in pain on his withdrawal last night, and the last thing he wanted was to hurt her even more.

Her hands firmed on his face and then the cheeky minx flicked her tongue out to tangle with his in his mouth. He drew her under him on the soft cushions, fighting arousal even while building the passion higher with their kiss. Anna was delightfully warm when in his arms; he could pleasure her and deny himself. He'd enjoy watching her come again if could be sure they would not be disturbed.

He drew back, looking down into her flushed face. "Now that is a good morning kiss."

She grinned back at him. "It is. Good morning, handsome."

He eased back a few strands of hair from her cheek. "Carmichael will be here soon, I'm afraid."

Anna blinked in surprise. "Today?"

"He is usually here by this hour. He is late actually, a concession, I suppose, to our status as newlyweds."

A frown line appeared between her brows and she struggled to sit up. "Surely he wouldn't call on us today of all days?"

He sat too but reached to brush his thumb across her soft cheek. "One of those newlyweds still has a murderer to catch."

"Yes, but—"

A timid knock sounded on the door. "Is it safe to come in yet?"

"Good morning, Carmichael. We were just speaking of you, in fact," he called and stood to straighten his coat.

Carmichael peeked into the room slowly. "Sorry about this, Anna. But there has been an unexpected development this morning."

"What has happened?"

"It's Miss Hayes," he said.

Anna cried out, "No, she can't be dead!"

He held up one hand to halt her panic. "She's only missing, as far as I know. I know you care for her, and I didn't want you to hear of it from anyone else, so I came straight away to tell you myself. I've called at her home already, at her father's invitation. There are no signs of a struggle and not a drop of blood to be found anywhere, inside or out. I searched the nearby mews too, just to be sure."

Anna sank into a chair with a moan. "I can't lose Miss Hayes, too."

Gilbert squeezed her shoulder and then addressed Carmichael. "Tell me what you know?"

"Her father came to see me this morning, asking for help in locating her. He'd read about our investigation in the papers and assumes the worst. Apparently, Portia went to bed at one o'clock, along with everyone else in the household. Morning came and she didn't ring for her breakfast. Strangely, her maid is missing, too. Nothing was seen or heard that gives any clue about a likely abductor or the time she was taken."

"We have to find her before she is harmed," Anna demanded.

"Yes, I agree, but where to begin a search?" Gilbert reached for her hand even as he searched his memory for the details of his investigation. "This is out of character for what we know of our killer's habits. In all other cases, they lured the victim to another part of the same property and killed them there. If Portia Hayes has vanished into thin air, it may well be someone else entirely has taken her."

"Or perhaps the release of our information has made them desperate," Carmichael worried out loud.

"Where could Portia be?" Anna looked at Carmichael.

"How would I know?" Carmichael complained.

Time was of the essence. "Would anyone besides a suitor have a motive for kidnapping Miss Hayes?"

"No," both Lord Carmichael and Anna agreed.

"How much was her dowry again?"

"Four thousand pounds," Anna told him. "Including property."

He considered the trouble it would take to kidnap an heiress and make it to the border without being stopped. It might be more likely that she was taken with the intention of simply forcing an expedient marriage. "Tell me who had the best chance of winning her hand."

"Carmichael or Grindlewood," Anna tossed out without any hesitation. "If either one had asked, her father would have agreed. There would be no need to kidnap her."

"She'll never have a proposal from me," Carmichael countered. "She had shown an interest in Lord Bellows as well last year. Bellows went back to his estate last week. I already called on Grindlewood. He is home and his movements accounted for."

Gilbert turned to Anna, stunned by a sudden idea. "What chance did Lord Wade have?"

"None. I told you. Portia can barely stand him." She sighed. "He might want to help us find her though."

He might if fear hadn't driven him away. "Lord Wade left London the day before we married."

"So that's why he never answered my invitation to come to our wedding." She frowned severely at that. "He never said anything about leaving London the last time we spoke though."

Carmichael laughed suddenly.

Gilbert stared at his friend. Now was not the time to recover his sense of humor. "What?"

Carmichael smiled slowly. "You don't think Lord Wade abducted Miss Hayes, do you?"

"He left in broad daylight days ago. Alone, I'm sure."

"He wouldn't just take Portia!" Anna protested.

"Why not? And who's to say he hasn't turned around and come back by now to abduct her? Now I think about it, he's shown a particular interest in Miss Hayes for some time. Practically glowers at me every time I dance with her because he saw me kiss her last year," Carmichael said, frowning. "He's a bachelor, and she's a very eligible young woman. Plus, there is a murderer on the loose, and Miss Hayes is exactly the type of young woman to foolishly place herself in harm's way. She could be on her way to Gretna Green even now."

"Or he could have abducted her just to keep her safe from the murderer and has not fled anywhere," Anna argued, looking worried about that prospect, too. "And Portia's maid could be with them to act as chaperone so her reputation remains beyond reproach."

He thought about the likelihood. Either scenario had merit but he wasn't keen to pursue an elopement to the border. "I say, what property comes attached to winning Miss Hayes' hand in marriage?"

"Why?"

"Well, we know Wade is not in his home. The house has been closed up for the season. I had someone watching in case he came back, but they said all was quiet still as of yesterday morning. If Wade needed to tuck Miss Hayes away somewhere, he might just use one of her own properties to hide her in."

"I know of one," Anna offered suddenly. "Portia has a favorite, and it isn't far."

"Let's go," Carmichael suggested.

Gilbert turned to his wife. Their first day as husband and wife was not supposed to be like this. "Do you mind?"

"If Wade has taken Portia, I'm coming with you to ring a peal over his head."

Gilbert smiled grimly. "I'll have a carriage brought round."

"It will be quicker to hail a hack," Anna argued.

"You are quite right, my dear." He kissed her quickly and rushed from the room, collected his small pistol just in case Wade proved resistant and ordered his butler to flag down a hack. By the time he returned from donning his hat and gloves, Anna was ready to go. She and Carmichael appeared congenial enough, for which he was grateful—until they spoke.

"I can't believe you fell for it," Carmichael complained.

"I was fourteen," she countered.

He looked between them. "Arguing again?"

"Reexamining the past," Carmichael explained. "She's like a dog with a bone about her first kiss."

"It is an important moment for any young woman," Anna argued.

"I see that now."

Anna snatched her parasol from where it now hung on the stand by the front door and brandished it. "Never touch my possessions again."

"I replaced the blasted parasol," Carmichael protested. "Years ago."

"Six months later," she complained, and then turned toward the front door smiling widely, despite the argument. He suspected she was enjoying herself berating Carmichael like that.

"I'm starting to have second thoughts about you marrying her," Carmichael confided, as they both watched Anna stroll to the top of the steps and outside. "This will not end well for me."

Gilbert smiled. "I'm not unhappy if you have to apologize for every wrong you ever did to her. You went above and beyond gentlemanly conduct to make her dislike you."

He followed his wife to the carriage, relayed the address they wished to visit to the driver and helped Anna inside. He took a place beside her, and then Carmichael joined them.

"What do we do if she's there, and he's there too?" Carmichael asked. "Do we force a marriage between them even if she has a maid?"

Anna hefted her parasol and waved it about as if it were a sword. "I have my weapon of choice."

Gilbert lowered the tip back to the floor when she swung too close to Carmichael for comfort. "No bloodshed."

"Oh, very well. But she's my very good friend. He claimed to be one, too. I reserve the right to be outraged."

Gilbert collected her hand and pressed a kiss to the back. "I won't stop you there."

They were soon at the Soho Square property Anna had described. Gilbert told the driver to keep moving as he saw a curtain twitch when the carriage drew level with the front door. He turned his face away so he was not recognized by anyone within.

Anna tugged on his sleeve. "Why are we not stopping?"

"He's not going to open the front door to us if he has her," Gilbert warned. "We'll enter discreetly from the rear lane and see if we can surprise him," he suddenly decided. Stealth and surprise were useful tools when hunting wary prey.

Gilbert had the driver stop around the corner on the next street. They alighted, slipped quietly along the rear mews and into the small cobbled yard attached to the rear of the property. They paused before a heavy-looking door. "It will be locked."

He looked at the windows facing the lane, and then noticed one lower down had been boarded up from the inside with new timbers. He crouched down and studied how they might enter that way.

Anna leaned over him and whispered, "A locked door is not a problem when you know where a key to open it might be found."

Gilbert looked up at her in surprise. "There's a key just lying around outside?"

Anna nodded. "The spare. Portia showed me where it was

kept herself when we came here together, but it is not easy to reach."

"Does your father know about this?"

She shook her head quickly. "Instead of going shopping, as her parents had believed we had, we—Portia and our maids and I—came here to spend an hour without chaperones or callers of any kind the other week."

"Defying your father?" Carmichael whistled. "I'm impressed."

"I'm not always good." She shrugged. "Portia once said that if she ever couldn't be found, she'd most likely be hiding here—dreaming of a life where she was her own mistress."

She moved toward the boundary wall, crept close to the corner of the house, and reached deep into the darkness. Gilbert cringed at her location and would have offered to replace her, if he'd thought a man his size could fit in the gap.

Anna withdrew slowly, brandishing a key in triumph. "Portia usually keeps one in her reticule at all times, too—for emergencies, she'd claimed. That one is for the front door only. She said if I ever had dire need of a safe haven, to come here and let myself in."

"This situation sounds exactly like the sort of emergency anyone would run from, and there is nowhere better to hide I think than an abandoned dwelling she already owned," Carmichael mused. "Very smart, really."

Anna unlocked the rear door quietly, warning them to step widely over the threshold to avoid the board that squeaked.

The house was silent but not empty, it seemed. The dark was cluttered with things Portia's uncle must have collected over the years. Even though these were the servants' domain, the hallways seemed to be piled high and required careful navigation.

He stayed close to his wife, anxious that they not stumble upon anyone, trusting that Carmichael would close the door behind them and follow just as quietly.

He considered putting Anna between them for safety's sake

but he didn't think she would agree. She was as anxious as he was to find Miss Hayes and save her from Lord Wade's abduction, if that was what had happened. Besides, only Anna knew where she was going in the near total dark. It would be quicker to let her direct them until the way forward became clearer.

He remembered the drapes twitching on a high front window on the right. Portia Hayes or Lord Wade would not be downstairs, unless one of them needed water or food to eat.

Speaking of food. He leaned down to whisper in his wife's ear. "Where are the kitchens in this house?"

Anna pointed to the side and they moved there in near silence. Gilbert eased around her when she leaned aside. "The lower halls gave me the creeps when I was here," she confessed.

At the kitchen doorway, he stopped and glanced inside. There were signs of recent habitation. Plates and cups set out on the old wooden work table—three of them. And a familiar picnic basket.

He shook his head, realizing their fears were spot on. Lord Wade was keeping Portia Hayes his unwilling prisoner in this house.

Carmichael squeezed past them both, going to the fire, hand outstretched, and then to the tea things on the table.

"Stone cold," Carmichael whispered as he put the china teapot back down.

Anna's sigh of relief was too loud, and Gilbert tensed as she spoke. "She wouldn't ever leave a mess behind. She's still here."

"You really are much too clever, you know, Lady Sorenson," Lord Wade complained as he grabbed Anna's arm and jerked her against his chest before Gilbert could stop him.

CHAPTER 24

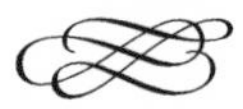

Anna yelped as cold metal pressed to her temple. She froze momentarily and then twisted in an attempt to flee. "Let me go!"

Wade hissed but his hold on her only tightened. "Not until your husband sets aside the pistol he's pointing at me."

She looked at Gilbert in surprise. He had a pistol in hand and was slowly prowling closer. "You carry a pistol?"

He nodded curtly. "Seemed a wise precaution. Let my wife go now, Wade, if you wish to be treated fairly."

"Not until you listen to me," Wade demanded.

"Oh, for heaven's sake, this is ridiculous!" Portia exclaimed loudly from some distant part of the house. There was a rumble of something crashing and breaking beneath their feet. "Oh, bother," Portia complained.

"Portia!"

"This house will kill her before anyone else stands a chance," Lord Wade grumbled under his breath. "Will you be careful down there," he yelled.

"Portia!" Anna twisted again in Lord Wade's grip, struggling to break his hold. "Where are you?"

"In the wine cellar," Portia called. "Give me a moment to find a way out again."

Anna turned to look at Lord Wade. "What have you done?"

He didn't answer but kept his attention on Gilbert. "The pistol, or I'll steal a kiss from your bride before you shoot me."

Gilbert lowered the point of the weapon slightly, frowning. "Touch your lips to any part of her and you will die, slowly, painfully."

Lord Wade chuckled. "Told you he was the jealous sort. Put the pistol on the floor and kick it farther into the kitchen, my lord. Then follow us after you shut the door," he said as he edged backward, dragging Anna with him as a shield and out into the hall again.

Anna remembered the layout of the house fairly well. He was leading her toward the entranceway to the cellar, where Portia was trapped.

Gilbert and Carmichael were out of sight for a moment but they quickly followed, stalking after them with matching grim expressions. Gilbert still held his pistol but loosely at his side now.

"If you hurt her, I will skin you alive, Wade," Carmichael threatened.

"Goodness!" Portia exclaimed as she suddenly appeared at Anna's side, unbound and grinning. Her hair was half falling down and she had a smudge of dirt across her cheek. "You're certainly a bloodthirsty one these days." She smiled at Lord Wade next. "Put the pistol down, Wade. You know it's not loaded. Didn't I say my best friend would be the one to find me?"

The press of cold metal vanished from her temple. To Anna's relief, Gilbert immediately turned the point of his weapon away too.

"So you did," Wade grumbled, sliding the pistol into his coat pocket, looking decidedly unhappy about that. "But her new husband brought a pistol along to your tea party, too. I'm sure it *is* loaded."

"Shame on you, my lord," Portia chided Gilbert. "That is the height of bad manners."

"A pistol seemed appropriate since your father was under the impression you were abducted by a murderer," Gilbert told her.

"So was Wade, unfortunately." Portia shrugged. "He followed us here."

"Us?"

"Did you really think I'd stand to be abducted?" She giggled behind her hand. "I ran away from home with my maid."

Wade's grip loosened on Anna and she flew across the room into the safety of Gilbert's arms. She looked back at Lord Wade, but he was grinning at her now.

"What a pretty sight," Lord Wade said as Gilbert hugged Anna tightly against him. He smiled as he turned his attention back to Portia. "Damn foolish idea anyway, to think you could hide in the city. Everyone seems to have deduced where you'd gone."

Gilbert set Anna aside but kept hold of her hand. "You followed Portia to protect her?"

He nodded. "Trying to. Her father certainly wasn't up to the job."

Portia's maid appeared from the cellar. "Miss Hayes, do you want another bottle of claret brought up or not?"

The maid was just as dusty but appeared happy enough.

"Yes, thank you. Since we have guests, we might as well bring a pair of bottles, don't you think?"

"Yes, Miss." The maid disappeared into the murky downstairs again.

"It is so dreary down here. The drawing room is much nicer. Come on." Portia pulled Anna away from Gilbert and moved toward the obscured staircase that would lead them up to the drawing room. "I'm so glad to see you. What is it like being a married woman?" Portia whispered as the men fell behind.

"Wonderful. What *were* you running away from?"

"My parents, of course," she said blithely, as if it were something she did every day.

"You would be safer with them than here," Anna promised. "Don't you realize the danger exists only at night? Fridays in particular."

"Of course I know that. I read the papers, too. And if you might think I'm safer at home then you would be very wrong."

"I don't understand."

"My father had the most brilliant idea after watching you wed Lord Sorenson. He has decided to marry me off too before the very next Friday ball." Portia crossed her arms over her chest. "Absolutely intolerable."

Carmichael laughed suddenly. "I heard him talking about that. He *was* quite taken with the notion, wasn't he? Unfortunately, he kept looking at me, for some reason."

Portia aimed a warm smile at him. "Well, you are known to be unmatched and available now."

"So you came here?" Anna continued when Carmichael's face paled. "With just your maid for company?"

"Last night, as soon as my father finished his little speech about my future, I began to plot my escape. We were intending to stay here, in very happy solitude I might add, until this one broke in and started bleeding all over the place," she said, pointing at Lord Wade.

"Bleeding?" She looked at Lord Wade more closely, and only then noticed his left hand was bandaged. That explained why he'd hissed when he'd held her. "You're hurt?"

"A scratch that will heal soon enough."

"He fainted," Portia confessed with another giggle. "I never before met a man who would."

Anna glanced up at her husband, one brow raised in question. "How could Lord Wade ever be a suspect if he faints at the sight of blood? There's always so much of it."

"I concede to your greater wisdom, sweetheart," Gilbert

murmured, crossing the room to press a kiss to the top of her head.

Anna blushed a little at the endearment and burrowed into his embrace once more. All this handholding and touching in public would make her swoon soon. "Of course Lord Wade isn't the killer. He's not at all vicious enough."

Portia shook her head, a teasing smile on her lips as she watched Anna enjoy the embrace of her new husband. "Wade told me you probably suspected him, so I let him stay, provided he made himself useful."

"I do apologize for suspecting you, Lord Wade, and beg your forgiveness," Gilbert offered, holding out one hand.

Wade held up his bandaged hand rather than offer it to shake. "Granted." Wade glanced at Portia. "If you're not expecting any other callers for a while, you will excuse me. I'd better get back to my work before my brother tries to fall asleep again."

He spun about and stalked from the room.

"What work?"

"Oh, he's keeping busy clearing out my uncle's study. It's the only room I don't wish to sort through, not after the first love letter I found. So I left him and his brother to clean it up in return for feeding them."

Anna laughed softly. "Not a bad idea to give someone else the task."

Portia shrugged. "He finds it amusing."

"This sounds intriguing. I think I'll join them in the study," Carmichael murmured, and left, too.

"Up the stairs, down the hall and to the front of the house," Portia called. "Make yourself at home."

Once they were gone, Gilbert rounded on Portia.

"You have scared your parents almost to death, young lady," he scolded.

"Mother knows where I am," Portia told them, appearing unconcerned.

"She does?"

"I told her where I was bound, but not my father. Couldn't have him knowing our secret hideaway, too." When Gilbert gaped at her, she rushed to add, "Where do you think I got the idea to come here? When she and father are at odds, you can almost always find her here, wishing she'd never married most likely."

Gilbert nodded. "And Lord Wade?"

"Mother does not know about Lord Wade, and I wish to keep it that way," Portia said, eyes pleading Gilbert to silence. "Besides, his aunt would tan his hide if he so much as put a foot wrong in this house."

Anna gaped. "His aunt came too?"

"Aunt and brother. Chaperoned the whole time, and vastly entertained I have been, too." Portia laughed softly. "She's not quite as frightening after you see her fall asleep ten minutes after she arrives. She drinks like a fish every other moment, though," Portia muttered under her breath. "My uncle's wine cellar will be cleared out by the end of the week."

Gilbert inhaled and exhaled very slowly. "Where is she?"

"Drawing room. Drinking her way through another bottle from my late uncle's cellar. They were old friends, she says." Portia's eyes twinkled with mirth. "In their youth, they might have been more, I suspect, given the way she describes him in such glowing terms."

They all trouped upstairs, interrupting Mrs. Lenthall from imbibing a glass of claret.

The old lady saluted them with it. "It's a tiresome prospect, chaperoning this one, Lady Sorenson. I'll be more than happy to hand the chore over to you in the future."

"Thank you for being here," Anna told her sincerely. The old lady's presence added a layer of protection around Portia's reputation that could not be matched.

"Couldn't have my Wade compromising the chit." She nodded sagely. "I told him she was just as headstrong as her uncle. Best to have her bedevil some other gentleman first before she's worth pursuing."

Portia's eyes narrowed. "Yes, so you have said already."

Mrs. Lenthall looked up at Anna and gestured to a vacant chair. "Sit and have a drink with us, Lady Sorenson. The gel and I were just speculating on the murderer's identity."

"The matter is under investigation," Gilbert promised as Anna settled into a chair and accepted a glass of claret. Just to be sociable. Ordinarily, she'd never touch a drop at this hour.

"Yes, I'm sure you have interrogated every possible suspect and still failed to see the most likely culprit is right under your nose all along," Mrs. Lenthall declared, and then took a hearty sip from her glass. "Drink up, gels."

Anna dutifully took a small sip.

Gilbert leaned against the back of Anna's chair. "Why do you say that, madam?"

The old woman's eyes lit up. "After you have studied all the evidence at hand, you concluded the killer is a man, yes?"

Carmichael returned at that moment, his expression as troubled as it always was when suspects were discussed in front of him. "Yes. Someone with an interest in Lord Carmichael's future."

"Yes, an easy enough conclusion, given the way his past amours have met their grisly ends. But why conclude it is a man?"

"The methods used to dispatch the victims. It takes great strength to kill someone the way it was done."

"That is where you are quite wrong." Mrs. Lenthall smiled sadly. "When I was a girl, we had a visitor come to our home. He took an unnatural interest, un-encouraged, in one of our little housemaids. He caught her alone one day in the garden. He would have had his way with her, too, without a doubt."

"What happened to stop him?"

"She caved his head in with a marble garden statue. Ordinarily, much too heavy for such a slight little thing to lift."

"Rage could make a difference," Gilbert whispered, appearing shocked as he looked about the room. "You suggest the killer is a lady."

"And a furious one at that, though she must hide it well to have escaped detection for so long." The old lady sipped her wine. "I bet you've spent the bulk of your investigation studying the male members of the *ton*. You're after a fiend who befriends her victims, not an outcast. She doesn't have to hunt them, they come to her for their end."

Anna covered her mouth. "But why?"

"Who can say why anyone does anything? Perhaps she was disappointed in her youth, married poorly, and now out of misguided concern, seeks to ensure Lord Carmichael makes the right match. Perhaps she was born to kill."

"My right match was Angela Berry. Whoever believes she wasn't does not care about my happiness at all," Carmichael protested.

"Many men love more than once in their lives," Mrs. Lenthall offered sympathetically. "Some never get over heartbreak."

"I will not," Carmichael declared, furious.

"Every love is different." The old lady held her empty wine glass to her cheek and closed her eyes. "What we need is a guaranteed way to draw this lioness out into the light, and quickly, before anyone else gets hurt. Make them think you have already moved on to another pretty face. It would have to be just the right woman, too, to make the ruse believable. Someone daring and brave and, well…rather obviously smitten by your pretty self, Lord Carmichael."

Lord Wade stepped into the room, scowling. "Aunt, don't you dare make such a suggestion," he warned.

"I haven't suggested anything yet, my dear boy. I'm sure these young people will reach the same conclusion as *we* have in due time."

Portia sighed, and then looked over at Lord Carmichael.

He was shaking his head. "I won't put anyone else in danger."

A sense of foreboding filled Anna as Portia's expression changed to one of grim determination. She turned to Gilbert. "What is being suggested?"

"Baiting the killer," Lord Wade answered sourly. "She will not hesitate to strike down another woman that gets in her way. Not if she read that article in the paper."

"The article suggested a male villain at work, not a woman," Gilbert said slowly. "She might still believe herself undetected and safe from suspicion. What if the potential victim knew what might happen and agreed to accept the risk?"

Lord Wade shook his head. "Foolishness, and I'll have no part of it."

Portia scowled at him. "But if you're watching, too, they stand a better chance of catching her in the act. Proof will be required and you will make an exceptional witness."

"The last time was a blade across the throat and a stab to the heart," Lord Wade growled. "You do not know how to protect yourself from that."

"But you can help me prepare," Portia decided, standing. "We have time to practice together."

"No." Lord Wade spun about and stalked off into the house.

"He'll do it," Portia promised, seating herself again. "He'll do what I want in the end."

"Portia, are you sure?"

"Oh, yes. I want revenge for Angela, Lydia, Myra and all the others."

"You'll need to do more than deflect a blade," Gilbert suggested. "If it's a woman, it will be well hidden. The timing must be just right to catch them in the act of attacking you. Carmichael?"

Carmichael stood motionless, staring at nothing. He hadn't added much to the conversation, and Anna worried that he was completely against the plan.

"Carmichael?" She went to him when he didn't answer. "Price, what is it?"

He blinked slowly and focused on her face as if he'd not even been listening. "I'll stop her."

He glanced at Gilbert, and then dropped his eyes. "I'll stop her."

"We'll all stop her," she told him. "This will draw her out, but it will be dangerous for you, too. I want you to be careful."

Carmichael smiled sadly. "I'm not the one in danger."

"I'll be watching you both the whole night," Gilbert promised.

"So will I," Anna insisted.

"I'll need a little time to arrange things," Carmichael murmured, shaking his head. He looked at Portia, frowning. "You'll have to be very convincing."

"Oh, I'm halfway in love with you already, don't you know?" She grinned. "Everyone will believe I've thrown myself at you by the end of the evening."

"I have already sent my acceptance to the Bertram ball. I will speak to the hosts to make sure that you all have been invited, too, Miss Hayes. Reserve me two dances on your dance card, make sure the most important ladies, the ones who gossip, know that I have." He clenched his jaw. "Be flirtatious with me, even from across the dance floor. A footman will hand you a note early in the evening. Blank paper is all we need for this game. Make sure you blush when you pretend to read it. If anyone asks, it is a love note from an ardent admirer. Keep it and then slip away to Lord Bertram's library, as if you intend to meet with me there. We spring our trap while everyone else is at supper."

"This is madness!" Lord Wade insisted, having returned to hear the last of the discussion.

Carmichael turned about. "You must shadow Miss Hayes wherever she goes."

Wade's jaw clenched. "If one hair on her head is harmed, I'll hold you accountable."

"I hold myself responsible already. This *is* my fault. If there is nothing else," Carmichael asked, looking around at everyone. "I'm expected at a luncheon today and cannot be late. It would be best not to give the game away to anyone, so act naturally around friends and family, especially. I will see you all again on Friday night."

"Be careful," Anna called after Carmichael, but he was gone before she heard any answer.

"I suppose I will have to return to my parents' house before the ball arrives," Portia said glumly, looking about the room with longing. "I do love it here."

"Carmichael might call on you at home, too, so his singling you out won't seem so sudden at the ball. Society does love to gossip about budding romances," Mrs. Lenthall remarked to Portia, as if that would cheer her up.

"Indeed they do." Portia grimaced. "I'll go home early tomorrow. I'll slip into the house before sunrise and convince my father I've been at home all along," she promised. "He's fallen for that before."

"He's not that foolish," Gilbert protested.

"You have no idea how dumb he can be," Lord Wade muttered under his breath. "It's staggering what she gets away with."

Portia approached Lord Wade, her lower lip trembling a little. She set her hand on his folded arms. "I'll be counting on you."

"Don't do that," he said, looking away quickly. "Don't pretend that you're not happy to know you'll have Carmichael's attention all night long. Your agreement in this little trap has very little to do with catching a killer."

"Fine," she said, dropping her hand. "You think you know me so well. Just don't get distracted by the other pretty faces you like to watch."

He scowled thunderously then. His jaw worked but he kept his mouth shut.

Portia shrugged. "You're so stubborn."

"So are you." Anna punctuated that statement by poking her friend's arm. "Are you not afraid?"

"Yes, and no." She chewed on her lip. "This is the right thing to do. Flirting with Carmichael will bring the killer out of hiding. Mrs. Lenthall and I discussed it over tea this morning, and we both agree it is worth the risk."

"But you could be hurt, killed even. I couldn't bear to lose all my friends this season." Anna hugged her tightly. "You must be careful."

Portia drew back, nodding. "Wade will teach me to defend myself. He'll be in the shadows as he always is. I'll be as safe as I can be."

"And after?"

Portia kissed her cheek and turned Anna toward the staircase. "We will see what happens after the ball. We'll talk again after this is all behind us."

"If you survive, we might," Wade muttered as they passed.

She glanced back at Gilbert. He'd stopped behind them, staring off into space. "Gilbert? Is something wrong?"

He looked at her sharply. "Yes, and no. Let's get home. We have a lot to do before the next ball."

CHAPTER 25

So many things could go wrong tonight.

Gilbert could have fixated on the wrong suspect, but he didn't think he'd made a mistake. Davis was still gathering proof and would bring it to him here.

They had reassessed everybody connected to the murder victims and to Carmichael. The conversation with Mrs. Lenthall had sparked an unpleasant memory that he could not shake. Carmichael had another confidant. Someone he told everything to, even things that were not strictly true.

Gilbert strode into the ballroom with Anna on his arm, aware his wife was nearly shaking with tension. Gilbert tried to project a calm he didn't quite feel, for her sake. His concerns ran deep. Miss Hayes might be defenseless should her protection fail her tonight. He could not let the killer escape again.

A woman.

A *lady* whose reputation was touted to be beyond reproach, beyond suspicion.

He'd had no reason to suspect her of Angela Berry's murder, because he'd believed the lie she lived.

The jealousy of a woman thwarted by love was a terrible thing, even more so in this case.

Not since Jane Peabody's killer had been uncovered had he felt so sickened by his suspicions.

The Bertram ball was already awash with guests and laughter, but to him the sound was strained. Anna was anxious to find Portia in the crowd, and she kept stretching up on her toes to look for her.

"You know no matter how often you do that, you will still be painfully short," Carmichael murmured behind them.

Gilbert turned lightly, spotting Carmichael moving to Anna's other side. He looked like he'd not slept again, despite the smile on his lips. Carmichael's teasing of Anna, apparently an unceasing habit, annoyed the hell out of him. "Carmichael, do you not have something better to do?"

"Not right now." He looked across the room and nodded. "Lady Scott is here."

Gilbert looked at him quickly to see if he was worried about that, but his comment seemed nothing more than a commonplace observation rather than a warning.

Anna smiled widely. "Do excuse me while I go and say hello to her."

"Yes, better run along and keep her happy," Carmichael said quietly.

Gilbert kept an eye on Anna, even though now as a married woman, she should be safe.

"I haven't seen you for a few days," he remarked to Carmichael. "Where have you been?"

"You know that." Carmichael smiled. "You've had men following me and my staff for days."

"How did you know?"

"I've learned a thing or two about following people these past weeks."

"I need to tell you something."

"It can wait. Miss Hayes and her parents have arrived." He began to smile widely to the group across the room.

Portia Hayes responded with her own smile and fluttered her fan before she turned back to her parents.

Well, that seemed to be an un-missable flirtation. He glanced about the room, wondering how many people might have noticed. "You called on her."

"Oh, yes. Took her driving in Hyde Park too." He grinned again. "Miss Hayes put on a good show, waving to everyone we passed and leaning into me time and again."

"So people are talking already?"

"I imagine so."

Carmichael turned his back on Portia, craning his neck over the crowd. "Can you see a footman with drinks anywhere?"

"Might be a better idea to keep a clear head tonight."

"Keeping in character," he promised. Carmichael waved over a footman who hurried to his side with a tray of drinks. The fellow moved away after a few words, leaving Carmichael with nothing to drink.

"What was that about?"

"Wait for it." He grinned, glancing toward Miss Hayes as the footman stopped at her side with a tray filled with champagne. She took one, blushing brightly.

"There we go."

"Don't get too carried away on this false flirtation. We don't want her reputation in tatters."

"A bit of smudging is inevitable," he conceded. "She knows that."

Anna hurried over, apparently done with her little chat with Lady Scott. She pulled Carmichael down to whisper in his ear. Even so he managed to hear every word. "Did Portia mention who else her father had in mind for her to marry the other day?"

"No, she never said. Why?"

Anna frowned. "He keeps gesturing toward Lord Grindlewood to join them."

Portia Hayes' expression appeared downright hostile as she stood beside her father. "She's supposed to look like she's smitten," he worried.

"Grindlewood will not get in the way," Carmichael promised. "I know how to deal with him."

"What will you do?"

Carmichael tugged down his waistcoat. "What I must. Excuse me."

Gilbert watched him go, striding across the room to convince others he was pursuing Portia Hayes. Anna curled her arm through his, worrying her lip. "I do hope he doesn't get carried away with this," Anna promised.

"He won't but this has to stop tonight."

Anna looked up him. "I can barely breathe."

He placed a hand at the small of her back and drew a soothing circle. "Shall we dance? There's time."

Anna shook her head. "I fear I am too nervous to dance well."

"A stroll about the ballroom then? We could step out onto the terrace for a moment to look at the stars above."

She nodded. "I've always wanted to do that."

"Hmm, I think that is easily the finest idea I've ever had. Come with me."

Gilbert escorted her about the room at a slow pace, pausing to accept congratulations on their marriage. He kept an eye on Carmichael and Miss Hayes, as well as their friends. Gilbert couldn't stop grinning but when he glanced at his wife after leaving another group of well-wishers, he saw he'd lost her attention.

"You're not looking at me," he whispered.

Anna looked up, startled. "Oh, I do beg your pardon."

"Quite all right." He smiled gently. "I now have some inkling of how you must have felt the first time we danced together."

Anna laughed softly, too. "Then, I had no notion you might have liked to know me better. It is different now."

It *was* different. He couldn't take his eyes from Anna no matter where they were. He felt extraordinarily proud to be her husband, to have discovered a rare jewel to keep for his own. But he wanted to know how Anna felt about him, too. "How so?"

"Well, we are married, and I know we will return home together when this night is over."

"To *our* bed," he stressed in a tone that was decidedly husky. He couldn't wait to be alone with his wife after this was done. He might just keep her in bed all day. She had shown a delightful inclination toward bedroom sports. Would it shock her if they dallied in other parts of the house, too? He couldn't wait to find out.

He drew her toward the terrace doors and the moonlight. He stopped within viewing distance of the doors and noticed Davis lurking in the shadows. He held Davis back a moment so Anna could enjoy the view. "There."

Anna looked up into the heavens, a smile playing over her lips. "When I was a girl, I always thought it would be romantic to marry under a moonlit sky."

"Well, it might not be strictly official but I do happen to know the marriage vows by heart. When this is over we could slip away and speak our vows again by moonlight."

"Married by Moonlight? You'd do that for me?"

"Anything for you." Gilbert pulled her close, considering his chances of stealing a kiss from her lips, but Davis was watching. He bent down and brushed his lips across her cheek instead. "As many times as you want"

Her eyes lit up and she leaned against him, her hands resting on his chest. "How did I get so lucky as to marry such a romantic?"

He cupped her face. "I'm lucky too."

Davis chose that moment to clear his throat.

Gilbert turned away from his wife. "You wanted to see me?"

"Yes, my lord. I do apologize for the interruption but it is rather urgent."

"Go," Anna urged, nudging him away.

He hurried into the shadows, keeping an eye on his wife. "I take it you have news for me."

Davis nodded, casting a worried glance at Anna.

"She will learn the truth eventually."

"Yes, my lord. Our investigation of Lord Carmichael is complete."

"And." Gilbert shuffled his feet, anxious to have his suspicions confirmed or disproved.

"The earl is without question innocent, however, an irregularity was uncovered that implicates the person you mentioned."

"Such as?"

"Purchases made from a silversmith of a rather pointed design. Several of them over the years…and another just yesterday."

"So she will strike again. How is the weapon concealed?"

"A fan, my lord." Davis frowned. "I have compared the blades and they are a match. The silversmith also recognizes his own work and has described the lady in precise detail. There can be no doubt."

Gilbert raked his hand through his hair. Part of him had hoped to be wrong. "Hell."

"Indeed my lord." Davis reached inside his pocket and extracted an elegant ladies fan of his own. "The handle detaches like so."

Silver flashed in the moonlight but Gilbert heard voices coming close. "Put that away quickly."

"Given the evidence, should we detain the lady?"

He considered what to do. "Arresting my wife's friend in such a setting will be problematic. Remember, she is armed."

Davis looked beyond him toward the ballroom. "The fewer guests around, the easier it will be to prevent accidental injury."

"We will continue with the plan we have. Watch her. Do not lose sight of her. Be ready to enter the library at the first hint of alarm."

"Very good, my lord." Davis backed into the shadows and disappeared without a sound.

Gilbert returned to Anna's side and put his arm around her.

Anna shivered as the dance before supper was called and looked up to him. "It's almost time.

Gilbert took her hand in his. "Carmichael's note will have already been delivered."

"Can you see Portia?"

"Gone already, I think."

"We should go, too." She looked at him. "Gilbert, do you know who it is now?"

"Yes." He raised her hand to his lips and kissed her knuckles. "Which makes what I have to say all the more difficult. Do you know why women are being killed?"

"Because they allowed Carmichael to steal a kiss."

"Yes and no. I suspect there has always been a preferred bride for him," he confessed.

She wet her lips. "Me?"

"Yes, you." He let her digest that suspicion before he spoke again. "I know our plan depends on catching the killer in the act, but you must prepare yourself for the shock and do nothing to prevent her making the attempt."

She seemed to breathe very fast. "Why?"

"We spoke of a woman with Mrs. Lenthall the other day. My investigation has focused on one person ever since. I know your father has never hidden the fact he wanted, *expected*, Carmichael to marry you. You know there is someone else who wanted that too, don't you."

Anna gasped. "No. She wouldn't!"

"She is ruthless and clever and very angry at anyone who gets in her way. And I am in her way now that we have married. I want you to stay away from her at all costs, no matter what happens to me."

She stared at him in shock. "Nothing will happen to you. I won't allow it."

It was nice to be the recipient of such sweet words, even if she'd not the power to prevent him being harmed. "I've been shot before."

"Where? I saw no wound."

"My leg," he replied and kissed her brow. "I will show you the scar when this is over."

"I'll protect you."

He believed she meant her promise. However, he would not allow her to put herself in harm's way. She and Carmichael were, most likely, the only two souls safe from this killer's wrath. They were destined to be together—or so the killer believed.

Gilbert was determined to stop her by any means, including putting his own life at risk.

He tucked Anna against his side and slowly strolled toward the library via the deserted terrace. They had a very short time before the supper bell rang. That was the signal to enter the room. They needed to be ready to sweep in and save Miss Hayes.

Once they reached the terrace door to the library, Anna shivered. He brought her hand to his lips for luck and kissed her knuckles once more.

The door to the library had been left unlocked on purpose to allow them easy entry.

He pressed a finger to his lips, and then slipped into the room first, knowing Anna would follow.

Instantly, he sensed the presence of others…breathing and the rustle of cloth. He could not identify anyone, but he saw two bodies standing in the moonlight. One small, the other towering over her.

Carmichael had his hands wrapped around his godmother's throat.

"What the devil are you doing? Stop!"

"No," Carmichael replied in a shockingly deadly tone. There was another sound in the room, the gasp of someone being choked. "She has to die."

Bow Street's men, led by Davis, charged into the room from

every doorway and encircled them. Gilbert looked around for Portia Hayes, sighing as he saw her whole and healthy with Lord Wade at her side.

"Not by your hand, my lord!" Davis cried out.

"You won't stop me. The ladies will be safe now. I promise you that!" Carmichael swore.

Gilbert moved quickly to intercept his friend, as did Davis.

"It was Bess all along," he answered without releasing his grip. "She killed Lydia and Myra and my Angela. Perhaps more. I'll *never* forgive her for this betrayal. I confided in her! Trusted her!"

Lady Scott's eyes were bulging, her hands growing limp on Carmichael's crushing hands. If Carmichael killed her, the other victims' families would never see her live to be charged. Carmichael would suffer for killing her, too, and he'd suffered quite enough already.

Gilbert pried them apart, keeping hold of Lady Scott when she was free. Davis held Carmichael back.

Gilbert dumped Lady Scott, still alive and gasping for air, into the closest chair.

Before he could speak, Anna had stepped between Lady Scott and Carmichael but her attention was only for their friend. "You cannot kill her. You're nothing like her."

"I could for what she did to Angela!" Carmichael cried, fighting against Davis.

"Angela would not want such a revenge," Anna promised him, patting his chest. "She was a gentle soul and would want you to live a long and happy life without a death on your conscience, no matter how much it might be deserved."

Lady Scott coughed and then lifted her fan, holding it with two hands.

Gilbert wrestled the weapon from her grip, revealing to all that the handle was attached to a long sharp blade. "An exact match to the blade found in Miss Lacy's breast."

Carmichael paled and took a pace back.

"How could you do this to him?" Anna stared at her mentor with tears in her eyes. "You had to know how much Angela meant to him? They were in love!"

"Empty word, love. Said many times and never meant." Lady Scott turned eyes as cold as winter on Anna. "What could *you* know of love yet?"

"I know enough to be sure I couldn't live without it," she whispered.

Lady Scott shrugged. "They were unfit for the distinction they craved. They would have ruined him."

Anna gasped. "Angela was perfect for him."

"Nonsense! Carmichael told me all about his little amours." Lady Scott nodded quickly. "You'll both be free to make the right decision now."

"I'll be free when you're hanged!" Carmichael insisted, taking a threatening step forward.

"You will see that I am right soon enough. I will help you, as I always do."

"Help me? You've torn my heart from my chest and I'll never find a love like that again!" Carmichael cried, turning away.

"I did it for you," Lady Scott whispered as she lowered her head to her hand. "I freed you."

"Did everyone hear her confess?" Gilbert asked.

"Indeed."

Lady Scott looked up sharply. Fever-bright eyes turned toward Anna as her hair slowly tumbled down from its moorings. "I saw to her instruction personally. She will never behave anything less than a lady. She'll always be loyal to him. She'd never be seduced by a pretty face."

"I was," Anna murmured softly.

Gilbert wanted to smile, but instinct had him tensing as Lady Scott's eyes narrowed on him. "Husbands come and go."

He saw metal glint in Lady Scott's hand, the moment before she lurched toward him and sank another blade into his side.

CHAPTER 26

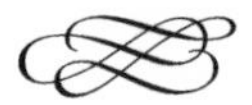

Anna flew toward her husband as he hit the ground hard. The others tackled Lady Scott, but she had no time to see what became of her former mentor when her husband had been obviously attacked.

She found Gilbert's handkerchief even as she sought the location of an injury. "You're all right," she told him.

Gilbert had his hand pressed to his side and she replaced his hand with the handkerchief and pushed firmly upon the wound.

She shifted to cradle Gilbert's head on her lap as the sounds of struggle rose beyond them. Gilbert might have predicted someone would be hurt tonight, but she wouldn't lose him. She couldn't bear the idea. "Don't you dare not be all right!" Anna whispered.

Gilbert struggled to lift his head, and Anna looked too when she realized silence had fallen in the room.

The Bow Street Runners moved back. Carmichael and Lord Wade were sprawled on either side of Lady Scott, who was lying flat on the floor. The lady was struggling for breath, and the short blade she'd attacked Gilbert with protruded from her chest. It was impossible to know which man had stabbed Lady Scott.

Her mentor, the woman she'd sought to make proud, had killed her closest friends. She had no words to express her shock and outrage.

"You could have done so much better, Anna," Lady Scott gasped, and then reached for Carmichael's hand. "It was all for you, my dear."

Carmichael knocked her hand aside roughly. "Get away from me!"

Portia edged closer, standing near Lord Wade, wringing her hands. "Are you all right?" she asked.

"Yes," Wade replied, turning away from Lady Scott.

The pair drew closer together and it seemed they touched, but Anna couldn't be sure from this angle. "You're not going to faint, are you?"

"I'm never going to live that down, am I?"

"Never," she said, grinning at him.

Anna turned back to Lady Scott as she continued talking.

"When I heard you talk of the women you were courting, I couldn't let you make the same mistake your father made. They'd never have made you proud. I saved you from making a terrible mistake."

"The only mistake I ever made was listening to your advice about the dangers of marrying too young," Carmichael told her. "The title will become extinct when I die, thanks to you."

"I won't allow…" Lady Scott's breathing became ragged. She made one more sound, and then fell utterly silent all of a sudden. When Anna looked closely, she noticed her eyes were open, staring at Carmichael, but her chest did not rise and fall anymore.

She had drawn her last breath, still convinced her way had been the right one.

Carmichael closed her eyes and then collapsed onto his back with a groan.

Davis checked Lady Scott's wrist for a pulse. After a moment, he stood and brushed himself off. "She's dead. It's over."

Gilbert rested his head back on Anna's lap and lifted a bloody hand toward her. "It *is* over, beautiful. Never again. I promise."

"Thank heavens for that." Anna caught his hand and bent over her husband to kiss his lips. "How badly are you hurt?"

"Not as badly as I first feared, but it stings like the very devil now."

"Fetch a doctor, Wade," she begged of her friend.

"At once," Lord Wade replied. "Portia?"

Portia ran to him and together they hurried from the room.

Anna sagged and brushed his hair back from his brow. "I love you," she whispered against his lips before kissing him.

He was smiling when she drew back. "You do?"

"I do," she promised. She removed the cloth she'd wadded over the wound and noticed very little blood had flowed from it. "I was afraid she'd truly hurt you. The blade seemed so bright."

"And sharp, but it's a shallow wound I think." He peered at the wound, too. "I'll still need a doctor though. Carmichael?"

"You'll need to find her maid and question her," Carmichael suggested in a quiet voice. "The woman has been cleaning blood from her mistress' clothing for two years at least that we know of. She'll know when it started and why. I'm going to let Bow Street handle the rest."

Gilbert rolled off her lap toward Carmichael, groaning in pain. "You knew it was her before tonight?"

"That day with Mrs. Lenthall. She came out the same year as Lady Scott." Carmichael groaned. "I remember wondering why she'd never once mentioned those murders."

Her husband suddenly dragged himself across the floor toward Carmichael and wrenched Carmichael's hand away from his stomach. "Damn it, why did you not say you were injured?"

Anna crawled to Carmichael. "Price!"

"She *was* quicker and stronger than I ever imagined," Carmichael complained. He looked down at his stomach. "It's all right, Anna. It doesn't hurt so much now."

"You're bleeding, you idiot." She found a clean handkerchief in her friend's coat pocket and pressed it to the wound. Carmichael groaned piteously. She cast a worried glance at her husband, who was holding his side again. "You lie down again. Help is coming."

"Little Miss Perfect needs to work on her bedside manner," Carmichael complained.

"That's *Lady* Perfect to you," Anna told Carmichael primly, then noticed how his blood was already soaking through the handkerchief and wetting her fingers. "He really needs that doctor."

The doors burst open and a man hurried to join them, urging Anna to relinquish her position over Carmichael's wound. She moved to hold his head, determined to be any comfort she could be. "You can't die. You said we would be friends now."

"I'll try not to disappoint you by dying then." Carmichael reached for her hand. Anna held his cold fingers as his wound was examined, probed and ultimately pronounced safe to be bound. Thankfully Carmichael fainted when the pain grew too great.

When he'd been bandaged enough, the gentlemen lifted him up.

"Where are you taking him?"

"Home to recover," one said.

"But there is no one at his home to look after him properly. Not even a decent chef." She glanced back to her husband, who was bandaged too but on his feet now. "He can come home with us, can't he?"

Carmichael had almost been living at Gilbert's home before their marriage anyway, she'd learned. She would much rather know where Carmichael was than run back and forth between their houses making sure he would be all right.

Gilbert nodded. "We'll look after him, but I need to stay and tie up any loose ends."

"But you're hurt too," she protested.

"Just a scratch," he promised, revealing his newly bandaged side was free of bloodstain.

He did seem to be moving freely so she hoped agreeing wouldn't be a mistake. "Very well."

"I'll keep an eye on him and deliver your husband home to you safe and sound, my lady," Lord Wade promised her as he returned to the room with his aunt on his arm.

"Where is Portia?"

His smile grew tense. "Where she's always wanted to be."

Mrs. Lenthall came to stand over Lady Scott's body. "No surprise here. Never did like each other."

"She nearly fooled us all," Gilbert confessed.

"You got there in the end," Mrs. Lenthall offered graciously. "Carmichael will need you both more than ever after this betrayal. Don't let him dwell too much."

"He will always have our support and my father's."

Lady Scott's face was covered to await the decision of what to do with her body. Anna didn't care where she was buried. The woman had harmed her husband, killed her friends, and destroyed her godson's happiness. That could not be forgiven. She was glad the nightmare was over.

Gilbert came closer, his expression serious.

She lifted up on her toes and kissed his lips to wipe the expression away. "How long will you be?"

"A few hours, I suspect. As Carmichael suggested, her maid and all her household staff must be questioned. Her home searched for further evidence, too, although we have witnesses and those blades she carried as evidence."

"I'll be waiting for you at home then," she promised.

"Good. Anna, before you go, I have one more thing to say to you."

"What is it?"

He caressed her cheek. "I love you so much."

Anna kissed her husband deeply, blushing even as she did so. And then she kissed him again because she could. There was no reason to stop. They were married and in love with each other. "I think I fell for you the first night we kissed. So romantic." She met his gaze boldly. She would have done anything he'd wanted that night. "Hurry home so I can kiss you some more."

"Nothing will keep me from you ever again," he promised, and she believed he meant it, too.

EPILOGUE

Late summer, Kent

Anna sorted through the day's mail. There were letters for herself, letters for their current houseguest and letters for her husband. Their guest's letters gave off the most dreadful perfume, and she held them away from her nose. "Will you take these out to the terrace, please, Jane? Another of Lord Carmichael's admirers has found out where he's staying for the summer."

"Very good," Jane replied, although sounding rather annoyed by the chore.

Anna watched her companion leave, hiding her concern over how transparently in love the woman was with their guest. Not that Lord Carmichael saw Jane Lord's devotion to him, nor would he act upon it if he did. Carmichael, for his part, seemed oblivious to most everything these days—everything beyond the absence of spirits at his elbow day and night.

There wasn't anything she could do for Carmichael. His loss was deep and his trust in others might never be fully recovered.

What Anna *could* do was help her husband, however. She

read the return addresses on the letters and knew what she must do.

Gilbert had been out of sorts for days and she believed she knew why.

She went to his study and entered without knocking. As she hoped, she managed to startle Gilbert from the papers and maps he rushed to hide from her. She took a deep breath and sat, watching his embarrassment grow. "I have today's mail with me."

He stretched for them. "Good."

He read the inscriptions on all the letters, and then stared at one longer than any other. If she wasn't mistaken, that was another letter from Mr. Davis, the Bow Street Runner.

He set the letters aside.

Anna wasn't about to let him dismiss the problem without a fight. "Are you going to open that?"

He wet his lips.

"Gilbert, you promised we wouldn't have secrets from each other," she complained.

"There are no secrets when my wife sees the mail before I do," he grumbled, finally looking up at her. "I asked for it to be brought to me first. You know what he wants from me."

Help. "I do, and you know you want to go and see what you can do to assist his investigation," she replied.

"No, I don't," he countered, shoving the letters in the drawer roughly. "My responsibilities are here with my wife and the estate now."

Anna got up again and hurried around the desk. She forced her way onto his lap and hugged him tightly. "Of course you want to go and help the man. I've known for days you would go. I can manage here without you for a few weeks or months while you investigate."

He hugged her back. "It can be done without me."

She believed the task would be completed quicker with him than without, though. "Who better knows the criminal mind than the Almighty's bloodhound?"

"Don't call me that," he chided, trying to escape the title he had earned long ago. Her husband was a skilled investigator, and she couldn't be prouder. Because she loved him, she could never hold him back.

Anna hugged him. "You'll write every day you're gone?"

He sighed against her throat. His fingers rose to cup her face and he pulled her closer against him. "Every morning and every night, I swear."

"Good. Now, I have your valet already packing for your trip. The carriage will be before the house in an hour. Do you need anything from me?"

He shook his head, smiling. "I vowed to give up this grisly business when we married."

"I never asked you to." She smiled and ran her fingers through his hair, soaking up the sight of him.

"You could," he suggested. He moved his hand down her leg and back up. "I would do anything you wanted of me."

She smiled. "My love is without conditions, but if you wanted to do something for me, you could take Carmichael with you."

"Is he annoying you again?"

"Not yet, but he cuts such a tragic figure that he's in danger of breaking a heart very close to me without knowing it."

"Your companion?"

Anna nodded, toying with the buttons on his waistcoat. "I'm worried about her interest in him. About him, too. He's drinking far too much."

"Then he comes with me, and perhaps I'll drop him off at your father's before I come home." He smiled suddenly. "I have the very best idea, too. Let's delay the carriage one more hour."

"Why?"

He caught her tight against his chest and stood, making her gasp from the sudden movement. He grinned down at her. "I'm afraid that I'm going to need to make love to my beautiful wife just one more time before she makes me leave her behind to consort with the criminal class."

"With Bow Street. It is an honest calling," Anna corrected him. She loved him so much, and she would remind him what he would come home to when the investigation was over. "I was hoping you would want me."

"From the very moment our eyes met, my lady," he vowed.

The Distinguished Rogues will continue with
The Duke's Heart.

MORE REGENCY ROMANCE FROM HEATHER BOYD...

Rebel Hearts Series

Book 1: The Wedding Affair (Felix and Sally)
Book 2: An Affair of Honor (William and Matilda)
Book 3: The Christmas Affair (Amy and Harper)
Book 4: An Affair so Right (Quinn and Theodora)

Wild Randalls Series

Book 1: Engaging the Enemy (Leopold and Mercy)
Book 2: Forsaking the Prize (Tobias and Blythe)
Book 3: Guarding the Spoils (Oliver and Elizabeth)
Book 4: Hunting the Hero (Constantine and Rosemary)

And many more

www.Heather-Boyd.com

ABOUT HEATHER BOYD

Determined to escape the Aussie sun on a scorching camping holiday, Heather picked up a pen and notebook from a corner store and started writing her very first novel—Chills. Eight years later, she is the author of over thirty romances and publisher of several anthologies too. Addicted to all things tech (never again will Heather write a novel longhand) and fascinated by English society of the early 1800's, Heather spends her days getting her characters in and out of trouble and into bed together (if they make it that far). She lives on the edge of beautiful Lake Macquarie, Australia with her trio of mischievous rogues (husband and two sons) along with one rescued cat whose only interest in her career is that it provides him with food on demand.

You can find details of her writing at www.Heather-Boyd.com